About the author

Born in New York in 1916, Harold Robbins grew up during the Depression. He left school at 15½ to go to work, and by the time he was 21 had made his first fortune and lost it: he went bankrupt for over a million dollars and had to begin all over again. When he was 30, and having risen to the position of executive director of budget and planning for Universal Pictures, Harold Robbins began to write. NEVER LOVE A STRANGER (1947) became an immediate bestseller. Five novels later, in 1960, Robbins faced a decision: his writing or a business career. For him there could be only one choice. He has since become one of the world's best-selling writers, many of his novels have been filmed, and his books have been translated into almost every language.

Also by Harold Robbins and published by New English Library:

THE ADVENTURERS
THE BETSY
THE CARPETBAGGERS
DESCENT FROM XANADU
DREAMS DIE FIRST
THE DREAM MERCHANTS
GOODBYE, JANETTE
THE INHERITORS
THE LONELY LADY
MEMORIES OF ANOTHER DAY
NEVER LEAVE ME
NEVER LOVE A STRANGER
THE PIRATE
79 PARK AVENUE
SPELLBINDER
STILETTO
A STONE FOR DANNY FISHER
THE STORYTELLER
WHERE LOVE HAS GONE

HAROLD ROBBINS

THE PIRANHAS

NEW ENGLISH LIBRARY
Hodder and Stoughton

First published in Great Britain in 1991 by New English Library Hardbacks

New English Library paperback edition 1992

Printed and bound in Great Britain for Hodder and Stoughton Paperbacks, a division of Hodder and Stoughton Ltd, Mill Road, Dunton Green, Sevenoaks, Kent TN13 2YA. (Editorial Office: 47 Bedford Square, London WC1B 3DP) by Clays Ltd, St Ives plc. Photoset by Rowland Phototypesetting Ltd, Bury St Edmunds, Suffolk.

British Library C.I.P.

Robbins, Harold
   The piranhas.
   I. Title
   823[F]

   ISBN 0-450-41737-9

FOR JANN

WITH ALL MY LOVE
AND GRATITUDE

THE FUNERAL

It was pissing rain at eleven o'clock in the morning in front of St. Patrick's Cathedral. The police had blocked all traffic down Fifth Avenue from 54th Street to 49th Street except buses and they were only in a single line close to the sidewalk near Rockefeller Center across from the Cathedral. The street itself was crowded with blackened window stretchouts. The sidewalk and the steps leading up to the entrance of the Cathedral were jammed with television cameras, reporters and the morbid curious crowd that always managed to show up for death and destruction.

Inside the Cathedral all the pews were filled with black-dressed mourners. Some very expensively dressed and others in threadbare black but each looked down toward the altar to the front of the ornate gold coffin with a simple wreath of flowers at the foot. There was an expectant air as they waited to hear the mass that would be given by Cardinal Fitzsimmons. They wanted to hear what he had to say, because he had always hated him.

I was seated in the first seat off the aisle reserved only for relatives of the deceased. I looked over at the open coffin. My uncle looked fit and relaxed. Better, actually, than he usually did in life. Even as a child I realized that he was taut and always thinking. But most of all, I could always see the Angel of Death peering over his left shoulder, who would disappear the moment my uncle would talk to me. There were five other members of the family in the pew with me. My aunt, Rosa, the sister of my uncle and my father who had been his brother. Then there were Rosa's married daughters and their husbands. I had trouble remembering their names because over the many years we had rarely seen each other. I think their

1

names were Cristina and her husband, Pietro, and Luciana and her husband, Thomas, who had two young children of their own.

Across the aisle also in the front pew were the important people and close friends of my uncle. My uncle had many friends. He had to have many friends because he died in bed of a massive cardiac seizure and not by a bullet as was the usual form of death for his compatriots. I looked across the aisle. I recognized some of the men, somber in the black suits, white shirts, and black ties. Next to the aisles, Danny and Samuel were seated. They were young, maybe about my age, fortyish. They were my uncle's bodyguard and secretary. The man sitting next to them I recognized from his photographs in newspapers and magazines. He was very handsome, silver gray white hair, in a carefully tailored suit. A black handkerchief in his breast pocket matching his tie falling neatly across the front of his white silk shirt. The CEO. The Chairman of the Board. Fifteen, twenty years ago, they would have called him The Godfather. The *Capo di tutti Capi*. That was what they used to call my uncle. But that was forty years ago, they used to kiss his hand. But not today. The CEO was fourth generation American. And it was not the Mafia. The Mafia, maybe, still in Sicily. But here in America it was a conglomerate comprised of Sicilians, Blacks, Latin Americans, South Americans and Asians. But the CEO held the reins tightly in hand with the board consisting of the five original families. The head of each of the families sat next to the CEO. In the few pews behind them were the others. The Latins, the Blacks, the Asians. The pecking order never changed. Not in all the years.

The Cardinal rushed the mass. The whole thing was over in less than ten minutes. He made the sign of the cross over the coffin then turned his back and started to walk away from the altar. At the same time, a thin, small, black-suited man, seated toward the middle of the church, began running down the aisle toward the coffin waving a gun wildly over his head.

I heard my Aunt Rosa scream and saw the Cardinal diving quickly down behind the altar, his robes flapping. I went out of the pew after the man and I saw others running after him.

But none of us caught him before he emptied his gun into the coffin, then the man stood there and cried loudly, 'One death is not enough for traitors!'

My uncle's bodyguards wrestled the man to the ground. I was just in time to see them begin to break the man's neck but the CEO was already there. He gestured with his hand and shook his head. 'No,' he said.

The bodyguards rose to their feet and by that time the coffin was surrounded with uniformed police. Two plain-clothes detectives were in charge of the officers. One of them pointed to the small man still on the floor. 'Get him out of here.' The other detective picked up the gun lying on the floor and dropped it in his pocket. He turned to me because I was the closest to the coffin. 'Who's in charge here?'

I glanced around. The Chairman and my uncle's body-guards were back in their front line pew. My aunt was crying loudly and broke away from her two sons-in-law and ran to the coffin and screamed again as she saw the mess inside the coffin. My uncle's head had been obliterated, more a gargoyle than a man's face. The silk sheet in the coffin stained and spattered with brains, pieces of torn skin and a pale pink colored fluid that the embalmer had used to replace the blood in my uncle's body.

I pulled her back and pushed her into the sons-in-laws' arms. 'Get her away from here,' I said.

Aunt Rosa did the right thing. She fainted and the two men dragged her back to the pew, as her daughters rushed to her aid. At least now she was quiet. I turned to one of the undertakers. 'Close the coffin.'

'Don't you want us to take him back and clean him up?' one of them asked.

'No,' I said. 'We go right to the cemetery.'

'But he looks terrible,' the man protested.

'It doesn't matter now,' I said. 'I'm sure that God will recognize his face.'

The detective looked at me. 'Who are you?' he asked.

'I'm his nephew. My father was his brother.'

'I don't know you,' the detective said curiously. 'I thought I knew all of his family.'

3

'I live in California and just came in for the funeral.' I took out a business card and handed it to him. 'Now, let me get the funeral on the road. I'll be at the Waldorf Towers if you want to get in touch with me this evening.'

'Just one question. Do you know anything about the nut who pulled this stunt?'

'Nothing,' I said.

The Cardinal came toward us. His face was pale and drawn. 'Sacrilegious,' he said huskily.

'Yes, Father,' I agreed.

'I'm very upset,' the Cardinal said. 'Nothing like this has ever happened in here.'

'I'm sorry, Father,' I said. 'But if damages have occurred, please give me the bill and it will be taken care of.'

'Thank you, son.' The Cardinal looked at me. 'I've never met you?' he asked.

'No, Father,' I answered. 'I'm the prodigal nephew. I'm from California.'

'But you are his nephew, I understand,' he said.

'True,' I replied. 'But I never have been baptized, my mother was Jewish.'

'But your father was Catholic,' the Cardinal said. 'It is not too late for you to come back to the faith.'

'Thank you, Father,' I said. 'But there is nothing to come back to because I have never been a Catholic.'

The Cardinal looked curious. 'Are you of the Hebrew faith?'

'No, sir,' I answered.

'What Faith do you profess to?' he asked.

I smiled. 'I'm an atheist.'

He shook his head sadly. 'I am sorry for you.' He paused a moment, then gestured to a young priest to join us. 'This is Father Brannigan who will accompany you to the cemetery.'

There were two flower cars and five limousines following the hearse down Second Avenue, under the Mid-Town tunnel to Long Island, through the gates of First Calvary. The family mausoleum shone brightly in the noon day sunlight, the white marble columns in front of the iron grill works in the doors set with stained glass windows. Over the door the family was chiseled in white Italian marble. Di STEFANO. The doors were open wide as the cortège came to a stop in the narrow roadway.

We stepped out of the cars in the narrow roadway and waited for the men to roll the coffin onto a four-wheeled trolley and push it up the pathway toward the mausoleum. The flower cars were immediately unloaded and followed the coffin up the pathway. Aunt Rosa, her family and Father Brannigan were in the first car of the procession. The priest led the way to the coffin. I was in the second car with my uncle's bodyguard and secretary, and we followed Aunt Rosa and her family. In the three cars behind us were the Chairman, his bodyguards, then my uncle's attorneys and accountants. Following them were six men, all older Italian men, probably friends of my uncle.

The flowers were piled high at the side of the open mausoleum doors as we entered the chilled cool of the mausoleum. The coffin was still on the trolley in the middle of the room. In the far corner there was a small altar over which the Christ looked sadly down at the coffin as it sat at the foot of the cross upon which He agonized.

Quickly the priest, his voice echoing hollowly in the room, gave the Blessed Sacrament and the last rites over the coffin, then made the gesture of the cross and stepped back. One of the undertakers handed each of us a rose and after Aunt Rosa placed her rose on the coffin we followed with our own.

Quietly, four men raised the coffin and slid it into its place in the wall. A moment later, two men fastened the bronze plaque over the opening. In the light streaming in from the stained glass windows, I could see the etched lettering: ROCCO Di STEFANO. Born 1908. Died ——. R I P

Aunt Rosa began crying again and her sons-in-law took her out. I glanced around at the walls of the mausoleum. There were names of other relatives I had never known. But my father and mother were not there. They were buried in an interdenominational cemetery north of New York City on the banks of the Hudson River.

I was the last man to leave the mausoleum. I watched for

a moment while one of the cemetery workmen turned the big brass key to lock the door. He looked at me. I caught the message. I took a hundred dollar bill and pressed it into his hand. He touched his cap as acknowledgement. Then I followed down the path to the narrow roadway.

The hearse and the flower cars were already gone. I went to Aunt Rosa and kissed her cheek. 'I'll call you tomorrow.'

She nodded, her eyes still filled with tears. I shook hands with her sons-in-law, kissed the cheeks of my cousins and waited until their limousine took off.

I turned to my car where the two bodyguards were still waiting. One of them opened the car door for me deferentially. The Chairman's quiet voice came from behind me. 'I'll take you into the city.'

I looked at him.

'We have many things to discuss,' he said.

I nodded and gestured to the bodyguards to go on. I followed the Chairman to his stretchout. This was his own car. Black all over and blackened windows in the passenger compartment. I followed him into the car. A dark-suited man closed the door behind me and got into the front seat next to the chauffeur. Slowly the automobile began to move.

The Chairman pressed a button and the blackened window between the passenger compartment and the front seat closed shut. 'Now we can speak,' the Chairman said. 'We are soundproofed. They cannot hear anything we say.'

I looked at him without speaking.

He smiled, his blue eyes crinkling. 'If I may call you Jed, you can call me John.' He held out his hand.

I took his hand. It was firm and strong. 'Fine, John. Now what do we have to talk about?'

'First, I want to tell you that I had much respect for your uncle. He was an honorable man and never went back on his word.'

'Thank you,' I said.

'I'm also sorry about that stupid incident in the church. Salvatore Anselmo is an old man and hasn't all his marbles. For thirty years he has been saying he would kill your uncle

6

but never had the balls to try. Now it was too late. He couldn't kill a dead man.'

'What was the vendetta about?' I asked.

'It happened so long ago I don't think anyone remembers or knows.'

'What happens to him now?' I asked.

'Nothing,' he said casually. 'They'll probably put him into the Bellevue psycho ward. Disturbing the peace or something. But no one will bother to press charges. They'll send him home to his family.'

'Poor bastard,' I said.

John leaned forward and opened the bar behind the front seat. 'I have a good scotch. Could you join me in a drink?'

I nodded. 'With ice and water.'

Quickly he picked up a bottle of Glenlivet and poured some into two glasses. He added the ice cubes and water from the small bottles of Evian lined up at the back of the small bar. We held up our glasses. 'Cheers,' he said.

I nodded and sipped the drink. It was good. I didn't know how much I needed it. 'Thank you,' I said.

He smiled. 'Now down to business. Tomorrow the lawyers will inform you that you're the executor of your uncle's estate. That estate, except for several personal bequests to your aunt and her family, is placed into a foundation that will distribute to various charities. A grave responsibility. About two hundred million dollars.'

I was silent. I knew Uncle Rocco had a great deal of money but I didn't realize that much.

'Your uncle didn't think he had to leave you any money because for one – you are rich in your own right, and two – as executor of the estate you will earn between 5 and 10 percent of the distribution of the funds from the foundation as ordered by the probate court.'

'I don't want any of the money,' I said.

'Your uncle said you would say that, but it is simply a matter of the law,' John said.

I thought for a moment. 'Okay,' I said. 'Now how do you fit into this?'

'In his estate – nothing,' he said. 'But there are other

considerations. Fifteen years ago when your uncle retired and moved to Atlantic City he made an agreement with the De Longo family and the Anastasia family that they would give him Atlantic City as his territory. That was long before gambling had ever been thought of there. Since then all the unions and various other businesses have been under your uncle's control. Now they would like to take over that part of his business.'

I looked at him. 'It's a lot of money?'

He nodded.

'How much?' I asked.

'Fifteen, twenty million a year,' he said.

I sat silent.

John stared at me. 'You're not interested in taking it over?'

'No,' I said. 'That's not my game. But I feel they ought to contribute something to Uncle Rocco's foundation. If for nothing other than respect of his memory. After all, if I understand it, Uncle Rocco took over that business when it was nothing but a broken down town and helped it grow to its own importance.'

John smiled. 'You're not stupid. If you wanted to keep his organization you would be dead in a year.'

'Probably,' I answered. 'But I have my own business to attend to and am not interested in Uncle Rocco's affairs. But I do think that they should donate something to his foundation.'

'How much?' John asked.

'Twenty million dollars would be about fair,' I said.

'Ten million,' John bargained.

'Fifteen and you have an agreement,' I said.

'Done,' he smiled, holding out his hand.

I shook his hand. 'The money has to be placed in the foundation before we go into probate,' I said.

'I understand,' he said. 'The money will be transferred tomorrow.'

He refilled our drinks. 'You are very much like your uncle,' he said. 'How come you never did go into the family business?'

'My father didn't like it,' I said. 'And I had a touch of it when I was young and I realized it was not my game as well.'

'You might have been in my place,' he said.

I shook my head. 'In that case, one of us would be dead.' I was silent for a moment and then nodded my head. 'I was very young then,' I said, remembering going up the Amazon with my cousin, Angelo, many years ago.

Book One

ANGELO AND ME

1

I was pouring sweat from every pore even though it was supposed to be cooler in the late afternoon. I wiped myself with the soaking cheap towel, dipped in warm Amazon river water. It didn't help. Nothing helped. It wasn't the heat, it was the humidity. But, this wasn't humidity, this was wet. And hot. I stretched out on the shelf of the stern.

I fucked myself. I never should have listened to my cousin Angelo. It was two months ago, June to be exact. We sat in the Four Seasons Restaurant in New York, at a poolside table. Just Angelo and me. I had just graduated from Wharton School. 'You don't have to go to work right now,' Angelo said. 'What you need is a vacation, an adventure.'

'You're full of shit,' I said. 'I have two offers from the best stockbrokers on Wall Street. They want me right away.'

'What are they offering you?' he asked, finishing his vodka rocks and ordering another.

'Forty grand a year for starters.'

'Chicken shit,' Angelo said. 'You can get that anytime.' He looked at me. 'You hurtin' for money?'

'No,' I said. He knew as well as I that my father had left me more than a million dollars.

'Then what's the rush?' Angelo looked across the pool at a girl on the other side. 'That's class,' he said appreciatively.

I looked at her. I didn't know what he was talking about. She was ordinary Radcliffe. Long brown hair, large eyeglasses making her eyes seem enormous, no brassière, soft titties. I didn't say anything.

He turned back to me. 'I'm going to South America next month,' he said. 'I would like you to come with me.'

'What the hell for?' I asked.

'Emeralds,' he said. 'Worth more than diamonds in today's market. And I have a line on a suitcase full of them for pennies.'

'Illegal?' I asked.

'Shit, of course,' he said. 'But I have arranged everything. Transportation. Customs. We walk through.'

'That's not my game,' I said.

'We could split two million,' he said. 'No hassle. The family's covering me. Blanket all the way.'

'My father walked away from that many years ago. I don't think I should go into it.'

'You're not going into anything,' he said. 'You're just being company for me. You're family. Anybody else I might take along might get some big ideas.' He looked across at the girl again. 'You think it's okay if I send a bottle of Dom Perignon to her?'

'Forget it,' I said. 'I know that type. Cold ass.'

'That's what I like. Warm them up and turn them on.' He laughed. He turned back to me. Serious. 'Coming with me?'

I hesitated. 'Let me think about it.' But even while I said that, I knew I would go with him. Burying my nose in books for the last few years wasn't my idea of great living. It was fucking dull. Wharton was not excitement, no action. Not like it was in Vietnam.

My father was pissed off when I enlisted. I was nineteen and had just finished two years in college. I told him that the draft would get me even if I didn't beat them to it. At least this way I had the choice of services. That's what I thought but that was not the Army's idea. They didn't need PR men. There were enough people shoving bullshit to the media. What they wanted was grunts and that was me. Grunt number 1. Asshole.

I took all four months of basic training. I jumped out of planes and helicopters, dug foxholes until I was sure that South Carolina was slipping into the ocean. Then to Saigon. Three whores and five million units of penicillin. Seventy pounds of armament. An automatic rifle, two Colt automatic 45 caliber, a dissembled bazooka and six hand grenades.

I jumped into the middle of the night, four hours away

from Saigon. The night was quiet. Silent. Not a sound except for us assholes groaning as we hit the ground. I got up and looked for the Lieutenant. He was nowhere to be found. The grunt in front of me turned around. 'This is a cinch,' he said. 'Ain't nobody here.' Then he stepped into a field mine and pieces of him and shrapnel blew back in my face.

That was the end of my career in the army. Four months later after I got out of the hospital where they fixed up my face, leaving only two small scars on either side of my chin, I walked into my father's office.

He sat behind his big desk. He was a small man and he loved his big desk. He looked up at me. 'You're a hero,' he said without expression.

'I wasn't a hero,' I said. 'I was an asshole.'

'At least you're admitting it. That's a step in the right direction.' He rose from his desk. 'Now what are you going to do?'

'I haven't thought about it,' I said.

'You had your turn, you went into the army.' He looked up at me. 'Now it's my turn.'

I didn't answer.

'When I go, you'll be rich,' he said. 'Maybe a million or more. I want you to go to Wharton School.'

'I haven't the credits to get into it,' I said.

'I've already got you in,' he said. 'You start in September. I figure that's the place to learn how to handle your money.'

'There's no rush, Dad,' I said. 'You're going to live a long time.'

'Nobody knows,' he said. 'I thought your mother would live forever.'

It was ten years since my mother had gone but my father still hurt for her. 'Mother's cancer is not your fault,' I said. 'Don't be so Italian.'

'I'm not Italian, I'm Sicilian,' he said.

'They're the same thing to me.'

'Don't tell that to my brother,' he said.

I looked at him. 'What's happening to the Godfather?'

'He's okay,' my father answered. 'The Feds couldn't lay a hand on him.'

'He's something else,' I said.

'Yes,' my father said disapprovingly. When my father was young he split with the family. It was not his way of life. He went into the car rental business and in a short while had thirty locations in airports around the country. It wasn't Hertz or Avis, but it wasn't bad. Twenty million gross a year. He hadn't heard from his brother for years, and didn't hear from him until my mother died. Then he sent a roomful of flowers. My father threw them all out. My mother was Jewish and the Jews don't have flowers at their funerals.

'Do you know what Angelo is doing?' I asked. Angelo was my first cousin, just a few years older than I.

'I hear he's working for his father.'

'That figures,' I said. 'Good Italian boys go into their father's business.' I looked at him. 'Do you expect me to go into your business?'

My father shook his head. 'No, I'm selling out.'

'Why?' I was surprised.

'Too many years,' he said. 'I thought I would travel around a little bit. I never saw anything of the world and I plan to start from where I was born. Sicily.'

'You got a girl to go with you?' I asked.

My father flushed. 'I don't need anyone to travel with me.'

'It would be good company,' I said.

'I'm too old,' he said. 'I wouldn't know what to do with a girl.'

'Find the right one and she will show you,' I said.

'Is that any way to talk to your father?' he asked indignantly.

It happened. I went off to Wharton and my father sold his business and went off to Sicily. But something went wrong. His car went off the curving, winding road coming down from Mt Trapani to Marsala.

My uncle called me before I left for Sicily to bring my father's body home. 'I'm going to send two bodyguards with you.'

'What for?' I asked. 'Nobody's going to bother me.'

'You don't know,' he said heavily. 'I loved your father. Maybe we didn't agree but that doesn't matter. Blood is blood.

Besides I heard that somebody had tampered with the brakes on your father's car.'

I was silent for a moment. 'Why? Everyone knows that he was straight.'

'That doesn't mean anything in Sicily. They don't know about those things, all they know is that he was family. My family. I don't want them to get to you. You're goin' to have two bodyguards.'

'No way,' I said. 'I can take care of myself. At least I learned that in the Army.'

'You learned how to get your ass blown off,' he said.

'That was something else,' I said.

'Okay,' he said. 'Then would you let Angelo go with you?'

'If I'm hot,' I said. 'Then he'll be hotter. He's your son.'

'But he knows the game and besides that he speaks Sicilian. Anyway he wants to go with you. He loved your father too.'

'Okay,' I said. Then I had a question. 'Angelo's not doing any business over there?'

My uncle was lying. 'Of course not.'

I thought for a moment. It really didn't make any difference. 'Okay,' I said. 'We'll go together.'

My uncle was smarter than I was. I didn't need any bodyguards. But Angelo always had four men with bulged armpits under their jackets and since he was always with me, we had bodyguards. There was no trouble in Sicily. The small funeral service we had in the church in Marsala was quiet with only a few people attending, none of whom I knew even though we were supposed to be relatives. I received their condolences and embraces as the hearse carried the coffin to Palermo where it was then transported by plane to New York. My father's wishes were to be buried beside my mother. It was done.

A week later I stood in the cemetery as the coffin was placed in the ground. Silently I threw a handful of dirt down to the coffin and turned away. My uncle and Angelo followed me.

'Your father was a good man,' my uncle said heavily.

'Yes,' I said.

'What will you do now?' he asked.

17

'Finish school. I'll get my degree in business administration next June.'

'Then what will you do?' my uncle asked.

'Get a job,' I answered.

My uncle was silent. Angelo looked at me. 'You're an ass-hole,' he said. 'We have many businesses that you could fit into.'

'Legitimate business,' my uncle added.

'My father wanted me to go my own way,' I said. 'But, I thank you for the offer.'

'You're exactly like your father,' my uncle growled.

I laughed. 'Exactly. As Angelo is exactly like you. Like father, like son.'

My uncle embraced me. 'You are my family. I love you.'

'And I love you,' I said and watched him go to his car, then turned to Angelo. 'What are your plans?'

'I have a date in town,' he said. He gestured to the limousine. 'I'll go in with you if you don't mind.'

'Okay,' I nodded. We sat silently as the limo drove back into Manhattan. Not until we had gone into the Mid-Town tunnel did I speak. 'I want to thank you for coming to Sicily with me. I didn't know it then but I needed your support. Thank you.'

'It's nothing,' he said. 'You're family.'

I nodded without speaking.

'My father means it,' he said. 'He would like you to be with us.'

'I appreciate that,' I said. 'And I'm grateful but it's not the way I'm going.'

'Okay,' Angelo smiled. 'I was always curious. Why did your father change the name from Di Stefano to Stevens?'

'That was far enough from the family name,' I answered.

'But Stevens, that's an Irish name. I don't get it.'

'My father explained to me,' I said. 'All Italians changed their names to Irish.'

'And your name, that's not Irish.'

'It was my father's idea. He wanted me to be as American as I could.' I laughed.

The limo came out of the tunnel. He looked out the

18

window. 'Drop me off on Park and Fiftieth.'

'Okay.'

'Want to have dinner tonight? I have a couple of cute chicks.'

'I'm packing tonight. I'm going up to school tomorrow. But thanks anyway.'

'You'll graduate in June?' he questioned.

'Yes.'

'I'll be in touch with you,' he said. And he did it. Almost before I knew it, I was sweating on the back of a dilapidated old river boat on the Amazon while he was down in the cabin screwing a crazy beautiful Peruvian girl he had hired as a translator in Lima.

I stared up at the sunlight shining through the trees hanging over the river bank. I was soaking wet with perspiration. I reached for a cigarette. Angelo had to be a better man than I if he could fuck in heat like this.

2

From the bench on the stern of the boat, I watched as the monkey moved expertly through the dense greenery on the shore. He swung gracefully from vine to vine. Suddenly, he stopped and sat down on his haunches. He eyeballed me. He knew I was an amateur. Then he quickly disappeared when Angelo came up from the cabin. He was naked except for his designer bikini shorts, and the hair over his chest, shoulders and back was matted with sweat. He took a bottle of beer and sucked on it. Disgustedly he threw it overboard. 'Crap,' he said.

'No ice,' I said looking up at him.

'Balls,' he said, throwing himself down beside me on the bench. He stared at me. 'The bitch fucked me out,' he said, unbelieving.

I smiled and reached for another beer without speaking.

'Why are you laughing?' he said angrily.

'I wasn't laughing,' I said.

'I don't believe it,' he said.

'She's used to the heat. You're not,' I said.

'Got a cigarette?' he asked.

I gave him the pack and watched him light up. 'When **are** we getting out of here?' I asked.

'In the morning,' he said. 'We should be loaded by ten o'clock then we'll take off.'

'I thought we were coming up for emeralds,' I said. 'Now we're sitting on two tons of coca leaves.'

'The Colombians don't want our money, they want coca. We give them the leaves and they'll give us the emeralds.'

I made his eyes. 'You're full of shit,' I said. 'Now that I'm into it, why don't you give me the straight story.'

21

'You won't like it,' he said, meeting my eyes.

'Try me,' I answered.

'It's the difference between two million and twenty,' he said.

'How do you figure that?' I asked.

He didn't answer.

'There were never any emeralds?' I accused.

He shook his head. 'You're family,' he said. 'The only one I could trust.'

'Did your father know about it?'

'He didn't want you to go. But it was my idea.' He shot his cigarette overboard. It hissed as it hit the water. 'Besides, you owed me one for Sicily.'

'Nothing happened there,' I said.

'Because I was there. I had four men to keep a blanket over us. Alone, you would have been wasted.'

I was silent. I didn't know whether to believe him or not. Maybe I would never know. But it was over. 'Now what do we do?'

'We go down river to Iquitos. I have a DC3 to take us to Panama. From there a Cessna Twin takes us to Miami where we make the drop. We're booked on Eastern to New York.'

I shook my head. 'I was really an asshole.'

'I'll never tell anybody,' he grinned. 'It's all in the family.'

'Do you know the people we're meeting?' I asked.

'Not personally,' he said.

'How will you find them?' I asked.

'They'll find us. It's all been arranged. Customs has been paid off through Miami.'

'I want out,' I said, shaking my head. 'It's not my game.'

'You can't quit now,' he said. 'All the charters are in your name. I had to do it. My name is on too many lists.'

'I still don't like it. Too much could go wrong. We could be hijacked, we could be fingered by some snitch. It makes me nervous.'

Angelo looked at me then went back into the cabin. He came up a moment later and placed a Colt automatic in my hand. 'That's insurance,' he said. 'Do you know how to handle it?'

22

'I had one of these in Vietnam.'

'If anyone looks even suspicious, waste them.'

I handed the gun back to him. 'No,' I said.

'Okay,' he said. He put the gun on the bench beside me. 'I'm going in for a swim,' he said and dove off the back of the boat.

Alma came up from the cabin as he dove into the water. Angelo's cotton shirt covered her down to her thighs. She looked at the gun then at me. 'Why did he bring a gun?' Her voice reflecting only a faint Spanish accent.

'He wanted me to have it,' I answered.

She was a pretty girl but her face looked worried. 'Does he expect any trouble?'

'No,' I answered. I looked at him swimming in the water. 'How is it?' I called.

'Great,' he yelled back. 'Come on in.'

'No, thanks,' I said.

He called to Alma. 'Come on, baby. The water's fine.'

She hesitated, looking at me, then dropped his shirt to the deck and posed for me. 'You like?' she asked in a teasing voice.

I laughed. 'You're a cunt.'

She laughed. 'I think you're a fag.'

'You're not my girl,' I said.

'But you never even look,' she said.

'I have rules.' I reached for another cigarette.

She laughed and dove into the water. She disappeared beneath the surface and came up in front of Angelo about twenty yards from the boat. She grabbed him and pulled him down under the water.

'Loco,' the heavy-set Peruvian captain of the boat spoke from behind me.

I looked at him.

'Tell your friends to get in the boat,' he said in his halting English. 'It is not safe.'

Something in the sound of his voice meant business. 'Angelo!' I yelled. 'The capitano wants you to get back in the boat.'

'What the hell for?' Angelo yelled.

23

'He says it's dangerous.'

'Horseshit,' he laughed. 'The water is as calm –' He turned in the water, searching for the girl. 'You bitch! Stop trying to grab my balls!'

'I'm not anywhere near you,' she called back to him from five yards away.

'Christ!' Angelo yelled. Then screamed in pain. 'What the hell is going on?' He thrashed about in the water trying to swim back to the boat.

'Piranhas!' the boatman shouted, picking up a boathook and holding it out into the water.

Alma began swimming back to us. 'They're after me!' she screamed. She grabbed the end of the boathook and the sailor pulled her toward us then pulled her onto the boat. Her legs were punctured with tiny bites from which the blood was already oozing.

The sailor left her lying on the deck and tried to reach Angelo with the hook. I looked at him. Angelo was still thrashing and screaming but was moving more slowly toward us. I grabbed the boathook from the sailor and took his arm so that I could lean further toward Angelo. 'Grab the hook, Angelo!' I yelled.

Still screaming in pain, he reached and grabbed the hook. The sailor and I pulled him heavily toward the boat, then the sailor grabbed him under the armpits and onto the boat.

I had seen terrible things in 'Nam but never anything like this. His right leg was eaten away almost to the naked bone, his left leg with flesh hanging in tatters to the bones of his feet. Angelo was staring at me, his eyes clouded with pain and fear. He looked down at himself. He couldn't make any words, only a moaning screaming sound. His groin was a puddle of torn flesh and blood, his penis and testicles gone. He turned his head back up toward me and tried to speak but no words came from his mouth.

'He will die,' the captain said without emotion. 'I have seen this before. It will take one hour, maybe two, but he will die.'

'Isn't there something we can do?'

The captain shook his head. 'Kill him,' he said impassively. 'Or let him die by himself in agony.'

24

I turned to Angelo. He talked with his eyes. He knew what the captain had said. He managed a word. 'Family.'

I knew what he meant. I turned and reached behind me to the bench and took the automatic in my hand. With the gun still behind me, I flipped the safety off with one hand. Then I kissed him on the forehead. 'Family,' I said and covered his eyes with my hand. Then I pulled the trigger.

Slowly I rose to my feet and looked down at him. Angelo was gone. And part of me was also gone. But another part of me was reborn. Family.

'What shall we do with him?' the captain asked.

For the first time I realized that the two other sailors were standing near us. 'There is nothing we can do,' I said, gesturing over the side.

'The watch,' the captain said, pointing to the Rolex on Angelo's hand.

'Give it to me,' I said. I knew my uncle would want it. I turned to the girl lying on the deck, her eyes staring in fear. I heard the splash of Angelo's body as it hit the water. I paused a moment, and then spoke to her. 'How do you feel?'

She was frightened. 'You're not going to kill me?'

Then I realized I was still holding the gun. I closed the safety and stuck it in my belt. 'No,' I said. I turned to the captain. 'What can we do for her?'

The Captain knelt beside her. 'She has not too many bites. The piranhas were too busy with your cousin. We will wrap some wet coca leaves on her, it will stop the pain and she will heal.'

'Take her down to the cabin and take care of her. Then come back to me.'

'Si, señor,' the captain said.

I watched as he lifted her in his arms and took her down to the cabin and one of the sailors followed him with a sheaf of coca leaves. I sat down again on the stern bench.

A few moments later the captain came up. 'My sailor is taking care of her. What can I do for you?'

I looked up at him. 'Do you have a bottle of whiskey?'

'I have rum,' he said.

'Bring it,' I said. 'I need a drink.'

3

There was only one large cabin below deck. A curtain pulled across the middle to separate my bunk from the larger bunk that Angelo and Alma had shared. Despite the half bottle of rum I had swallowed I was straight, not even the slightest buzz. The curtain was now pulled back and I looked over toward Alma lying on the bed. She appeared to be sleeping, her eyes closed. A faint whisper of breath seemed to be passing her lips.

I crossed the cabin and stood next to her bed. I touched her forehead with my palm. She didn't have any fever. Then her eyes opened.

'How do you feel?' I asked.

'Numb,' she said. 'No feeling in my legs at all.'

'It's the coca leaves,' I said. 'The captain told me. It's natural cocaine, a real painkiller. He said you only have small nicks, you'll be okay in a day or two.'

'I feel heavy,' she said.

'He gave you some coca-leaf tea,' I said. 'It will let you rest.'

She nodded. Then tears came to her eyes. 'I feel sorry about your cousin.'

I was silent.

'I liked him,' she said. 'He was crazy, but nice.'

'Yes,' I said.

'What will you do now?' she asked.

'I'll go on I guess,' I answered. 'There is nothing else I can do.'

She looked into my eyes. 'You don't cry.'

'Crying won't help. He is gone. It's over.' I turned and

walked back to my bunk. 'Why don't you try to sleep? You will feel better in the morning.'

'I am afraid I will have bad dreams,' she said.

'Don't be frightened,' I said. 'I will be right here.'

She nodded faintly and closed her eyes. In a moment, I heard the faint whisper of her breath. I pulled out the attaché bag Angelo had placed under my bunk. It was locked. I found the key in a pair of pants he had thrown over a chair.

The attaché case was filled with bank-sealed packages of one hundred dollar bills. Quickly I checked it. One hundred thousand dollars. On the open top cover was a typewritten note:

'Pucalipa to Iquitos – Boat	10m
Iquitos to Medellin – DC3	20m
Medellin to Panama – DC3	20m
Panama to Miami – Cessna	35m

I stared at the money. Angelo had it all laid out. He was not as crazy as he pretended. I took out a package of ten thousand dollars and closed up the attaché case. I put the case under my bunk and opened Angelo's valise which was leaning against the wall. Under his clothing was another automatic and ten clips of cartridges were in the valise. I pushed the gun and clips under my bunk next to the attaché case then closed Angelo's valise and placed it back against the wall.

I stretched out on my bunk and put my hands behind my head on the pillow. I stared up at the ceiling, then it hit me. Angelo was gone. And whether I liked it or not I had to go through with it. And even worse than that, at the end of it all I had to tell his father. And all I could give him of his son was a gold Rolex watch. It would not be easy. Angelo was the apple of his father's eye. I dozed.

I opened my eyes when I heard soft steps running on the deck over my head, and the soft whispering voices of two men. Quietly I slipped out of my bunk and onto the deck, the gun in my hand. The captain and another man were talking quietly on the stern of the boat. I watched them silently. The stranger gestured his hand and two more men came aboard behind him and bent down to the hold, picking up two bales, and started to take them off the boat.

I turned off the safety of the automatic and stepped around the cabin entrance toward them. 'What's happening?' I asked.

The strangers stopped talking and stared at me. I spoke to the captain. 'What the hell's going on?'

'The señor says that the deal is off. He hasn't gotten the money to be paid by your cousin.' The captain was very nervous.

'Tell him that I already know the money has been paid. If not the coca would never have been placed aboard,' I said.

The captain spoke quickly. The man replied in Spanish to him, then the captain turned back to me. 'Only part of the money. There was still one thousand dollars to be paid when all the coca has been delivered.'

'Tell him that he will get the money as promised when he has delivered the rest of the coca.'

The stranger understood me. He spoke quickly to the captain and the captain translated. 'He says that he is a simple farmer and he has worked hard for his crops and he does not want his labor to be stolen from him.'

I looked at the captain. 'How much is he paying you for this bullshit?'

'Nada, señor. Nothing,' the captain said nervously. 'On my family's honor I tell you the truth.'

I stared at him for a moment, then at the stranger. 'Tell the son of a bitch to get off this boat or I will kill him. He can come back tomorrow with the rest of the coca and we will pay whatever else he is due.'

The captain spoke quickly. The stranger looked at me then nodded. He spoke to the captain and nodded. 'He will be back in the morning,' the captain said.

I nodded and gestured with the gun. 'Off.'

The stranger and his two men scrambled from the boat. I watched them disappear into the trees around the lagoon. I turned to the captain. 'How did he learn that my cousin had died?'

'They are watching. They are always watching us,' he said.

'Why did you allow him to come aboard to take back the coca?'

'He is Indian. Mestizo. Very dangerous. He would have killed me, if I didn't let him on the boat,' he said.

'I see,' I said, thinking for a moment. 'Then he will come back tomorrow and kill us.'

The captain was silent.

'But not if we are not here tomorrow,' I said.

The captain looked at me. 'They are in the trees hiding and watching,' he said. 'They will hear the engines if we try to leave.'

'Then we don't start the engines. We use boathooks. It is not deep and we can push us far enough so that the river current can take us downstream until it is safe to start the engines.'

The captain stared at me with new respect. 'You know about such things?'

'In Vietnam. Many times.' I lied, I had only heard about it. I never really believed it until now.

'Si, señor,' he said. 'When shall we start?'

'Give them about an hour to fall asleep,' I said. 'Then we go.'

'And if they come after us?'

'You have guns?' I asked.

'Two pistols, two rifles,' he answered.

'Then we kill them,' I said. 'Bring the guns up to the deck and have your men get ready to cast off.'

He nodded and climbed into the hatchway that opened to his quarters. I went back to the cabin and got the other gun and stuck it into my belt beside the other. Quickly, I stuffed several cartridge clips into my pockets.

Alma's voice sounded across the cabin. 'What is happening?'

'We're taking off,' I said.

She sat up on the bunk. 'But we were supposed to get ten more bales of coca leaves in the morning.'

'We're not waiting for it,' I said. 'The farmer was already aboard and wanted to take the bales back. He said that Angelo hadn't paid him.'

'It's not true,' she said. 'I saw him give him the money in front of the captain.'

'The captain saw it?'

She nodded. 'He arranged it. He spoke to the farmer in Indian.'

My hunch was right. The captain had already made his deal. 'How long will it take us to get downriver to Iquitos?'

'Five, six days,' she said. 'It's down on the Uyacali river where it joins the Amazon.'

'Okay,' I said.

'Will there be trouble?' she asked.

'I don't know,' I said.

She looked up at me. 'Maybe I can help. I can use a gun.' She got out of bed.

I gave her one of Angelo's guns. 'You keep it,' I said. 'I don't expect any trouble tonight, but if there is any I'll holler.' She kept looking at me.

'But you are worried about something?'

'Not about the Mestizo, it's the captain, I don't trust him. He was ready to let the others take off the bales without even letting me know.' I suddenly remembered. 'Didn't we meet the captain in the market in Tingo Maria?'

'That's right,' she answered. 'Tingo Maria is the main source of coca and marijuana. It was the captain who made the deal with the Mestizo to bring the coca over the mountain road to Pucalipa. The same road we came down on.'

'It was also the captain that had us move the boat downstream, about ten kilometers from the Pucalipa docks.' It began to fall in place. 'It was safer, he had said, we would not be found by the police.'

'Yes,' she nodded. 'I hadn't thought about it but the Mestizo came right to us. The captain had it all arranged before we left Tingo Maria.'

'Okay,' I said. 'You stay down here. I feel we'll have no trouble here. If he makes a move it will be when we are further downstream when he thinks that I believe we are safe.'

'You'll have to watch him,' she said.

'I will.' I reached across her bunk to the shelf where Angelo had left his small bag. I opened it and took out a vial of coke.

Quickly, I had a snort. I felt my head open and my eyes went wide. 'I'll be awake now.'

'You'll be stoned,' she said.

'I'll be careful,' I said and went up on the deck.

The captain and his two sailors were waiting for me. He gestured and I saw the guns lying on the shelf in front of the wheel house. I nodded. 'Now pick up the gangplank,' I said. 'But carefully. No sound.'

The captain motioned to the sailors. Quickly and quietly they pulled the gangplank aboard. Then the sailor picked up the boathooks and began to pole us out of the small lagoon into the main current of the river while the captain held the wheel. I could feel the boat move with the current. It seemed strong and we moved quickly downstream.

The captain turned to me. 'Start the engine now?' he asked.

'Not yet,' I said. 'Another fifteen minutes.'

'The water is strong,' he said. 'I don't know if I can keep it straight.'

'Have your men use the boathooks on the stern. They'll hold us straight long enough.' I looked back to the lagoon. There was no motion on the bank. 'Keep going,' I said.

The captain held up a hand and one of the sailors came and took the wheel. The captain walked around and went down into the hatch to the engine room. Fifteen minutes later I heard the engine roar and the boat began to move faster in the water. I looked at the sailor at the wheel. He turned to look back at me. Mistake. When you have a wheel in your hand, whether you're driving a car or boat, you always keep your eyes on the road.

I spun sideways turning back. The captain was out of the hatchway, a rifle pointed toward me in his hands. I could almost see the surprise on his face as the automatic spat angrily at him. Then slowly his arms stretched out and he tumbled from the stern of the boat into the water.

I pointed the gun at the sailors and gestured toward the wheel. Alma had come from the cabin, the gun in her hands. 'What happened?' she called.

'We lost the captain,' I said.

She stared at me.

'Ask the sailor if he can get the boat down to Iquitos,' I told her. 'Tell him if he does, he gets a thousand dollars, if he doesn't he goes swimming with the captain.'

Quickly she spoke to the sailor. The second sailor came to the wheel house and spoke to her. She turned to me. 'They are captains in their own right, he says. And if they do what we say, the two should get money.'

'They can divide the money,' I said. 'I will also give them the boat for themselves.'

She spoke again. They looked at each other, then nodded. They spoke to her and she translated again.

'They want to know if you would give them the papers for the boat?'

'They will have them,' I said.

She spoke to them again then turned back to me after listening another moment for their answer. 'They want you to know that they are not bandidos like the captain, they are honest men and all they want to do is their job.'

'Fine,' I said and shook their hands. 'It's a deal.'

They grinned and smiled at me. 'Deal,' they both said.

4

I stared down at my plate. Rice and beans covered with a sickly brown tomato sauce and greasy yellow oil. I'd had it. Day and night. It had been four nights since we left Pucalipa. Rice and beans. Rice and greasy yellow fish. Rice and canned meat that preserved the maggots the moment the can was opened. My stomach was either exploding with gas or heaving with expectant nausea that never quite came.

I looked at Alma. 'How can you handle it?'

'Drink more beer,' she said simply. 'We have no choice.'

I opened a bottle of beer and gulped half of it down my throat. 'Are there restaurants in Iquitos?'

'Iquitos is a big city,' she said. 'Relax, we'll be there tomorrow.'

I pointed at my plate. 'Throw this shit overboard.'

'You'll eat it,' she said firmly. 'You're not eating enough as it is. You look like you've lost ten pounds.'

'I'm okay,' I said.

'You'll need your strength,' she said. 'Nobody knows what you'll have to face tomorrow. We've been lucky so far but you're like a babe in the woods. You don't even know what we'll be facing up there. Angelo never told you anything.'

I took a large spoonful of rice and swallowed it. I followed it with a mouthful of beer. Even though it was warm, it killed the taste of the grease in my mouth. I looked over at her. 'Did he ever tell you anything about Iquitos?'

'Only that he was meeting a red-bearded man who would be waiting on the docks when we came in.'

'Did he say anything else?'

She shook her head. 'Angelo didn't talk much about his business.'

I nodded. Angelo didn't talk to anyone. Even me. 'Has Iquitos an airport?'

'Yes,' she said. 'Iquitos is the second biggest city in Peru but the only way to get out is either by boat up the Amazon or by air over the mountains. They are too high to cross any other way.'

'How did the city get so big?' I asked.

'Years ago it was the center of rubber plantations and was important until they brought the rubber trees into Malaysia. When that business had been lost, the city barely existed on produce until they discovered oil. Now tankers can go down to the ocean by the Amazon.'

'Is it a big port?'

'I've never been there,' she answered. 'But I think it has to be pretty big because ocean-going ships go in there from Brazil.'

I was just going for another spoonful of rice when I heard the small engine stop and the boat began to wallow slowly in the water. I reached for the rifle and climbed out of the cabin with Alma right behind me. I saw the two sailors on the bow dropping the anchor, the long rope slipping into the water behind it. I moved up behind the sailors. 'Ask them what they're doing,' I told Alma.

She spoke rapidly in Spanish. The sailors looked up at us nervously, both of them speaking at the same time. She asked them another question. Then the older one answered her. He seemed to be explaining something to us.

She turned to me. 'They thought it would be better for us to anchor in this cove until morning. It is only thirty kilometers to Iquitos and it would be better if we went in early in the morning.'

'Why not now?' I asked.

Pablo, the older sailor, answered her. She relayed his words to me. 'The fishermen are all going out in the channel. Their nets will be everywhere and we could become snarled in them. Many of them are Mestizos and thieves. Look over at the channel and you will already see them. They have bright searchlights aiming at the river to attract the fish and if we have trouble with them, they would all gang up on us.'

36

'What time can we get in?' I asked.

'The fishermen go in at four in the morning. By five o'clock we could begin. We should be in Belen by eleven o'clock and be tied up to the dock a half hour later.'

'What's Belen?' I asked.

'It's where the Pucalipa boats dock. The smaller boats like ours. They also live on the houseboats there. The big ships are ten kilometers beyond at the other end of the city.'

'Where did the captain tell them they would dock?' I asked.

They shook their heads. 'He never told them,' she said.

I looked out at the channel in the center of the river. Their searchlights were like lightning bugs bobbing up and down in the water about three quarters of a mile outside of our cove. It seemed as if there were hundreds of them. I turned back to them. 'Okay,' I said to Alma. 'Tell them I want to get underway as soon as the fishermen are gone. And to stay out in the river as far away as possible from Belen and we will go in where the big ships dock.'

Alma translated. Pablo shook his head. He said something angrily. She turned to me. 'He says it would be dangerous. That is where the customs and police are stationed.'

'I'll worry about it when we get there,' I said. I turned again and looked at the fishermen. 'Keep your eyes out for them,' nodding out toward the river. 'If any of them come toward us, let me know.'

She told them and then followed me to the stern where we sat down on the small bench. 'What are you thinking?'

'I don't trust any of them,' I said. 'But if we are to meet someone, it makes more sense that they would meet us at the more important docks than at the docks for crappy riverboats and fishermen.'

'I would think that would be safer than the big docks,' she said.

'I remember something that Angelo once told me. The best place to hide is out in the open. No one ever thinks you would be doing anything wrong.'

'Angelo was crazy,' she said

'Not that crazy,' I said. 'He got me down here. What did he promise you to come with him?'

She looked down at me. 'I liked him.'

I smiled. 'Nothing else?'

She laughed. 'Money. A lot of it.'

I nodded. 'How much?'

'A thousand dollars US.'

'You just got a raise,' I said. 'We get out of this you get ten grand.'

She was silent for a moment, then she laughed. 'Now we have to fuck,' she said.

'First, we get out of here,' I said, looking out at the fishermen's boats, their lights bobbing up and down in the channel.

'What are you watching for?' she asked.

'I don't feel right,' I said. I pointed around the cove. 'We may be hidden from the fishermen but we're less than a hundred yards from the shore around us. And on top of it, the forest is right up to the water and there is no way we can see into it.'

She stared at the shoreline. 'Do you think the Mestizos have followed us along the river?'

'I don't know,' I said. 'Do you think they could?'

'There are really no roads,' she answered.

'But they have horses,' I said. 'They could have made it on footpaths.'

She gestured forward to the sailors. 'Do you think they might know anything about them?'

'I don't know,' I shrugged. 'They weren't very upset about the captain. I'm sure they knew what he was planning and were part of it.'

She turned and stared at the shore. Night had fallen swiftly and the only lights we had were from the sparkling stars and the yellowish full moon. 'I can't see a damn thing in there.'

I nodded. 'Bring the rifles and the gun I gave you and let's keep them up here with us.'

'You're going to stay up all night?' she asked.

'I'll feel safer,' I said.

'I'll stay up with you,' she said. 'I'll feel safer with you.'

I looked at her. 'Then put on a pair of jeans instead of your shorts and get a hat and a bug veil as well as the bottle of citronella. I don't want the bugs to get us if the Mestizos don't.'

She laughed. 'I'll be up in a few minutes,' she said going down into the cabin.

She wasn't stupid. She came up from the cabin with blankets and pillows. 'If we wrap up in these blankets the damp will make us feel soaked as if we are in a bath. If we stretch out on the deck, it will be dryer than sitting on the bench.'

'Good idea,' I said. 'We'll also be less of a target.' I watched her spread the blankets on the deck. The pillows almost made it look comfortable. Too comfortable. I had an idea. 'There's a round three-foot wicker basket next to my bunk. Bring it up with another blanket.'

She didn't ask any questions. When she returned, I sat the basket on the bench where I had been sitting, wrapped a blanket around it and stuck my old panama hat on the head. I turned to her. 'What do you think?'

She giggled. 'He looks exactly like you.'

'Thanks,' I said and slipped down to the deck beside her. 'Now you can get some sleep. I'll keep watch.'

'You're not tired?' she asked.

'I'm okay.'

'If you need a lift, I've got a vial in my pocket.'

'I'll keep it in mind,' I said. 'I might need it.'

I watched her wrap herself in the blanket and turned back up to look at the basket and smiled to myself. She was right. In the black of night it looked exactly like me.

5

I felt her hand on my shoulder and came wide-eyed awake. She pressed a finger against my lips so that I would not speak and pointed forward to the bow of the boat. Keeping my head down I peered behind the overhang of the cabin.

A man was climbing aboard from a rowboat tied to a stanchion near the bow. In the dark I could not see his face but I saw our sailors gesturing to him. He nodded and began walking silently on bare feet across the narrow deck to where we were sleeping.

I pushed her into the cabin doorway behind me and raised the rifle against my shoulder. The man moved quickly now. I saw the gleam of the machete as he held it over his head and brought it down viciously into the basket I had placed on the bench. The machete was tangled in the blanket as the wicker basket collapsed around it. I didn't wait for the man to turn toward us. I pumped two shots into his back between his shoulders. He bent forward and slumped over the stern. I kicked him in the ass and he fell awkwardly over the small railing and into the water.

Alma's automatic roared in a series of staccato explosions. I whirled toward her. She had the gun held stiff-armed in front of her, pointing at the sailor running toward us on the narrow deck. He was still moving toward us as I pushed her out of the way as he fell forward. I pushed him away. A revolver fell to the deck from his lifeless hands. I shoved him off the deck into the water.

'It was Pablo,' she said in a trembling voice. 'He was trying to kill us.'

'That's right,' I said.

'Is he dead?' she asked apprehensively.

'Yes,' I said.

She crossed herself quickly. 'I have sinned. I have never killed a man before.'

'You would have sinned more if you let him kill you,' I said. I took the gun from her hand and replaced the cartridge. 'Keep this. You might need it again.'

I gestured to her. 'Follow me,' I said and started along the narrow deck toward the bow.

Just as I came in front of the cabin, I heard the splash of oars and the rowboat moving away. In the prow of the boat was the younger sailor, still holding a six-pronged grappling hook with the rope trailing behind it. He stared, almost frozen with fear. Slowly I raised the muzzle of the rifle at him. He didn't hesitate. In one motion, he dove from the boat and thrashed swimming through the water after the rowboat.

I watched him for a moment, then turned to Alma. 'I guess we lost our crew.'

Alma looked at me. 'Now what do we do?'

'We'll figure out something,' I answered, sounding more confident than I felt. I touched her hand. It was trembling. I pressed her palm into mine. 'Take it easy,' I said. 'We'll manage. We survived this far.'

Her eyes filled with tears. 'I killed a man.'

'He would have killed you,' I said. 'It's okay.'

She began to cry and I pulled her head to my chest. 'Calm down,' I said softly, stroking her head. 'It couldn't be helped.'

She clung to me. 'When we get to Iquitos, I will go to confession.'

I felt her body pressing warmly against me. 'Whatever you say,' I said.

A note of surprise came into her voice. She looked up at me. 'You have a hard on.'

I tried to move away from her but she held tightly to me. 'I'm normal,' I said.

'I thought you didn't like me,' she said.

'I told you. You were Angelo's girl.' I moved away from her and she turned her face up to me. I kissed her quickly, then stepped back. 'I like you. But we have other things to do before we begin to play.'

She began to smile confidently. 'Did you ever have any Peruvian pussy?' she asked teasingly.

'No,' I answered, smiling back at her. 'The only thing Peruvian I've ever had is Peruvian blue.'

'You're in for a treat. Peruvian pussy is even better than Peruvian blue. You'll never have a better high than that.'

I laughed. 'Stop. You'll get me crazy.' I walked down the deck to the stern of the boat. I opened the small hatch to the engine room. I looked up at her. 'Keep your eyes open and call me if any of them try to come over here. I'm going to check out the engine.'

'Okay,' she said.

There were only three steps to the ladder into the engine room and the room was no more than three feet high. I hunched over and found a small electric bulb next to the wall. There was no switch to turn it on with, so I turned the bulb into the socket and it lit dimly. I turned to look at the engine. It was a simple old-fashioned, two-cylinder Harvester motor that had probably once belonged to a small tractor. The motor could be started by a flywheel pulled by a cord much like an outboard. Next to the motor was a bank of six twelve-volt car batteries and above them was a gas tank. I peered at the gauge of the tank. It showed almost half full. I then checked the gears. There were only two positions. Forward and rear. Simple enough, I thought, I could handle it. I unscrewed the bulb slightly and climbed out of the engine room.

She was standing at the stern and watching the land around the cove. 'I don't see anything moving.'

'Good,' I said. I smiled. 'I think we'll be okay. I can handle the engine and piloting the boat should be easy.'

'Fine,' she replied. 'But do you know where we're going?'

'Iquitos downstream,' I said.

'Great,' she said sarcastically. 'But do you know anything about the waterfront down there? What docks would be safe, which would not?'

I looked at her. 'Don't you know anything about Iquitos?'

'I've never been there,' she answered. 'Why should I? It's the fucking ass end of the world. No one in Lima would ever go there except for business. Like I told you, there are no roads out of there because of the mountains. You get in by plane or by riverboat from Brazil and Colombia, and I've never had a reason to be there.'

'Angelo had arranged for us to get out by plane,' I said. 'He had a contact.'

'Do you know the contact?' she asked.

'No,' I said. 'But once we're in town, I figure we'll be able to make him.'

She was silent for a moment. 'You don't know Peru,' she said. 'Iquitos's a rough town and they'll make you long before you make them.'

'We have to take our chances,' I said. 'There are no other places to go.'

She pointed out toward the river. 'The fishermen are going in.'

I watched them moving downriver toward Iquitos. They were leaving in a group. Only a few seemed to be laying back. Maybe they were trying to fill up their nets. 'As soon as they're all going we'll start,' I said.

'We'll be traveling in daylight,' she said.

'We have no choice,' I said. 'We can't stay here. The fucking Indians will be coming after us.'

She shook her head. 'I'm frightened,' she said in a tight voice.

'We'll be all right,' I said, wishing I could feel as sure as I sounded.

She seemed embarrassed. 'I have to change. I peed in my pants.'

I laughed. 'Don't feel bad. It's normal. You go below and clean up. I'll stay up here.'

I stepped into the small wheelhouse. It was only two steps higher than the deck but it gave a good vantage point to see anything moving toward us. I found a pack of cigarettes I had left yesterday on the bench and took one out and dragged on it. The smoke helped even though it was old and damp I coughed and kept my eyes on the cove.

My eyes were burning by the time she came up. I kept thinking that I had seen lights flashing in the forest against the shore but then there was nothing.

44

'I feel better,' she said. 'I washed up. And fresh clothes help.'

'You look good,' I said. I rubbed my eyes. 'I must look like hell.'

'Not too bad,' she smiled. 'You didn't have much sleep.'

I nodded. I looked out toward the river. There were about three or four fishing boats still out there. 'I wish they'd get the hell out,' I said.

'It will be dawn soon,' she said. 'They'll be gone then.'

I grunted and didn't answer.

She took a vial from the pocket of her jeans. 'Peruvian blue,' she said. 'I need some help.' Quickly she took two snorts then handed the vial to me. 'We both need the help,' she said.

I took the vial from her. Quickly I took two hits in each nostril. I felt my head open up and my eyes stopped burning. I was wide awake. Who needs sleep? I gave the vial back to her and laughed. 'Party time,' I said.

She laughed. 'You're feeling better.'

'Check,' I said.

'Look!' She pointed at the river.

One of the fishing boats was coming into the cove, its searchlight pointing at us. I picked up the automatic rifle. We watched the boat coming slowly toward us.

I pressed her shoulder. 'Get down on the deck,' I said. 'I don't want anyone to see you.'

She stretched out on the deck, her automatic held closely between her hands. I waited until the fishing boat was near then blew out its searchlight with a rifle shot.

The voice was in English. 'What the hell are you doing?' the man said angrily.

'Who the hell are you?' I shouted back.

'Angelo?' the man questioned.

'He's not here,' I answered.

'Jed Stevens?' the man asked.

I waited for a moment. 'Right,' I said.

'Vince Campanella,' the man replied. 'I have the deal with Angelo to take him to Medellin.'

'You have the plane?' I asked.

'That's my business,' he said. 'Where's Angelo? You were supposed to meet me in the next cove downriver toward Iquito. What the hell are you doing here?'

'Nobody told me,' I said.

'Get Angelo,' he said. 'We have to get moving.'

'Angelo is dead,' I said. I didn't want to tell him how Angelo had died. 'Our crew tried to jump us.'

'Where are they?' he asked.

'Dead and gone,' I said.

'Is the girl with you?' he asked.

'She's here,' I said.

'Can I come aboard?' he asked.

I kept the rifle pointed at his belly. 'Only you.'

He climbed over the small railing and stood up straight when he reached the deck. He was a tall man, six feet two, wearing green khaki shirt and pants, with blue eyes and red hair and beard. 'I spoke to your uncle yesterday, he wanted to know if I had heard from Angelo. You were supposed to be in yesterday, that's why I started out to look for you.'

Alma got to her feet, she still held the gun in her hands. 'Now, what do we do?' she asked.

'We get you out of here,' he said. 'We're going to give you a tow and move into the next cove. Then we unload the cargo and I take you into Iquitos and put you on a plane to Lima; from there you go to New York.'

'Angelo had a plan,' I said. 'What happens with that?'

'I'll take care of it,' he said. 'Your uncle told me to handle it.'

'When can I call him?' I asked.

'This evening when we get into the hotel,' he said.

'What happens with me?' Alma said.

'You go to Lima with him,' he said. 'You can be his tour guide.'

46

6

It was early morning and the sun was rising over the trees as we entered the other cove. There was a rickety old dock that came out from the shore. The men jumped quickly over the side of the boat and tied up to the dock. Vince took out a walkie talkie and spoke into it. Ten minutes later an open two-ton truck pulled up beside the dock. Right behind it came a jeep with two men and parked next to it.

Vince called out to his men in Spanish. One of them climbed up on the cab of the truck and sat there, a light sub machine gun cradled in his arm as he kept watch. Then the four men, two from the fishing boat and the other two from the jeep, began to unload the bales of coca leaves from the boat and load them onto the truck.

He turned to me. 'Get your bags together, we're moving out of here.'

I looked at him. 'But what about the boat?'

He shook his head. 'Screw it. Two of my men will pull it out into the middle of the river and scuttle it. I'm not taking any chances of that boat being seen in Iquito. I have a hunch that the captain had also tipped off customs. He would have gotten a reward if he had turned in the cargo.'

'Wouldn't it be dangerous if we showed up there?' I asked.

'We are not going into the Iquitos airport. I have the plane on an airstrip not far from here. It's cut out from a former rubber plantation. We're organized. We've been working out of here a long time.'

I turned to Alma. 'How do you feel about it?'

'Okay,' she said. 'I'll be happy to get home.'

'We won't be landing in Juan Chavez International. There is too much paperwork for Police and Customs. We'll put you

47

down at an airstrip about sixty kilometers from Lima. I'll come in low behind the mountains so that radar doesn't pick us up.'

'Then how do we get in town?' she asked.

'Don't worry. We'll have a car there to take you in on the Pan American Highway. You'll be okay.' He smiled. 'Now get yourself packed, we need to be moving fast.'

He watched her disappear into the cabin then he turned to me. 'Angelo told me I would collect the fare when we met.'

'Yes,' I said. 'Forty grand for you to Medellin and then to Panama.'

'Sixty now,' he said.

'You're being greedy, Vince,' I said.

'No,' he said. 'Forget that we had to find you, no charge for that. That's for the family. But you to Lima from here adds another two thousand kilometers to our flight. That costs money.'

'How much?' I asked.

'An extra twenty,' he said.

'I don't know if Uncle Rocco would like that,' I said.

'He told me if I got you out I would get a bonus,' he said. 'I'm just covering my extra expenses.'

I laughed. 'You're a hustler. You remind me of my cousin.'

He laughed with me. 'Do I get the money?'

'Do I have a choice?' I asked.

He laughed again. 'Your uncle wants you home.'

'Okay,' I said. Then I looked at him. 'Who pays for the plane from Panama to Miami?'

'If you have the cash I can handle it for you.'

'After the extra twenty I haven't got enough,' I said. 'I'll tell my uncle and he'll work it out.'

'Good enough for me,' he said. 'You can give me the money once we're airborne.'

It was a few minutes after six o'clock when we began our descent toward Lima. Five and a half hours in a hard plastic seat behind the pilot wasn't my idea of comfort. But the DC3 wasn't made for passengers. It was a freight carrier.

Vince looked back at us from the pilot's seat. 'We'll be on the ground in half an hour.'

I groaned and stretched. 'Thank God,' I said. 'I don't think I could take another hour in these seats.'

Vince laughed. 'This ain't no 707, that's for sure.' He turned serious. 'Do you have the fare?'

'I have it ready for you,' I answered. During the flight while he was busy taking care of business I managed to open the attaché case and get the sixty thousand out for him. There had been several large manila envelopes in the case and I had put the money in two of them. I reached over his shoulder and gave them to him.

He slipped them down into the map racks beside his seat. 'Thanks,' he said.

'Don't you want to check it?' I asked.

He smiled. 'You're part of the Family. I trust you.'

'Thank you,' I said. 'I don't know what I would have done without you.'

'We all have our jobs,' he said. 'You just tell your uncle what I've done.'

'I will,' I said. We seemed to be skimming down over the mountains. Below I could see what seemed like a small town. 'Where are we?'

'We're passing Huancavelica and heading toward the coast,' he said. 'If you look forward you can begin to see the Pacific.'

I stood behind him. I could see the blue waters of the ocean. I turned to Alma, who had stood up next to me. 'The water is sparkling like blue diamonds,' I said.

'Better get back into your seats and belt up. It usually gets turbulent coming down from the mountains to the ocean,' Vince said. 'You made it this far, I don't want you to break your skull in the plane.'

He hadn't been joking. The little plane tossed around like a leaf in the wind and then finally when I was almost ready to throw up, it suddenly straightened out and a few minutes later I felt the wheels touch the ground.

As soon as the plane had stopped, he opened the door and Alma and I rushed out. The cool evening air was great. I breathed in deeply. 'Jesus,' I said.

He smiled at me. 'You have to get used to it.'

'Not me,' I said. 'I'll stick with the big jets.'

He gestured to his co-pilot. 'Get their bags out.' Then he turned to one of the men standing near us. He spoke quickly in Spanish. The man nodded and ran off to the small building at the end of the runway.

He turned back to me. 'He's getting a car and driver for you and they're bringing a fuel truck over to me.'

In five minutes an old '65 Chevy four-door stopped in front of us. The men began to slam the luggage into the trunk.

I turned to Vince and held out my hand. 'Thank you.'

'It's okay,' he said. 'When you talk to your uncle please give him my condolences.'

'I will,' I said.

He turned to Alma and held out his hand. 'You're a good lady. Take care of him.'

She nodded and kissed his cheek. 'I will,' she said. 'Thank you.'

We got into the car as the fuel truck began rolling up. He waved his hand and we waved back and the driver kicked the car into gear and moved toward the highway.

It was dark and after eight o'clock when the driver placed our valises in front of the Hotel El Gran Bolivar. Alma whispered to me. 'Give him a tip.'

I gave the driver a hundred dollar bill. He touched his hand in a half salute. 'Gracias, señor,' he smiled.

'Okay,' I said and turned to pick up our bags.

She placed a hand on my arm. I looked at her. 'No,' she turned back to me. 'We won't stay here,' she said. 'There is always police hanging around in the lobby. And the way we are dressed they will be very curious.'

She had to be right. We were still wearing the same dirty clothing we had been wearing on the boat. 'Where do we go then?' I asked.

'My apartment,' she answered. 'It's not too far from here. I have a large apartment in a new building near the *Parque de Universario*.' She waved to a taxi waiting at the head of the line parked near the hotel entrance.

Twenty minutes later we got out of the elevator and walked

along the narrow marble-floor corridor to her apartment. She rang the doorbell.

I looked at her. 'You have someone living with you?'

She smiled nodding. 'My mother.'

I was curious. 'Won't she be upset that you are bringing a man with you?'

She laughed. 'My mother is very liberal.'

I looked puzzled.

She laughed again. 'She's not really my mother,' she explained. 'She's my maid but she's been with me so long I call her mother.'

The door opened and a small dark Indian-looking woman looked out at me. She smiled when she saw Alma. Alma hugged her and kissed her cheek. They spoke rapidly in Spanish, then the small woman held her hand out and smiled shyly. '*Encantada*,' she said.

'Thank you,' I said, reaching for the valises.

She shook her head quickly. 'No.'

'You come in with me,' Alma said. 'She'll bring the bags. Let me show you the apartment.'

It was a large apartment. The living-room wall was covered with photographs of Alma and framed magazine covers with pictures of Alma. I looked at her. 'You're really photogenic.'

She laughed. 'That's how I make my living. I'm a model.'

'I didn't know,' I said.

'You thought I was a whore,' she said wickedly.

'No,' I answered. 'I just thought you were a party girl.'

'I'm that too,' she laughed. 'Peruvian pussy.'

'Okay,' I said. 'Whatever you say.'

The living room was furnished with modern Italian furniture, plastic chairs, long white fabric couches, milk-white shaded lamps. 'Come here,' she said, gesturing to the long window. She opened a door and led me out on to a balcony.

We were on the seventh floor of the apartment house looking over a park. 'It's really beautiful, isn't it?' she asked.

'Very,' I said.

'Are you surprised that I could have an expensive place like this?' she asked.

'That's none of my business,' I answered.

'But, I want you to know,' she said. 'I like you and I don't want you to have the wrong idea.'

I was silent.

'When I was seventeen I fell in love with a wonderful man. He was much older than I and also married. I was his mistress for almost eight years. He sent me to school and gave me an education and helped me in my career. Last year he died. He left me this apartment and some money. I was not only grateful to him for what he did, I also loved him. It's only been in the last six months that I started going out again. But it wasn't much fun for me until your cousin asked me to go on this trip with him. I thought it would be a wonderful change.' She looked up at me. 'I really wanted to get away from here and forget my yesterdays.'

I took her hand. 'And did you?'

'After the last few days, I'm beginning to think I did,' she said.

'Good,' I said.

She led me back into the apartment. 'Let me show you to your room.' I followed her across the living room. 'Besides,' she said, 'I think you want a bath and a chance to clean up as much as I do.'

'I do,' I answered. 'But do you have a telephone? I have to call my uncle.'

'The telephone's in my room,' she said. 'You give me the number and I'll get it for you.'

I sat on the edge of her bed as she gave the operator the numbers. We waited a few minutes then she turned to me. 'The operator says the lines to the States are backed up. They'll call you back in a few hours.'

'Damn,' I said.

'That happens here all the time,' she said. 'You have to be patient. Take your bath and clean up then we will have some dinner and by that time the call will come through.'

7

I followed her from her room to the bathroom. She gestured to the door on the opposite wall. 'That's your bedroom,' she said. 'The bathroom is between us.' She opened a mirrored cabinet over the twin sinks set in a marble counter. 'You have everything you need here. Razor, shaving cream, cologne. I'll fill the tub for you.'

I opened the door into my bedroom. My valise was spread open on the bed but the clothing was gone. I turned back to her.

She anticipated my question. 'Mamacita is cleaning your things. She'll have them pressed and ready for you by the time you get out of the tub.'

'I can't believe it,' I smiled. 'This is better than any five star hotel.'

'It's only the beginning,' she laughed. She turned on the faucets in the large oval bathtub then took a bottle of multi-color bath salts and sprinkled them over the water. A strange exotic perfume began to fill the air. She found a small white wooden paddle and mixed the salts into the water then turned to me. 'Get out of your clothes,' she smiled. 'And shave. It must be at least three days since you have shaved.'

I stared at her. 'What should I do with these clothes?'

'Throw them on the floor,' she said. 'Mamacita will throw them away. They're no good for anything.'

I was still looking at her. 'Then what are you going to do?'

She began to take off her clothes. 'I need a bath too,' she laughed. 'It's a big tub, especially for two. Are you shy?'

'No,' I answered. 'But I am surprised.'

'I don't know why,' she laughed. 'You've seen me naked before and I've seen you.'

53

'How come you've seen me?' I asked.

'Don't be silly,' she answered. 'We were all in that tiny cabin. There was no place we could conceal ourselves. Now get going.' She crossed to the side of the bathroom and straddled the bidet. 'I'll have my pussy washed before you finish shaving.'

She was already in the tub by the time I began to step into the water. The water felt warm and soft. It felt good against my skin.

'Okay?' she asked.

'Perfect,' I said.

She smiled and stood up and took a large cream-colored plastic bottle with a plunger spout. 'Stand up,' she said. 'It's a special bath soap. I'll spread it over you. It will make your skin soft.'

Slowly she spread the soap over me with a light hand. 'Now it's my turn,' she said, handing me the soap.

I felt clumsy. My touch was not as light as hers. She turned slowly and let me do her back and then turned again to face me. I looked at her questioningly. She smiled. 'Don't be silly. Finish.' Quickly I spread the soap over her. Her breasts felt heavy in my hand and her belly strong and flat. Very lightly I spread the soap over her pubis.

'Harder,' she said. 'Get it into my hair.'

I did as she asked and then brought the soap down between her legs. She was looking into my eyes as I gave her the bottle. She squirted more soap over my penis and testicles.

She was breathing lightly. 'Did you feel my love button sticking out?'

I nodded.

She began massaging my genitals. 'You're getting hard,' she said.

'You keep on doing that and I'll come in your hands,' I said.

'I've come twice already,' she said. She put an arm over my shoulder and began to pull me down to her.

We made it to our knees then I couldn't hold it any longer. The spasm tore through my body. It felt as if it would never stop. 'Jesus!' I said. I looked down at her. 'I've come all over you.'

'That's beautiful,' she smiled. 'That's the best skin lotion ever made.'

In the distance I could hear the telephone ringing. Then I felt her hand shaking my shoulder. Slowly I sat up. We were both naked in the bed. 'Oh, boy,' I said. 'I really passed out.'

'You were entitled to it,' she smiled as she spoke in a soft voice. 'I thought you would never stop coming.'

I shook my head. 'Did I hear the telephone?'

'It's your States call,' she said. Quickly she held out a vial. 'Take a snort,' she said. 'You're still half asleep.'

I nodded. As I packed my nose, my head opened up. 'Where's the phone?' I asked.

'Here,' she said picking it up from her bedside table.

I held the receiver to my ear. It was an American voice I heard. 'Mr. Stevens?' she asked.

'Yes.'

'I have Mr. Di Stefano for you,' she said.

There was a click then I heard my uncle's voice. It sounded heavy and sad. '*Angelo è morto*,' he said. It wasn't a question, he already knew it.

'Yes,' I said. 'I'm sorry.'

'When did it happen?' he asked quietly.

'Almost a week ago,' I said. 'The captain tried to hijack us. He shot Angelo in the back. It was over in a minute.'

'Where were you?' he asked.

'I was down below, in the cabin. When I heard the shots I grabbed the automatic just in time to put the captain away as he came down the cabin steps. I took out one of the other sailors. We made it downstream into a cove with the other two sailors until they got ambitious. I got rid of them before Vince found us. If it weren't for him we would never have made it.'

'You said, "we", was there someone else with you?'

'Yes,' I said. 'Angelo brought a girl from Lima. He wanted an interpreter.'

'Angelo wanted to get laid,' my uncle said mirthlessly. 'Can we get him back to the States?'

'No, uncle,' I answered. 'He's five hundred kilometers up the Amazon in the jungle.'

My uncle was silent for a moment. 'I told him not to go,' he said. 'But he never listened to me. He always wanted to prove himself.'

I had no answer.

'I didn't want you to go. I told Angelo that you had no part in this,' he said.

'Angelo was my cousin and I loved him,' I said. 'Of course I would go with him. He came to Sicily with me.'

'I want you home,' he said. 'When can you get a plane?'

'It's night now,' I said. 'I'll check the first thing in the morning.'

'Get on Braniff,' he said. 'I don't trust any of the foreign airlines. You fly American.'

'Yes, uncle,' I said.

'You call me the moment you book your flight.'

'Yes, uncle,' I said.

'When you get home, we'll arrange for a mass for Angelo,' he said.

'I'll be there,' I said.

His voice was husky. 'The girl? Is she all right?'

'Yes, uncle.'

'Was she a nice girl?'

'Yes, uncle,' I said. 'Angelo had good taste. He didn't go with tramps.'

'Take care of her,' he said. 'Don't forget that you're the only man in the family that I have left.'

'Thank you, uncle,' I said.

'Take care of yourself, too,' he said. 'And call me tomorrow.'

'Yes, uncle,' I said.

'I love you,' he said.

'I love you too,' I said. The telephone clicked off in my hand. I gave her the receiver.

There were tears in her eyes. 'How is he?' she asked.

'Heartbroken,' I said. 'Angelo was the light in his eyes.'

8

We had breakfast on the balcony. The sky was blue, the sun bright and the air fresh. The old lady served a large plate of fried eggs, onions and tomatoes and slices of thin grilled meat covered with a spicy salsa. The bread was hot and dark and the slices were covered with butter. The coffee was strong and hot. I was starved. I ate like there was no tomorrow.

Alma laughed. 'Do you always eat like this?'

'Only when I'm hungry,' I mumbled through a mouthful. 'At least it's real food, not that shit we had on the river.'

'Mamacita is a great cook,' she said.

'I'll agree to that,' I said. I looked at her. 'You don't eat much.'

'Girls have to watch their diet,' she smiled. 'Peruvian women tend to get fat.'

'Like Peruvian pussy,' I laughed.

'That's good fat,' she laughed with me. 'You didn't seem to complain.'

'Beautiful,' I said. 'The best.'

She leaned across the table and kissed my cheek. 'You're sweet.'

The old lady stood at the balcony railing. She turned to Alma and spoke.

Alma rose from her chair and looked over the railing. She gestured to me and I joined her. 'Down there across the street. That car with two men standing next to it. They might be police.'

'You don't know?' I asked.

'It looks like a police car but I don't see any insignia,' she said. 'Could be plainclothes men. Their cars are not marked.'

'How do you know they're looking at us?' I asked.

'I don't know,' she said. 'But Vince said that the Iquitos police might have been tipped off about us. If they had, they would have notified Lima headquarters because it's the national headquarters.'

'And if they are not police?'

'Then they are the *cocainas* still looking for the property.' She raised her hand to mine and took my arm away from the railing. 'Get dressed,' she said. 'I have some friends in headquarters. My patron was a general in the army and once the *jefe* of police. At one time we were all close. I'll make a few calls and see what I can find out.'

I went to my room. The old lady was better than any valet. She had my clothes all laid out on the bed. A dark-blue blazer with gold buttons, gray flannel slacks, a light-blue shirt and a narrow black knit tie. My black oxfords were polished to a high shine and the silk socks carefully placed in each shoe. It took me less than five minutes to dress. There was only one thing I thought I might need. I opened the attaché case and took the automatic from it and slipped it into my jacket pocket. Then I took the ten thousand dollars I had promised Alma and put it into a manila envelope. I placed my passport and return air tickets in my breast pocket and few packages of bills in my pants pocket. I walked through the bathroom into her room.

She was still speaking on the telephone. The old lady was taking a dress from the closet and placing it out for her. I waited in the doorway until she put down the telephone.

'They are the police,' she said. 'But they are not looking for you.'

'Then we have nothing to worry about,' I said.

She shook her head. 'They are looking for Angelo. And they think that you are him.' She dropped her dressing-gown to the floor and stepped into lace bikini panties, then quickly she fastened a matching lace brassière between her breasts. She looked up at me as she sat on the edge of her bed and pulled up her nylons. 'You're staring,' she smiled.

'You're a tease,' I said. I tossed the manila envelope on the bed beside her.

'What's that?' she asked.

'The money I promised,' I answered.

She was silent for a moment then handed the envelope to me. 'You don't have to do it,' she said. 'I don't need the money.'

'I made the promise,' I said, returning it to her.

'But we were different then,' she said. 'Now we are friends and lovers.'

'I want you to keep the money,' I said. 'More now than I felt before, because of the way we feel about each other.'

She rose from the bed and kissed me. 'You're a lovely man,' she said softly.

I held her for a moment then let her go. 'Thank you.'

She took the dress from the bed and slipped it on over her body. 'Mamacita!' she called.

The old woman hurried into the bedroom. Alma spoke quickly to her. Mamacita nodded and fastened the snap of the dress near the base of her neck. Then she took the envelope from the bed and left the room.

Alma turned back to me. 'How do I look?' she asked.

'Beautiful,' I said.

'I'll fix my makeup,' she said. 'You pack your valise, we'll be leaving for the airport in a few minutes.'

'What about the police outside?' I asked.

'There won't be any problems,' she said. 'I spoke to the captain of police. He'll call them off and take us to the airport in his car.'

'He believed your story?'

She nodded. 'Of course. It was the truth anyway. But he will want to see your passport before we go. You have your visa, and it wouldn't hurt if you also left a thousand dollar bill with it.'

'I thought he was a friend of yours,' I said.

'If he wasn't a friend he wouldn't do this for us,' she answered. 'You don't understand. Our officials don't earn much money, they need much help.'

'We have the same thing in the States sometimes but we call it graft,' I said.

'You have no right to be sarcastic,' she said quietly. 'You've been breaking almost every law we have on the books.'

I stared at her. She was right. Who was I to cast stones? I took her hand. 'I apologize.'

She squeezed my hand. 'Now, hurry. Get packed.'

I closed the valise and locked it, then placed the attaché case on top of it. I left them on the bed and walked out onto the balcony. The small black Volkswagen was still parked across the street. While I was watching, a large four-door Ford Fairlane pulled into the street beside it. I couldn't see the driver but the two men who had been standing next to the Volks seemed to speak to the driver in the other car then the Ford moved and the men got into the Volks and moved away. I watched them all until they had turned the corner then went back into the apartment. I took my valise and attaché case and walked into the living room.

Alma was waiting for me. I stared at her. She had a dark mink coat loosely thrown over her shoulders and on the floor beside her were two large valises, a folded hanging bag and a small square compact jewelry bag. All Louis Vuitton. I smiled at her. 'You've got class. Planning a trip?'

She laughed. 'I'm going to New York with you.'

'Hey,' I said. 'I don't remember talking about it.'

'Don't be stupid,' she said. 'Do you think they would have believed me if I hadn't told him that you were taking me to New York with you?'

'It's not that easy,' I said. 'You need a visa.'

She laughed again. 'I have a multiple entry visa to the States. After all I went to school there.'

I was silent.

'I also went to school in Paris for a year,' she said.

'Are you planning to go there too?' I asked.

'Maybe,' she smiled. 'But I won't be any problem to you. My patron left me a small apartment in the Hotel Pierre.'

I started to laugh. 'Maybe you could take me in. I don't have an apartment in New York.'

'You can be my guest as long as you want,' she said.

The buzzer rang from the house phone near the door. She pressed a button and spoke into it. House phones always had a tinny sound and this was no exception. The man's voice sounded thin and excited. She spoke to him. His voice came through again. Finally she nodded and replied with the only word I could understand in English. 'Okay.'

'*El capitano* is downstairs in the garage under the apartment house. He has kept the two detectives with him. He says they tell him that there are three suspicious characters waiting in a car just outside the entrance to the garage. He thinks they are *pistoleros* because the car has Colombian license plates. He doesn't want us to open the door to anyone except himself.'

'Shit,' I said. I took the automatic from my pocket. 'Do you have another door to the apartment?'

'Service door through the kitchen,' she said.

'We better push a table against it,' I said. 'We don't want anybody to come in from the back.'

She called to Mamacita and I followed them into the kitchen and helped them move a heavy wooden table against the door then we walked back into the living room. She turned and spoke to the old woman. The old woman began weeping, she hugged Alma and kissed her. Alma kissed her and spoke more to her and finally Mamacita left the room.

Alma looked up at me. 'I told her to go to her room and lock the door behind her. That the police were here and they would take care of everything.'

'Good,' I said. 'Maybe you should go with her.'

She shook her head. 'I have to be there with you. You wouldn't recognize the captain's voice.'

'Why are you doing this for me?' I asked. 'I'd feel better if you could be safe.'

'I'm with you,' she said simply. 'You pulled me out of the water from the piranhas. Besides we are friends and lovers.'

I didn't speak. Just leaned over and kissed her. 'Friends and lovers,' I said.

9

'Ten minutes,' I said to her. 'He's taking his time.'

She looked at me. 'He's a very careful man. I'm sure he knows what he is doing.'

'Maybe,' I said. 'But I'm getting nervous.' I moved to the front door and peered through the wide-angle tiny glass peek hole. I could see down the hallway to the elevator door. There was nothing moving. I turned back to her. 'Can you reach him in the garage?'

'No,' she answered. 'It only works one way. When they call here.'

A moment later the tinny sound came through the house phone. The man's voice crackled through the speaker. Alma replied to him quickly. He spoke again, a nervous urgency in his voice. Alma turned and looked at me. There was a puzzled expression on her face, then she spoke to him. 'Okay.'

She let go of the speaker button and the house phone went quiet. 'I don't understand it,' she said. 'He called me Alma. He never called me by my first name before.'

'But that is your name,' I said.

'Yes,' she answered. 'But you don't understand. He is a very correct man. And this is not his kind of etiquette.'

'Okay,' I said. 'What else did he say?'

'First, he asked if we had our bags packed, and if you had your attaché case. I said we were ready then he said he's coming up in the elevator.' She shook her head. 'He didn't seem quite like himself.'

'I think he's in trouble. Otherwise, he would not have known or even asked about my attaché case,' I said. I turned to the peek hole in the door and called over my shoulder to her. 'You hadn't said anything about the attaché case, had you?'

'Don't be an asshole,' she said angrily. 'I am not stupid.'

I laughed. 'I never said that you were stupid. But we better find a quick way out of here.'

'This is the only way,' she answered. 'The kitchen door will only take us down the stairway.'

I looked through the peek hole. The elevator doors began to open. I gestured to her. 'Check. See if it's your friend.'

She glanced through the peek hole. 'It's him. But there is another man behind him.'

I looked through again. Her friend was not a tall man. But he wore a police uniform and high-heeled boots that gave some height to him. The flap on his leather holster was snapped open and no gun in it. There was also no gun in his hand. The man behind him was a head taller than him and his arm seemed to be pushing from the captain's back.

His voice came through the door. 'Alma! Estoy Felipe!'

'What do we do now?' she whispered quickly.

I slipped the safety from my gun and stepped behind the blind side of the door to hide myself. I held the gun tightly in my clasped hands and nodded, whispering to her. 'Let him in.'

She turned the knob and stepped back as the door began to open. The captain seemed to be pushed into the apartment. He stumbled against Alma. The other man was still on the other side of the door and I couldn't see him.

'The Americano!' the man said harshly.

Alma kept silent. She gestured to the bedroom behind her. The man shouted in Spanish at them. I didn't understand what he had said, but I could understand the tone of his voice. Alma shook her head. The man shouted at her again and started to move into the apartment toward her. Now it was my turn.

I slammed my heavy automatic against his gun-hand and wrist. His gun fell to the floor as he turned to me and tried to grab my arm. There were a few things I learned in the Army. I stepped back from him slightly, then kicked him in the balls. He grunted and bent over forward, this time I laid the gun over the side of his head. Now he was on the floor. He stared at me then tried to reach for the gun.

But this time the policeman was fast. He had picked the gun up from the floor. He looked at me and gestured with the gun. 'My revolver,' he said.

'Good,' I said.

The policeman bent over the man and quickly snapped a pair of handcuffs on his wrists behind his back. He rolled the man over on his back and angrily snapped at him in a harsh voice. The man snarled back at him silently. The policeman smashed his gun against the man's face. A trickle of blood began to come down from the man's mouth and nose. The policeman began to hit the man again.

Alma spoke quickly. 'Not on the white rug. It won't clean.'

The policeman stared at her then half smiled and nodded. He wasn't a big man but he was strong. Easily, he pulled the man across the floor out to the marble balcony, then he hit the man across the face again. This time the blood began flowing. The policeman growled at him. The man shook his head silently.

I spoke to the policeman. 'Do you know anything about him?'

The policeman answered me in English. 'Nothing, only that he's Colombian. We thought there were only three of them. We had watched them in the car. He was hiding in the garage and he got me when I got out of the car.'

'Where are your men?' I asked.

'In the street watching the others in the car,' he answered. He turned to Alma and spoke in Spanish.

She answered in English. 'I don't know anything about why they are after us. Maybe they had the same tip that you had about the other man.'

I looked at her admiringly. She didn't use Angelo's name. No reason she should bring attention to his name.

'But did you ever meet this Angelo Di Stefano?' the captain asked.

'Possibly,' she said. 'Maybe at one of the discos or a party. I meet many people.'

'And this man?' he asked, nodding toward me. 'How did you meet him?'

'One of my girlfriends from school in the States. She called me and said that he would be calling on me.'

He looked at her. 'But you went away for almost two weeks with him. Where were you?'

'I was at my small place in the country,' she said.

'And you're going to the States with him? It seems like a quick romance,' he said.

'Love comes in mysteriously sudden ways,' she said.

He turned to me. 'You know about guns?'

'I was in Special Forces in Vietnam,' I said.

'Where did you get the gun?' he asked.

Alma answered quickly. 'I gave it to him. It used to be the general's.'

He was silent for a moment then turned back to the Colombian. He spoke quickly to him in Spanish. Again the man wouldn't answer.

The captain picked the man up and turned him around, pushing his belly into the balcony railing. Holding his revolver against the back of the man's head, with his other hand he unlocked the handcuffs and pulled them off the man's hands. Still holding his revolver to the man's head he again snapped at him in Spanish. The Colombian snapped angrily back at him. It sounded to me like he was cursing at the captain.

The captain moved as if he were shrugging his shoulders. Then he slammed the revolver against the back of the Colombian's head. The man half slumped over the railing. The captain moved gracefully. He shoved his hand between the man's legs and lifted him under his groin. The Colombian flew up over the railing as the captain stepped backward, and he fell screaming down toward the street.

The captain looked over the railing for a few moments. A faint thump came up from the street. The captain turned to us. His face was expressionless. 'Clumsy, stupid son of a bitch,' he said noncommittally. 'He landed on the roof of a new car and ruined it.'

We didn't say anything.

The captain placed his revolver back into his holster. 'He would have killed all of us,' he said.

'I know,' I said.

'Do you want to take a look?' he asked.

I shook my head. 'I saw enough of that in Vietnam.'

He nodded. 'Very well. Let us go back inside. I will call for more men and while we wait for them, I will check your papers.'

There is nothing like a police escort to take you to the airport. Two motorcycles with sirens wailing in front of a white and black police car, then we in the captain's car with another black and white behind us. People watching us curiously as we sped through the streets.

Alma and I were in the back seat, a uniformed policeman drove the car and Captain Gonzales sat beside him in the passenger seat. The captain turned back to us. 'I think we're okay,' he said. 'There's no sign of the *Colombianos*.'

'I wonder where they went?' I asked.

'Who knows?' he answered. 'My men lost them in traffic when they took off after the accident.'

Accident was a polite way of expressing it. Especially since he pushed the bastard over the railing. He checked his watch. 'You missed the Braniff flight already,' he said. 'It took off at two o'clock and their next flight won't be until tomorrow.'

'Shit,' I said.

'Nothing to worry about,' he said comfortably. 'Air Peru takes off for New York at four o'clock. I can get you on that.'

I looked at Alma. She nodded. 'It's a good flight. They have a first class section. I've taken it a number of times.'

'Okay,' I said to the captain. 'We'll take it.'

'They won't accept your Braniff ticket,' he said. 'You'll have to buy a new ticket.' He reached his hand back to me. 'Give me the money and your papers. I'll arrange everything.'

I took my hand out of my inside jacket pocket. I laid two one-thousand dollar bills on him, and with it I gave him my passport and exit visa. 'Get a ticket for Alma while you're at it.'

'Of course,' he said and shoved it into his pocket. 'It's three o'clock now. I'll set you up in the VIP lounge.'

'Thank you,' I said.

He looked at Alma. 'When are you expecting to come back?'

'I haven't thought about it,' she answered. 'I might go over to Paris for a quick visit.'

'That's very nice,' he said politely. 'Send me a telex when you're ready to return. I'll pick you up at the airport.'

'You're very kind, Felipe,' she smiled. 'I'll let you know.'

He left us with a detective in the VIP lounge as he went to arrange the formalities for the flight. Alma lit a cigarette and a hostess brought us two glasses of champagne. 'Excuse me a moment,' I said. 'I have to go to the john.'

'Hurry back,' she smiled.

I went to the toilet and pressed myself against the urinal as I opened my fly. I was doing real good until I looked in the mirror in front of me then I almost lost it and pissed on my pants. Quickly, I zipped up my fly and turned. Vince was standing behind me, leaning against the door.

'What the hell are you doing here?' I asked. 'I thought you would be gone.'

'I had to stay over,' he said. 'Did you talk to your uncle?'

'Yes,' I said.

'Good,' he said. 'Then you told him what I did?'

'Of course,' I answered. 'He was very pleased.'

'Okay,' he said. He took an automatic fitted with a silencer from his pocket. 'Then you'll never be able to deny that you and Angelo were screwed over the coca, that it was all tobacco leaves.'

'You're crazy,' I said.

'Twenty million dollars crazy,' he said moving toward me.

I saw the door open behind his back then there was a cough of another silencer and I was quick enough to get out of Vince's way as he pitched forward, his gun falling to the floor, the back of his head torn open with blood and brains into the urinal.

Captain Gonzales was standing in the doorway. 'One of the *Colombianos*,' he said.

I couldn't talk, I nodded.

'Now, get out of here,' he said. 'I'll have one of my men clean this up.'

I was still silent.

He half smiled. 'You're a lucky man,' he said. 'It's time for you to board the plane.'

10

Captain Gonzales gestured to one of his policemen as we stepped from the men's room. The policeman came toward us. The captain spoke quickly in Spanish to him. The policeman nodded and placed himself in front of the men's room door so that no one could enter.

I looked at Captain Gonzales questioningly.

'I want to get you and Alma on the plane before we have to bring the airport police into it. Once they get here, they'll drag in Immigration and you'll be tied up in formalities, and it might be two or three days before you could leave.' He smiled. 'I'm sure you're anxious to get home.'

'Thank you,' I said.

'You're welcome,' he said. 'After all, you saved my life back in the apartment.'

'And you saved mine,' I said.

'That is my duty,' he said. 'To protect innocent people.'

I held my hand out to him. 'But thank you again.'

We began walking to the lounge where Alma was waiting. 'Strange,' he said. 'I don't understand why the *Colombianos* followed us.'

'They probably had the same information that your department received. The only problem is that I was not the man they were searching for,' I answered.

'You didn't recognize the man in the toilet?'

I shook my head. 'No.'

'But he was going to kill you,' he said.

'I don't know why,' I answered. 'But thanks to you, he didn't.'

He nodded solemnly. 'I will have two more men with me

71

to take you on the plane. I don't want anything to happen to Alma and you.'

'I feel safer already,' I replied.

He laughed suddenly. 'Do you plan to return to Lima again?'

I laughed with him. 'I don't think so. I've had enough excitement with this visit.'

He nodded. 'I think that is wise of you.' He glanced at me as we began to approach Alma. 'There is no reason for you to tell anything to her about the incident in the bathroom. She has been frightened enough over this affair.'

'You're just in time,' Alma said. 'I just ordered a bottle of champagne.'

The captain smiled at her. 'You won't have time for it. I arranged to preboard you.'

'What's the hurry?' she asked. 'We have forty minutes before takeoff.'

'I want you on the plane before any other passengers get on. We will escort you aboard the plane. Then I will have my two detectives at the foot of the ramp checking the other passengers boarding. They saw three men in the car with Colombian plates.'

'You don't think they would be here?' she asked.

'I don't want to take any chances,' he said. He picked up her compact valise and the other small valise that she was carrying on board. 'Come,' he said.

We left the airport through the employee door. Alma and I walked across the crossway to the plane, the captain leading us, two detectives, one at our side and one following behind. Silently we climbed the steps into the plane. It took a moment for my eyes to get adjusted to the dark after the bright sunlight outside.

A stewardess smiled at us. '*Bienvenido*, Señorita Marissa.'

Alma smiled at her. She spoke in Spanish. The stewardess nodded. Apparently they had known each other. The girl led us forward to our seats. We were seated in the last row of first class with our backs to a bulkhead.

'You should be comfortable,' the stewardess said. 'There are only two other passengers in first class.'

'Thank you,' I said.

'May I serve you some champagne?' she asked.

Alma laughed and answered her in Spanish. Then she looked up at Captain Gonzales as she slipped into the window seat. 'Will you join us, Captain?' she asked.

He shook his head as he placed her valises in the overhead rack. 'No, thanks, I'm still working.'

'I'm sure that there is nothing to worry about now,' she said.

'I'll stop worrying when you've taken off,' he said. 'Enjoy your champagne. They're starting to board the passengers and I want to check them out with my men. I'll be back in a few minutes.'

The stewardess placed a bottle of champagne and glasses before us. Quickly she filled our glasses then walked out to the entrance to greet the new passengers.

I held my glass to Alma. 'We're getting great service,' I said. 'Gonzales is keeping a close eye on us. I wonder what he knows that we don't.'

'He's a policeman,' she said. 'They like to make themselves important.'

'It's more than that,' I said, thinking about how quickly he followed me into the toilet. 'But I'm not complaining. If it wasn't for him we would be in the shithouse.'

'It's over now,' she said. 'We're on our way to the States.'

'Yes,' I said, then cursed. 'Damn, I didn't have time to call my uncle. He'll be worried.'

'You'll be in New York in ten hours,' she said. 'You can call him from JFK.' She refilled our glasses. 'Relax,' she smiled. 'We'll have a pleasant flight. Air Peru's DC8s are more comfortable than Braniff's 707s even if they are a little slower. We'll be able to stretch out.'

'I've never been able to stretch out on a plane,' I said.

She smiled. 'That's because you've never flown with me. I'll hold your prick all the way. I'll powder it with a little cocaine and you'll be flying on your own.'

'You're a real cunt,' I said.

'No,' she laughed. 'Peruvian pussy.'

73

I laughed and we touched our glasses again. I looked up as another couple was escorted up the aisle to their seats. They seemed like a middle-aged couple, very well dressed, the woman wore a mink coat and her hands sparkled with diamonds. The man took off his homburg, revealing thin curls of white hair and his eyes hidden with shaded French-type eyeglasses. I watched as they seated themselves and the stewardess served them champagne.

Captain Gonzales returned. 'Everything's in order,' he said. 'The passengers are all boarded. It's a very light flight. There are only forty-seven passengers in the back.'

'Maybe you can now join us in a glass of champagne?' Alma said.

'No, thanks again,' he said, apologetically. 'I will have to fill in papers at headquarters for hours,' he said. He held out his hand to me. 'Good luck, Mr. Stevens. It is an honor to have met you.'

'The honor is all mine, Captain Gonzales,' I said, pressing his hand. 'Thank you for everything you have done for us.'

'*De nada*,' he said to me then reached for Alma's hand and kissed it respectfully. '*Hasta luego*, Señorita Vargas.'

Alma nodded to him. '*Mil gracias*, Capitano,' she said. 'Is there one more favor I can ask of you?'

'Anything,' he said.

'We will arrive between two and three in the morning in New York. Would you be kind enough to send a telex to my hotel and have them send a limousine to the airport?'

'I will attend to it immediately, Señorita Vargas,' he smiled, then touching his hand to his cap in a half salute, he turned around and walked off the plane.

I heard the click of the doors close behind us and the whine of the jet engines began to whistle in my ears. I turned and watched her. Her face was turned toward the window and she was looking at the ground. I leaned over her shoulder and could see the captain and his men walking back to the terminal. The voice came through the intercom explaining the safety instructions in both Spanish and English as the plane rolled slowly onto the runway.

The plane turned slowly on to the head of the runway. The brakes held the plane and the jets began to rev up. Suddenly Alma's hand held mine. Her grip tightened on me as we began to race down the runway. There was a faint whine and then we were airborne. She turned to me, her face pale. 'It always frightens me,' she said.

But I wasn't thinking about what she was saying. I was thinking about her asking the captain to telex her hotel. It was just now that I realized she had never told the captain which hotel. She placed her hand on my thigh. 'The Hotel Pierre,' I said.

She looked at me. 'What about it?'

'You never told the captain its name.'

She laughed. 'I told you that we had been old friends. He knew many years ago that my patron had given me an apartment there.'

It was slightly more than three hours and two bottles of champagne into the flight and I was dozing when the stewardess placed her hand on my shoulder. I opened my eyes and looked up at her.

She held a fresh bottle of champagne and smiled. 'Congratulations,' she said. 'We are just passing over the equator.'

I turned to Alma. 'Did you sleep?' I asked.

'A little,' she answered as the stewardess gave us fresh glasses of champagne and went forward to the other passengers. Alma held her glass against mine and leaned over and kissed me.

'Congratulations to you, too,' I smiled and kissed her.

'I have a special present for you,' she said laughingly. She pressed something into my hand.

'What is it?' I asked.

'Smell it,' she said.

I held it to my nose. 'It smells like pussy and perfume.'

She laughed. 'You guessed right. It's my bikini panties. They are still damp. I slipped them off after you fell asleep. Put them into your breast jacket pocket. Everyone will think you are wearing a handkerchief.'

I stuck them in my pocket. 'You're crazy,' I said.

'Not really,' she answered. 'I just want to give you something that will remind you of when we crossed the equator at thirty thousand feet.'

'You took me higher than that without a plane,' I smiled.

The stewardess came back. 'Dinner will be served,' she said.

11

I felt her hand on my shoulder and I rolled over in the comfortable bed and opened my eyes. Daylight poured in through the window. She was already dressed, as she looked down at me and smiled. 'You were sleeping pretty good,' she said.

I shook the cobwebs out of my head. 'What time is it?'

'Twelve thirty,' she answered.

I bolted, half out of the bed. 'I have to call my uncle.'

'Don't worry,' she said. 'I already called him. I told him that you were sleeping. He asked that you call him at two o'clock.'

I stared at her. 'Where did you get his number?'

'Don't you remember?' she asked. 'You had me call him from Lima. I never forget telephone numbers.'

'How did he seem?' I asked.

'Okay, I guess,' she answered. 'Kind of sad though.'

'Was he surprised that it was you that called?' I asked.

'No,' she answered. She gestured to a table near the bed. 'We have orange juice, coffee and real American Danish.'

'I'll have the coffee,' I said, swinging my legs off the bed. The coffee felt good. Strong and hot. My head began to clear. 'What time did you wake up?'

'Eight,' she said.

'Why so early?' I asked. 'It had to be after four in the morning before we fell asleep.'

'I had some things to do, calls to make,' she answered.

A chime rang from the apartment door. 'That must be the valet,' she said hurriedly. 'I have a number of things they have to press. I'll get that arranged while you grab yourself a shave and shower.' She picked up two of her medium-sized valises

77

and took them into the room, closing the door behind her.

I filled my coffee cup again and took it into the bathroom with me. I sipped it again as I opened the medicine cabinet for a razor but there wasn't any there. I thought a moment, then wrapped a bath towel around me and walked to the door going to the living room.

Her back was to me as I opened the door. Two men were standing across the table from her. There were two leather valises on the table next to her Louis Vuittons. Her valises were open and she was handing cellophane packages of white powder to them as they were placing them into their leather valises.

'Twenty-two kilos,' she said and then one of the men saw me and took an automatic from his jacket.

She turned to me.

I felt stupid. 'I was looking for a razor,' I said.

'Put your gun away,' she said coolly. 'He's Di Stefano's nephew.'

The man looked at me. 'The one that went with Angelo?'

'Yes,' she said then turned back to me. 'The razor is in the drawer at the side of the sink.'

I nodded and closed the door behind me. I went back to the bathroom. Suddenly I felt sick and threw up into the toilet. Nothing made sense to me anymore.

I turned to the sink and stared at myself in the mirrored sliding doors of the medicine cabinet. I looked like shit. Pale and sweating and my mouth felt sour and acrid. I slid open the mirrored door and took out a bottle of Lavoris I had seen earlier.

I emptied the bottle until I was able to gargle out the taste in my mouth. I found the razor, an old double-edged Gillette, but there was no shaving cream so I covered my face heavily with the faintly feminine soap on the basin. The razor blade was not too bad but my hands were a little shaky so I wound up with a few nicks. I held a hot washcloth against my face to take off the small spots of blood then placed little pieces of damp toilet paper on them to stop the flow of blood.

I sat on the toilet until the toilet paper dried. Then went into the shower and hit myself with ice-cold water. I was shivering when I stepped out and wrapped myself with a heavy turkish bathsheet. I looked at the mirror again. I didn't look too bad this time. Quickly I combed my hair and opened the door to walk back into the bedroom.

Alma was seated at the edge of the bed, looking up at me. 'Are you all right?' she asked.

'Fine,' I said, reaching for my clothes from the closet. The only things I saw in the closet were my suits and shoes. I took my valise out and put it on the bed.

'Your shirts, underwear and socks are in the bottom drawer there,' she said, pointing to the chest of drawers.

I dressed while she sat there watching me silently. I began to throw my clothes into the empty valise. I didn't pack it very neatly, but I managed to close the valise and lock it. I picked it up off the bed and made for the door.

She was still seated at the edge of the bed. 'Where are you going?' she asked.

'I can use my father's old apartment,' I said.

'Wait. Please. I can explain things to you,' she said.

'What more can you explain? With more lies?' I said sarcastically.

'I thought we were friends and lovers,' she said.

'The only thing we had between us were friendly fucks,' I said.

'We were fighting for our lives,' she said.

'But we survived,' I said angrily. 'And you never told me where you fit into it. I thought you were coming to New York with me, not to carry in twenty-two kilos of cocaine.'

'That was delivered to your uncle's associates,' she said.

'And, of course, you got nothing for it.' I was still angry. 'I was a stupid fool.'

'No,' she said softly. 'Your uncle and the general had an agreement for many years. I was part of it. I continued working for your uncle after the general died, how else do you think I could live? The general left me everything but money.'

'Where did Angelo fit into it?' I asked.

'He was my contact for that last five years,' she answered. 'And I was his. He needed someone he could trust who could speak Spanish.'

'You were lovers?' I questioned.

'Not really,' she said. 'I would say that we were more like business associates. We had a fuck once in a while but it meant nothing to either of us.'

'My uncle knew about you?'

'Yes,' she said. 'Since I was seventeen. The first time the general brought me to New York.'

'And you've been carrying all that time?'

'It was arranged,' she said. 'They had everything on both sides, Lima and New York. And I was the perfect courier, first coming in and out for school, then as a model through the biggest agencies.'

'Why didn't you tell me?' I asked.

'I couldn't,' she said. 'I didn't know how much you knew, so I had to be quiet. Angelo also never told you anything.'

I shook my head. 'Jesus,' I said, then looked at her again. 'The captain, was he in on it too?'

'Yes,' she said. 'It was one of his jobs to protect you in the airport. You remember he followed you to the toilet?'

I nodded.

'It's good he did,' she said. 'I saw Vincent following you there and I told the captain.'

'Then you know what happened there?' I asked.

'Yes. Your uncle told me when I spoke to him this morning.'

'When you spoke to my uncle this morning, what else did he say?'

'He told me to call the captain and have him send the coca to a man named Ochoa in Medellin. That was the same man that Angelo was taking it to.' She took a cigarette from the night table. Slowly she dragged the smoke into her lungs. 'I told him that I should tell you. He said nothing. Just that you should call him at two o'clock.'

I looked at her. 'I don't know whether I want to talk to him.'

'But he loves you,' she said. 'And he needs you. More now since Angelo is gone.'

I was silent.

'And what about me?' she asked. 'We had something special. I need you too.'

I met her eyes and there was a hint of tears in them. 'It doesn't make sense to me anymore. You'll get along, you always have. But I don't know how to live in your world.'

'You have to feel something,' she said huskily. 'If not about me. Your uncle. After all, he's still your family.'

'The family has given me nothing but grief,' I said. 'Tell my uncle if he wants to talk to me I will be at my father's old apartment.'

Then I turned so that she could not see the tears in my eyes and picked up my valise and walked out the door.

12

My father's apartment was only a ten-minute taxi ride from the Pierre. Across 59th Street and up Central Park West to 70th Street. It was an old-fashioned apartment house nothing like the new apartments that were being built on the East Side. It was a comfortable apartment on the eleventh floor with high ceilings and two bedrooms, a living room, a dining room, a kitchen and two bathrooms. My father had bought it after my mother had died. He couldn't live in the house he had spent his life in with her. But when he moved to an apartment, he did get the second bedroom for me. Even though most of the time I was away at boarding school.

Barney, the doorman, greeted me as I stepped out of the taxi. He took my valise. 'Welcome home, Mr. Jed,' he smiled.

I paid the driver and turned to him. He had called me 'Mr. Jed' ever since I had been twelve years old, when we had moved in there. 'How are you, Barney?' I smiled.

'Getting on, Mr. Jed,' he said leading me through the lobby to the elevator. 'The arthritis is still bothering me. But I can handle it.'

'Good,' I said, slipping a ten dollar bill into his hand.

He put the valise on the elevator floor beside me and pressed the button to my floor for me. 'The apartment should be nice,' he said. 'The cleaning girl was just there yesterday.'

'Thank you,' I said as the doors began to close.

I dropped the valise in the entry hall as I entered the apartment. Barney was right. The apartment was neat and clean. I walked into the living room and opened the windows. The fresh air coming in from Central Park helped. The apartment didn't feel so close. I took my valise and went into my bedroom. I opened the windows and looked out across the park.

I could see the towers of the Sherry Netherland and the top of the Pierre next to it on Fifth Avenue.

It didn't make me feel that good. I turned and opened my valise and unpacked it. Then I threw the bag on the floor of the closet and took my jacket off and left it on a chair. I picked up the attaché case and went into the dining room and opened it on the table. I looked down at it.

I checked to see that the money was still there. Seventeen thousand dollars. Inside the flap I took out Angelo's passport and wallet with his credit cards and driver's license. I lifted Angelo's Rolex from the zippered slot. I looked at it for a moment. It had a dark blue face with three diamonds at the quarter hour and the date at three o'clock. I turned it over. It was engraved in thin script. 'To my beloved son, Angelo. On his 21st Birthday from Papa.'

I put the watch back into the zippered slot. I was still angry with my uncle because he was a part of all of them playing games with me. But, he was my father's brother and Angelo had been my cousin. And whether I liked it or not, they were family.

I closed the attaché case and took it into the living room and placed it on my father's desk. At the end of the desk there was a double silver frame, one side my father, the other, my mother. I stared at them. I was nine when my mother had died. I always felt guilty because I couldn't remember much about her. Then I looked at my father. I felt strange. For the first time I realized how much he looked like my uncle.

I took a deep breath and went into the kitchen and took down a bottle of Courvoisier and poured myself a good shot. The cognac burned down to my stomach. I began to feel warm. But not better.

I sat down at the desk and sipped another mouthful of cognac then I picked up the telephone. I didn't know Alma's private number so I called the Pierre.

The operator's voice was professionally cheerful. 'Miss Vargas is out.'

'Did she say what time she would return?' I asked.

'No, sir,' she answered.

'Then would you leave a message please that Mr. Stevens called. My number is –.'

The operator interrupted me. 'She left a message for you, sir. She wanted to let you know that she was leaving for France this afternoon.'

'Thank you,' I said and put down the telephone. I thought for a moment, then looked up at my father's photograph. 'What do I do now, Father?'

But photographs didn't answer questions. My father just smiled and looked wise. I sipped another bit of the cognac and stared at the photograph. Maybe I was getting drunk but I thought he looked even more like his brother than he had before. The house phone rang and I picked it up from the desk. 'Hello.'

'Mr. Jed, this is Barney,' he said. 'Your uncle, Mr. Di Stefano, is here.'

'Okay, Barney,' I said. 'Send him up.'

I left my glass of cognac on the desk and went to the entry hall and opened the door. I waited until he came out of the elevator. His two bodyguards were right behind him. They started toward me. I held up one hand. 'Not them,' I said. 'I want to talk to you alone.'

He gestured to them and they stayed in the corridor. I stepped back and let him into the apartment and closed the door.

My uncle was a big man and before I could turn, he put his arms around me in an embrace. Then he kissed me on both cheeks. 'My son,' he said.

'My uncle,' I said stiffly.

He sniffed. 'You've been drinking.'

'Just a cognac,' I said. 'Would you like one?'

'No,' he said. 'You know I don't drink cognac.'

'I forgot,' I said. I led him into the living room and opened the attaché case in front of him. 'This was Angelo's attaché case.'

He looked down at it silently.

'Everything in it belongs to Angelo.' I gestured to it. 'There is seventeen thousand dollars left.' I opened the flap. 'Here is his driver's license, passport and credit cards.' Then I unzipped the small slot and took out Angelo's Rolex.

Slowly he took it in his hand and turned to the engraving on the back. Then he began to cry. Hard, heaving sobs, the tears falling from his eyes down his cheeks.

I put my arm around his shaking shoulders and guided him into the chair beside the desk. My own voice was choking. 'I'm sorry, Uncle Rocco. I'm really sorry.'

He held his face in his hands. 'I really didn't believe it. I couldn't. Not until now.'

'Please, Uncle Rocco,' I said. 'You have to be strong.'

He shook his head, his face still in his hands. 'My beautiful son is lost. He is gone. And now I have no son. No heir who came forth from my loins. What have I done to him?'

'You have done nothing to him. All you did was to always love him,' I said.

He looked up at me. 'I should have stopped him. I told him not to go. I told him I didn't want you to go. But he had to do it his own way. He said if he didn't go, no one would ever respect him, he would always live in my shadow.'

I was silent. I didn't know what to say.

He looked at me. 'Was he in very much pain?'

'There was no pain. It was over in a second,' I said.

He nodded slowly. 'I thank God for that,' he said. 'And I also thank God that you were there with him. At least he had his family around him.'

I remembered holding his head in my arms. 'Family,' I said. Then I killed him. I looked at my uncle. 'His family was with him,' I said.

My uncle was quiet now. 'I will arrange for a mass.'

'Yes,' I said.

'You will be there?'

'Yes,' I answered.

'And you will be my son, my heir,' he said, taking my hand.

I held his hand. 'But I am not Angelo,' I said. 'I am not like him. I would not know how to live in his world.'

'But you will be rich,' my uncle said. 'More rich than you ever dreamed. Already you will receive twenty million from Angelo. He left it to you in his will. You were his only heir.'

'My father left me all I need. I do not want to be rich. We can give Angelo's gift to the poor.'

He looked at me. 'You are as crazy as your father. You come with me and a whole world will open up for you. In twenty years cocaine will make you a billionaire.'

'Or dead,' I said. 'The only thing I learned in all of this is that we cannot control this world. The South Americans in time will take over that business. They grow it, they manufacture it, soon they will want to distribute it. Then we will all be out of it or dead.'

He stared at me. 'Maybe you are not as crazy as I thought. Then what do you want to do?'

'My father had a good business. He rented automobiles. I have another ambition. Airlines are becoming greater each year. But I need capital to own the planes. And capital is difficult to get. I got the idea while traveling on TWA, and I began to notice that behind each cockpit there was a metal notice. "This plane is the property of Hughes Aircraft Corp. and leased from HAC."'

My uncle shook his head. 'I don't understand.'

'Hughes only owns TWA. I'm sure that many other airlines would like the same kind of deal,' I said.

'But that would take a great deal of money,' my uncle said.

'I'm sure that you have the connections to find the money. I think we can begin with two hundred million.' I laughed.

'I have to think about it,' he said.

'Forget it,' I said. 'You can't even get into this business. There are seven government agencies keeping close check on the airlines. I think you would have to retire before you get into anything like this.'

'Maybe you are really crazy after all,' my uncle said. 'Money has no name on where it comes from.'

'But people do,' I said.

My uncle rose to his feet. 'I will call you when I have the mass arranged.'

'I will be there,' I said.

He started to the door then turned back to me. 'You know the girl has gone to France?'

'I know,' I said.

'She was a nice girl but not for you,' he said.

'What kind of girl would you like me to marry?' I asked.

'Angelo had a nice girl, from a nice Sicilian family. I think he was thinking of marrying her in time.'

'A nice Sicilian family?'

'A very nice Sicilian family. Maybe sometime I can arrange for you to meet them,' he said.

'Thank you, Uncle Rocco,' I said. 'Maybe in time.'

Then we embraced and this time I kissed him also. I opened the door and watched as he walked to the elevator and his two bodyguards waiting out in the hall joined him.

CAPO DI TUTTI

CAPI EMERITUS I

There was no way they could kill Uncle Rocco. Not that they hadn't tried. Knives, guns and car bombs. Uncle Rocco had a sixth sense. He had made up his mind. That was not the way he was going to die. 'I'm fifty-six years old,' he told me. 'And now that Angelo is gone and you don't want to come into the business with me, I have no one to leave it to. So why should I have to fight anymore?'

I stared at him. We were seated in a small booth at the back of The Palms on Second Avenue. We sat alone, his bodyguards seated at another table nearby. Uncle Rocco still had his black mourning band for Angelo on the sleeve of his jacket. 'I don't know, Uncle Rocco,' I said. 'My father told me a long time ago that you never really get out of the business.'

'What did your father know?' he growled, rolling a large forkful of pasta from his plate. 'This is not the old days. This is the seventies. We're civilized, more businesslike. I've already made my agreement with the five families.'

'What does that mean?' I asked. 'They're not going to kill you?'

'You've been seeing too many movies,' Uncle Rocco said.

I cut into my sirloin. It was bloody rare, exactly the way I like it. 'You still haven't told me anything.'

'I'm moving to Atlantic City,' he said.

'Why Atlantic City?' I asked. 'I thought you always wanted to retire in Miami.'

'It doesn't work that way,' Uncle Rocco answered. 'Miami is controlled out of Chicago. Bonanno worked it out for me to take care of the hotel and restaurant unions in Atlantic

89

City. It's a simple operation, enough for me. I don't want to work hard anymore.'

I chewed another piece of my steak slowly. 'And what did you give them for it?'

'They're taking over my operations here. But that's okay. I'll have peace and quiet.'

'That's a lot of money,' I said.

'I have a lot of money,' he smiled. 'Maybe a half a billion dollars.'

I was silent. I could hardly believe it was that much. But I knew it had to be true. My uncle wouldn't lie to me. 'What else are you going to do?'

'I'll take care of my investments,' he said. 'Everything I have is clean money now, I can do whatever I want.' He finished his pasta and emptied his glass of red wine. He pointed his finger at me. 'You're not eating,' he said.

I sliced another piece from my steak. 'I don't understand. If you can do whatever you want, why do you stick yourself in a shithouse like Atlantic City and watch a couple of nickel and dime unions for them?'

He shook his head. 'You don't understand,' he said as if he were explaining to a child. 'I've spent my life with these people. I can't walk away when they ask me to help them.'

'You can be nailed for a small operation just as much as a big deal, maybe more. Why take the chance?' I said.

My uncle filled his wine glass. 'I know what I'm doing,' he said testily. 'I have connections better than the Bonanno and the other New York families. Ten years from now Atlantic City will be big business.'

I looked at him. 'Then you're really not retiring.'

He smiled. 'I'm retiring.'

I watched him sip at his wine. I had no idea what he had in his mind, but I knew my uncle. In his own way he was a genius. He knew exactly where he was going.

He looked over at me. 'How are you doing?'

'Fair,' I answered. 'I have five of the big banks ready to lend me ten million each. That with my own twenty, I am seventy million up.'

'Pretty good,' he nodded. 'Is that enough?'

'No,' I answered. 'I need a minimum of a quarter billion.'

'Where are you going to get that kind of money?' he asked.

I cut another slice of my steak. 'You,' I said and looked up.

He stared at me. 'Are you crazy?'

I laughed. 'You told me you have the money. And you want to use it legitimate. I'm legitimate.'

'I'm not crazy,' he growled. 'If I wanted to piss out my money, I'd throw it in the gutter.'

'You'll make 10 percent interest on your money and 15 percent of the profits. All in all you might wind up with forty million a year before taxes. Legitimate.'

'You gotta prove it,' he said.

'I'll bring you the papers tomorrow morning,' I said. 'You'll see it then.'

'I don't know,' he said.

'Check it out,' I said. 'You can always keep your money in the banks and live comfortably in Atlantic Shitty.'

'You're a little prick,' he said.

'Family,' I said.

He dropped a hundred dollar bill on the table. 'Let's go,' he said.

I looked for his bodyguards. Their table was empty. I gestured. 'Where are your friends, Uncle Rocco?'

He glanced at the table. 'They're probably getting the car.'

I felt a knot gathering in my gut. 'Wait a minute,' I said. 'Did you tell them to go out?'

'No,' he said. 'Why should I? They always get the car for me.'

'They know you are out of the business?' I asked.

'Of course,' he said gruffly. 'Everybody in the world knows that now.'

'And nobody complained?' I asked.

My uncle thought for a moment. 'Maybe, only one. 'Lilo' Galante, one of the underbosses of the Bonanno family. He never liked me. But there is nothing he can do. He is in jail.'

'Does he still have connections in the family?'

'Many,' my uncle answered. 'Many of them want him to be the *Capo* when he gets out.' He thought a moment. 'I heard he didn't want to give me any part of Atlantic City. He's a greedy bastard.'

I looked at Uncle Rocco. 'Are you thinking what I'm thinking?'

He nodded silently, then gestured. 'We'll go out through the kitchen, then into the hallway and up the staircase. We'll go over the roof to the next building.'

The hallway was dimly lit and we hurried up the old rickety staircase and on to the roof. I looked at Uncle Rocco, he was breathing heavily. 'Are you okay?' I asked.

'I'm not in condition,' he growled. He reached into his jacket and came up with two silver automatics. He held one out to me. 'You know how to use this?'

'Yes,' I said.

It was a dark night and we had to walk carefully across the roofs between the other buildings. Fortunately they were all old tenements, and there was little space between them. We began trying to open the roof doors of three of the buildings. It wasn't until the fourth building that the door pulled open.

We stepped into a completely black staircase. The moment we landed on the fifth floorway, we realized that the building was deserted. No lights flickered under doorways and I heard the scamper of rats or mice running as we slowly made our way down the steps. By the time we hit the top of the third staircase a pungent odor of Chinese food came to our nostrils.

'There is a Chinese restaurant on the first floor,' I said.

He grunted. 'And mice on the staircase. That's why I never eat Chinese.'

'It doesn't make sense to me,' I said. 'The building is closed but they still allow a restaurant to stay there.'

'That's normal,' my uncle said. 'Half the buildings down here are like this. For money you can do anything.'

There was a flickering light on the ceiling as we came down the first landing. Quietly we slipped through the opened door leading toward the Chinese kitchen. I looked into the kitchen; there were several men working there. They didn't see us. We walked out the hall door into the street.

'Don't step out too far,' my uncle said. 'Just see if my boys are out there.'

I peered around the corner of the building. There were a number of cars and limousines piled in front of The Palms and McCarthy's restaurant on the corner of Second and 45th Street. 'I don't see them,' I said.

'What about my car?' he asked.

'There are a few black limos,' I said. 'But they all look alike to me. I don't know which one is yours.'

'I'll look,' he said and peeked over my shoulder. He moved back. 'My car is there. Parked right on the corner under the streetlight.' He cursed. 'The sons of bitches are setting me up. They know better than to park my car under a streetlight.'

'What do we do now?' I asked.

'Fuck'em,' he said. 'I still have some friends in town. We'll go into the Chinks and I'll make a few phone calls.'

I followed him back into the hallway and we went into the Chinese restaurant through the kitchen. A few Chinamen looked surprised at us but did not say anything as we went into the restaurant. We sat ourselves at the bar and ordered a couple of scotches and my uncle went to the telephone. I watched him make two calls then he came back to the bar and drank his scotch and ordered another. 'We wait now,' he said quietly. 'They'll let me know when everything is straightened out.'

I stared at him. 'Just like that?'

'It's just business,' he said.

'But they were going to have you killed,' I said.

'That's one of the hazards of this business,' he smiled. 'I've been through it before. I'm still here.'

I finished my scotch and ordered another. 'What about your bodyguards?' I asked.

'They've lost their jobs,' he said.

'You're going to fire them?'

'I don't have to,' he said. 'Their new boss will take care of that. They quit the job with me the moment they walked out of the restaurant. They're not my problem anymore.'

I shook my head. 'I don't get it.'

My uncle smiled at me without humor. 'You don't need to,' he said. 'Now tell me more about your proposition.'

'It can keep,' I said. 'You have enough problems of your own just now.'

'Don't be stupid,' my uncle said harshly. 'I said it would all be straightened out. You tell me about your great idea.'

'It's simple,' I said. 'I have an arrangement with eleven small countries right now. They all want their own airlines but they don't have the money to pay for them. Still they feel it is important for their prestige. I rent them planes almost like my father leased automobiles.'

'How do you know you can get the planes?' he asked.

'I'll pay cash. Money talks,' I smiled. 'Besides, I hired General Haven Carter as the president of my company. He's a heavyweight, former head of the Air Force.'

'He's gotta cost you a bundle,' Uncle Rocco said.

'Two hundred thousand a year,' I said. 'And that's cheap, I would have given half a million if he asked.'

It was a big, deep voice that came from behind us. 'Mr. Di Stefano.'

Uncle Rocco and I turned on the bar stools in the Chinese restaurant. It was a big voice and it came from a big man. Black, six four and four feet wide, a banker-gray suit, white shirt and a black thin tie. A dark-gray snap-brim fedora sat on his shining black head as he smiled, showing large white teeth.

Uncle Rocco smiled at him. 'Joe,' he said. He turned to me. 'Sergeant Joe Hamilton, my nephew, Jed.'

The man's hand was the size of a catcher mitt. 'Nice to meet you, sir,' the sergeant nodded. He turned to my uncle. 'We located your boys,' he said.

'Where?' my uncle asked.

'Down the block, in a car between 43rd and 44th. They have two other men in the car with them. They were double parked on the other side of Second so they could see your car parked on the corner.'

'Damn,' Uncle Rocco said. He looked up at the policeman again. 'Do you recognize those men?'

'Out of town,' he said. 'Contract men. I figure that because we never saw either of them before.'

Uncle Rocco nodded. 'What did you do with them?'

94

'Nothing,' Hamilton answered. 'I didn't know what you had in mind. I just have them under watch.'

Rocco turned to me. 'There's always a greedy pig. I offered everyone a fair deal.'

'I learned something in business school. There's no such thing as a fair deal. Someone always wins and, someone always thinks they're losing.'

'Then you think there's no such thing as a fair deal,' my uncle said.

I shrugged my shoulders. 'Somebody thinks you were screwing them.'

'What do you think?' he asked.

'It's your business,' I said. 'I don't know anything about it. All I know is that someone was going to kill you.'

'Then what would you do?' He met my eyes.

'You're my uncle,' I said. 'And I love you. And I don't want anyone to ever hurt you. But these assholes are only errand boys. If they don't get you, somebody else will be sent after you. You have to get to the head of the snake and straighten him out.'

'It's not that easy,' Uncle Rocco said. '"Lilo" is in jail. I can't talk to him there.'

'Somebody can, I'm sure,' I said.

'Meanwhile, what do I do with these assholes, just let them off?' he said sarcastically.

'That could be the first step,' I said. 'Then you can find someone who can reach him.'

The black policeman turned to Uncle Rocco. 'I can talk to him. I can tell him that life is simple. There's eight blacks to two whites in that jail and if he doesn't behave he goes out in a box.'

Uncle Rocco turned to me. 'What do you think about that?'

Uncle Rocco thought silently for a moment. 'Okay,' he said finally. 'We'll go that way.'

'Good,' I said. 'I feel that your other friends would approve of what you're doing. No one wants to start another war.'

My uncle smiled. 'Frank Costello just died. After Lucky he took the job of being the judge. He kept things quiet for a very long while.'

'Maybe they'll give you that job,' I grinned. '*Capo di Tutti Capi Emeritus* I.'

My uncle stared at me. 'That's stupid,' he said, but I saw he liked the idea.

He turned to the policeman. 'Can you get to "Lilo"?'

'Easy,' he said. 'I own that can.'

'Okay, it's done,' my uncle said.

Sergeant Joe Hamilton nodded and asked one more question. 'What do you want us to do about the four guys out there?'

Uncle Rocco smiled and lifted up his scotch. 'Beat the shit out of those bastards and leave them in the gutter.'

We watched the policeman leave the restaurant and my uncle turned back to the bar and ordered us another round. 'You have a proposition for me, now I have one for you.'

'What?' I asked.

'You buy my brownstone on 60th Street. It's a great house and the right location for you. It's big enough for you to have office space as well as living space and in the upper class that you're going into, living on the West Side isn't the image you should have.'

'That's expensive,' I said. 'I haven't got my business organized yet.'

'You've got it organized,' he said. 'You meet me at my place tomorrow morning. Bring your lawyer and accountant and I'll have mine. I'll give you the money you need and you buy my house.'

I stared at him. 'Do you think I can afford it?'

'Three hundred thousand, fair enough?' my uncle laughed. 'In fifteen years it will be worth two million.'

I reached for his hand. He pulled me to him and hugged me. 'I love you,' he said.

'And I love you, Uncle Rocco,' I said and kissed his hand.

He stopped and took his hand from me. 'No,' he said quietly. 'We're family. We kiss on the cheek.'

Book Two

LOVE, MURDER, AND
THE RICO ACT

1

The hum of the twin-engined, four-passenger Beechcraft came softly into the cabin. Daniel Peachtree, president of Millennium Films Corporation, sat comfortably at the controls. He glanced down at the vector dial, then at the Sat-Nav indicator. 'We should be there in about twenty minutes,' he announced satisfactorily.

'I think you're a fuckin' nut,' Neal snapped.

'He's a bitch,' Daniel said quietly. 'Always complaining. Besides I'll get more publicity out of this than anyone else.' He turned to the beautifully gowned rock MTV stars seated in the seats behind him. 'How are you both doin'?'

'Scared shitless, darling,' Thyme replied, her voice sounding nothing like the video she brought up to the top of the hits list. 'Shouldn't you be looking out the window or something, darling, instead of looking back at us like a Roman taxi driver?'

Daniel smiled. 'We're on automatic right now. I have nothing to do until we begin to land.'

'Then get us down, darling,' Thyme said. She opened her purse and took out a vial of coke and turned to her girlfriend. 'Here, Methanie, a couple of snorts of this will straighten you out.'

Methanie nodded and snorted quickly. 'You're saving my life, baby.'

Thyme helped herself and then slipped the vial back into her purse. 'That really do help.'

Daniel looked at her. 'Don't get too stoned. We're having reporters and photographers at the airport, and remember this is zero tolerance time.'

'Fuck'em, they won't know the difference, darling,' Thyme replied. 'I've been stoned all my life, no one ever saw me any other way.' She leaned forward toward him. 'You sure Donald Trump will be there?'

'If you have the hots for him, forget it,' Daniel laughed. 'He's got a Russian wife. But maybe he'll give you a gig at his hotel in Atlantic City.'

'I can live without him or his hotel,' she snapped. 'I want him to get me next to Mike Tyson.'

Daniel stared at her. 'What makes you think Tyson will want to meet you?'

'I heard he was playing my albums all the time at his training camp,' she replied. 'He may be the champ, but he's nothing but an overgrown pussywhipped baby to me.'

'I never knew you really went for men anyway.'

'Never men,' she laughed. 'Only boys. They bring out the mother in me.'

'You're a real bitch,' Daniel smiled, as a buzzer sounded above his head. He pressed a button and reached for an earphone clip. 'We're coming in, kids. Remember, keep cool.'

'We cool,' Thyme said, with a smile. 'A little pale but cool.' She opened the coke vial again. This time she pinched Methanie's nipples then her own. 'This'll stick them out a little bit baby. Looks dynamite on black and white newspaper photos.'

Bradley Shepherd squeezed himself into the chair behind the small desk in his wife's bedroom and held the telephone to his ear. The music from the orchestra came up from downstairs so he covered his other ear against the noise of the voice in the telephone. 'The bank said they wouldn't advance us over twelve dollars a barrel for our crude.' Chuck's voice was nervous through the receiver. 'They also want us to make a six million payment against our loan because they have the federal and state auditors up their ass.'

'The fucking world is getting crazy,' Bradley said. 'This value is only temporary, oil will go up. It's the fucking Arabs blowing us out of the market.'

Chuck was silent.

Bradley spoke into the telephone again. 'Do we make any profit on the fifteen dollars a barrel we get?'

'Our own cost analysis brings it up to eleven dollars forty, that leaves us three dollars and forty cents. One hundred thousand barrels a month brings us only three hundred sixty thousand.'

'We can ship out ten times more than that,' Bradley said.

'Sure, we can,' Chuck said. 'But we have no one to buy it. You've been away from Oklahoma a long time. You don't realize what has been going on. All the high rollers have been wiped out and more than seventy banks have folded this year. There's no money around, not even with the shylocks.'

'Fuck the Ayatollah,' Bradley swore. 'I told Jimmy Carter that he would screw us. At least the Shah was on our side. He would have kept OPEC in line.'

'You better get back here,' Chuck said. 'You're the only man who could keep our set-up from going down the tube. In Oklahoma you're still the king.'

'I'm in the shit up to my ass right here. When I gave four hundred million back to the Swissman, I had to take Jarvis into the package. He paid off the Swissman. Now he's pushing me. I have to drop another eighty-five million into the pot for my share of the new movie and TV production.'

'Do you have that?'

'I got shit,' he said.

'Do you have to pay it?' Chuck asked.

'It's in the contract.'

'And if you don't pay it?'

'Then he has the right to buy me out,' Bradley answered.

'For how much?' Chuck asked.

'My half. Four hundred million.'

'Does he have that kind of money?' Chuck questioned.

'He's got more money than God,' Bradley said.

Chuck was silent for a moment. 'Then you haven't any choice. You're between the devil and the deep blue sea.'

'Don't tell me,' Bradley said gruffly. 'Give me some time, I'll call you back in a half hour. Tell them to hold their balls.' He lit a cigar and stared angrily across the room.

His wife's bedroom suite was beautiful. And so was the house. But for fifteen million dollars in cash it should be. He shook his head angrily. How could he ever have become so

101

stupid? And in the movie business especially.

Charlene came in from her dressing room. Thirty years married and she still looked like the best lady in town. Five six, long light-brown hair set in formal chignon, a diamond and emerald necklace around her throat with a matching bracelet on her left wrist, her simple gold wedding ring she had worn at their marriage and on her other hand a large twenty-five carat pure white diamond. She looked down at him. 'We better start going down to the party, about a hundred of our guests are already here.'

'How many are we expecting?' he asked in a hoarse voice.

'Close to five hundred,' she answered.

'Shit,' he exclaimed.

'What's wrong?' she asked, her eyes searching the lines on his face.

'How much money have you stashed in the kitchen box?' he asked.

She knew what he meant. When they were first married and had very little they used to hide the money in a box on a shelf behind the dishes in the kitchen. 'About twenty million,' she said quietly. 'Is it that bad?'

'Worse,' he said. 'The roof is falling down. Where do you have it?'

'Chase Manhattan in New York,' she said.

'I'll need ten million of it tomorrow,' he said.

She didn't ask any questions. 'You can have it all if you want.'

He managed a wry smile. 'I'll try to make that manage, Mama.'

'It's our money,' she said. 'I always said that.'

'I know, Mama, but I was hoping to make it better for you,' he said and rose from the desk and kissed her on the cheek. 'Thank you, Mama,' he said. 'Now we can go down to the fucking party.'

The long driveway leading to the expansive veranda entrance to the house was jammed with limousines, Rolls and occasionally a Mercedes which seemed out of place. The press and the photographers were exploding their flashes on their cameras and screaming to their favorite stars and actors to get an answer to their unheard questions as they swept through the double doors and handed their guest cards to the burly tuxedoed security guards standing there.

Reed Jarvis and Sherman Siddely, his personal attorney, walked by the guards without turning in any guest cards. One of the large men held them from entering. 'Can't enter without a card, gentlemen,' he said politely.

'This gentleman is Reed Jarvis,' Sherman explained. 'We don't have any cards.'

'Sorry,' the guard said with half a smile. 'No tickee, no shirtee. Out.'

'This is stupid,' Sherman said angrily. 'Mr. Jarvis is Shepherd's partner.'

'I have my orders,' the guard said. 'No one without the fancy gold card can enter.'

Jarvis was relaxed. Suddenly, in his hand, appeared a thousand dollar bill. 'If you can have a word with Mr. Shepherd, I'm sure you'll find everything in order.'

The guard glanced at the bill. Quickly it disappeared into his own hand. 'Wait here a moment, sir,' he said. 'I'll find Mr. Shepherd for you.'

'That was a thousand dollar bill you gave him,' Sherman said.

'That will be the most expensive dollar that prick ever made,' Jarvis said softly. 'He's going to be out of a job tomorrow morning.'

The guard earned his money. Bradley was right behind him. He held out his hand, smiling. 'Reed, I'm so glad you could make it. Come on in.'

He led Jarvis and Sherman into the giant party room. At the far end was an orchestra, along the side of the inside room was a long table, covered with a massive display of hors-d'oeuvres and hot food. On the other side, the large french doors opened onto a tented area completely covering the Olympic size swimming pool with beautiful tables decorated with gold and silver. Bradley smiled, 'Nobody would believe a redneck from Oklahoma can throw a party like this. It's putting them all away.'

'It's big,' Reed replied without enthusiasm.

Bradley stared at him. 'Something's bothering you,' he said shrewdly.

'We have the directors' meeting tomorrow,' Reed said.

'I know that,' Bradley said.

'I've heard some rumors that your oil companies are going down the tube. No money,' Jarvis said.

'Where did you hear that?' Bradley asked.

'Reliable sources.'

Bradley stared at him. 'What are you getting at?'

'You have to come up with eighty-five million tomorrow for the new production fund,' Reed answered.

'I haven't got it, I need time,' Bradley said.

'Sorry,' Jarvis said smoothly. 'We made a deal. But I don't want to embarrass you in front of the other directors. You simply sell your share of the controlling stock for 400 million. Then you can go back to your own business and straighten out your oil company.'

'And if I don't want to do that?' Bradley asked.

'You don't have any choice that I can see,' Jarvis' voice was cold.

Bradley kept his face impassive. 'Let me think on it a bit, Reed,' he said. 'I'll let you know before the party is over.'

'Fair enough,' Jarvis said.

Bradley waved his hand to the now crowded room. 'Enjoy yourselves. I have some other guests I have to greet.'

The long bar at the far end of the ball room was five deep with people getting a drink. Reed stared at it distastefully. 'I hate that. There has to be somewhere we can find a table with service.'

'From what I see all the tables are already taken up,' Sherman said.

Daniel came up behind them. 'I heard you,' he smiled. 'Follow me, I know about these affairs. If you don't get a table you're screwed.'

Silently, they followed him through the large french doors leading outside to the pool area which was covered by a giant circus tent. Daniel had a large table overlooking the stage built over the pool, on which a sixteen-piece orchestra was playing to a dance floor built across the remainder of the pool. Strobe colored lights and Japanese lanterns hung from wires strung tautly from tent pole to tent pole, making a strangely pleasant light.

Daniel made the introductions. 'You know Neal,' he gestured then to the others. 'Reed Jarvis, Sherman Siddely. This is Thyme and Methanie.' He waited until the two men were seated. 'We have scotch, vodka, and champagne, ice is on the table. If there is anything other than this you need, I'll call a waiter.'

'Scotch will do for me,' Reed said, sitting next to Thyme. 'You look very familiar to me,' he smiled. 'Have we met before?'

'I don't think so,' she laughed, pouring a scotch on the rocks for him. She lifted her champagne. 'Cheers.'

'Cheers,' Reed said, sipping his drink. 'You're quite beautiful. Are you an actress?'

She laughed again, teasing him. 'No.'

'What do you do then?' he asked.

'I make records,' she answered. 'I also like to party. What do you do?'

'I make money,' he laughed.

'That's lovely,' she said. 'I like money. Maybe we can party sometime.'

Reed turned to Daniel. 'This girl is delicious. Where did you ever find her?'

Daniel smiled. 'You really don't know her?'

Reed shook his head.

'She has the number one MTV video and record in the country. Her album has just gone platinum,' Daniel laughed.

Reed turned back to her. 'I apologize. I'm afraid I haven't much time for radio and TV.'

'That's okay,' Thyme replied. 'You do the important thing. Make money.' She rose to her feet. 'Could you all excuse me? I have to powder my nose.'

'You look perfect to me,' Reed nodded.

She kissed his cheek lightly. 'Silly boy,' she laughed, then turning to Methanie, 'Want to join me?'

Reed watched the girls as they walked away, then he turned to Daniel. 'I want to fuck her.'

Daniel shook his head. 'She's trouble. Completely crazy.'

'I like trouble. I can handle a woman like that,' Reed said.

'Besides, she's lez'. That's her girlfriend with her.'

'That makes it better,' Reed retorted. 'I can take care of both of them. It's only a matter of money.'

'Money doesn't mean a damn to her. She's in the two million a year class.'

'I'll get her,' Reed said flatly. 'I saw the glint in her eyes when I told her what I do. You just arrange for me to take her back to the city in my car after the party.'

'I'll try, but I can't guarantee anything,' he said.

'You'll manage it,' Reed said. 'After all, you're going to be the CEO of the company when I take over.'

'I didn't know that pimping is one of the duties of a CEO,' Daniel answered, trying to keep his temper in check.

'Your duties will be what I want you to do,' Reed said coldly, reading the anger beneath Daniel's words. 'For the three million a year plus stock and bonus I pay you, I have the right.'

Daniel was silent for a moment then glanced at Neal. 'Tell Reed and Sherman what we heard this weekend.'

Neal was nervous. He stammered. 'I noticed that Donald Trump, Marvin Davis, and Jed Stevens are here at the party. And there is a friend of mine, a commercial real estate broker, told me that they'd like to buy the seventy acres that Millennium owns on the far end of Marina Del Rey.'

'Were they together here tonight?' Sherman asked.

'I saw them separately,' Daniel said.

'Think they joined forces for this?' Reed asked.

'I don't know,' Daniel answered. 'But the one thing I do know, none of them like having partners.'

'What's the property worth?' Reed asked.

'Millennium bought the land just after the war for three million five. They were planning to move the studio there. But it never worked out. The latest idea that Shepherd has is to build a Fantasyland there. Something like a Disneyland and he's already asked several amusement park builders to develop some plans and costs,' Daniel answered. 'He hasn't brought me into it, so I don't know in which stage the plans are. The latest figure I heard from Arthur Young is that the land is worth ninety million even though it is still carried on the books at cost.'

'That means either of them would easily pay a hundred or more for it. They're accustomed to buy high and sell for even more,' Sherman said pompously.

'I'm not concerned about them. A hundred million isn't enough to get Shepherd out of the bag. I hear he needs 250 million to get even. He also has problems at his oil companies,' Reed said quietly. 'But I will still make contact with all of them, and let them know that I will protect them when I make the deal.'

'Have you spoken to Bradley yet?' Daniel asked.

'He's still thinking about our offer, but I'm not worried,' Reed said confidently. 'We'll get it.' Then he turned to Daniel with a smile. 'The only thing you have to worry about at this moment is that you get that nigger whore in my car tonight.'

'I'd better get right after her,' Daniel said, rising to his feet. 'Come on, Neal, I saw her heading to the garden. Let's try to catch her.'

2

Jed Stevens lifted a flap of the tent over the pool area and stepped out to the large manicured garden. The fresh night air came up from the green lawn. He breathed deeply, filling his lungs. All parties were the same no matter how large or small. They all smelled the same, a mixture of perfume, sweat, cigarettes, and grass. He let the flap fall down and walked down the pathway. He heard the stables were down that way. Even horseshit would smell better than what he was breathing at the party. There was no light on the path and he stumbled over a large bush and then tripped over two people kneeling in front of him. 'Oh, shit,' he said.

Neal stepped up in front of him. 'What the hell are you doing over here?' he asked in a husky angry voice.

'I'm sorry,' he answered, still not seeing Neal's face in the dark. 'I didn't know that anyone was here.'

Daniel stepped up next to Neal. 'Get your fucking ass out of here,' he said. 'Or I'll break your goddamn neck.'

Then Jed recognized the two men. Daniel Peachtree and his boyfriend, Neal. He tried to make light of the incident. 'Sorry, fellows,' he said. 'I didn't mean to disturb you. I'll go back to the party and we'll all forget about it.'

'You're going to forget nothing,' Daniel said harshly. 'I'm going to beat the shit out of you. I'm gonna make sure you keep your mouth shut.'

Jed felt his temper rising. 'Before you do anything you two better zip up your pants before you get AIDS from the cold night air.'

Neal moved toward him. 'I wouldn't try that if I were you,' Jed said quietly.

Neal's voice was flat as he zipped his fly. 'We're both black belts.'

'Congratulations,' Jed said. 'But I have something better. Two hundred million dollars in Jarvis' deal.'

He looked at the men staring at him in surprise. He stared coldly at them for a moment before he spoke. 'Just in case you two guys don't know it, we're all kind of partners,' he said as he turned and walked back up the path to the tent.

He lifted the tent flap and entered into the party. It wasn't until then he regretted what he had done. 'Damn,' he said to himself. Probably Uncle Rocco would be upset because he had opened his mouth.

Bradley was on the private telephone in his own library. Quickly, he punched in the telephone number on the computerized speed dialer on the desk. A moment later Chuck's voice answered in the receiver.

'I want you out here right away,' Bradley said.

'I'll get the first plane in the morning,' Chuck answered.

'I mean right away,' Bradley said. 'That means tonight.'

'How can I get there?' Chuck asked. 'You have the Lear in California with you.'

'An ordinary jet would never make it fast enough for me,' Bradley said. 'You call my cousin, Brig. Gen. Shepherd at the air base outside of town and tell him that I want him to lend us one of the new F-Zero-60 four-passenger fighters, to bring you and Judge Gitlin over to me "tout suite".'

'The judge is seventy years old,' Chuck said. 'He's probably in bed.'

'Wake him up then,' Bradley said. 'Besides his being my kin you tell him that he needs to get out here now if he wants to see the twenty-five million he loaned me, otherwise, he may never seen a penny of it. That'll wake him up.'

'And what do I tell the general?' Chuck asked.

'He's got a half million shares of my oil stock and that'll go down into the shithouse too, if he doesn't help us out. If you put everything together the F-Zero-60 will bring you all here in a little less than four hours. That baby can go better than Mach Two.'

'I'll try,' Chuck said.

'You'll be here,' Bradley said and put down the phone. He glanced at the desk clock. It was nine-thirty. If all goes well they should make it here by two in the morning.

He left his library and ran into Daniel Peachtree and Neal Shifrin walking across the landing to the bathroom. He stared at them. Their tuxedoes seemed rumpled. 'What the hell happened to you guys?' he asked.

Peachtree looked back at him. 'We were walking in the garden,' he said. 'And we tripped over a low cypress hedge we didn't see in the dark.'

'What were you doing out there?' he asked.

'I was on my way to the performers' set-up,' Daniel said. 'I wanted to talk to Rainbeau. We have a problem with his new album.'

'Did you find him?' Bradley asked.

'No,' Daniel answered angrily. 'We're trying to brush the grass off our clothes.'

'I saw you at the table with Jarvis and his lawyer. What were you talking about?' Bradley asked quietly.

Daniel was so surprised that Bradley had noticed them in the crowd, he blurted out the truth. 'Jarvis is thinking of making me CEO over everything.'

'He can't do that,' Bradley said calmly. 'I still have something to say about it.'

Peachtree stared at him, then he backed off. 'Maybe I didn't understand.'

'Maybe,' Bradley said succinctly. 'Meanwhile, you two better get yourselves straightened up.'

Bradley watched them walk to the bathroom then he started down the staircase.

Senator Patrick Beaufort of Louisiana was a little high. He reached for his fourth bourbon and water. 'This is a hell of a party.'

Roxane Darrieux, a beautiful creole girl, who was his executive assistant as well as his mistress, placed a calm hand on his wrist. 'Slow down, Senator. It's strong liquor.'

He looked at her. She shook her head. He put his drink

back on the table. He had learned a long time ago in their relationship that she had good instincts. He smiled at her. 'Do you have panties on?' he whispered.

She laughed. 'You know I never wear anything under my dresses.'

'I want to dip my fingers in your pussy,' he said.

'Later,' she said, looking past him. 'Bradley Shepherd's coming to talk to you.'

Senator Beaufort turned and rose as Bradley greeted him. 'My host,' he said warmly. 'I have to say that you throw a hell of a party.' He gestured to Roxane. 'You know Ms. Darrieux?'

Bradley took Roxane's hand. 'Nice to see you again, Roxane,' he smiled. 'I'm glad you could make it.'

'I wouldn't miss it for the world, Bradley,' she answered in a soft voice. 'Please join us for a drink.'

'For just a quickie,' Bradley nodded and dropped in the chair next to the Senator while Roxane quickly gave him a drink. 'What's the word from Washington, Senator?'

'Reagan's second term is just starting to set in but it will take a little while for them to get their bearing,' the Senator replied.

'What's the attitude on oil? Are the domestic producers going to get any relief?'

'Talk, but no action as yet,' the Senator said. 'Like I said it will take time. But I'm staying on top of it and the minute we have a chance to move we'll be on it. Don't forget my state is hurting too.'

'I know, Patrick,' Bradley said. 'And we all appreciate your concern and are ready to back you on anything you want to do.' He paused for a moment. 'Right up to the White House.'

The Senator nodded seriously. 'Thanks, Bradley. But it's too early to think about that.'

'Just remember, Senator, the independent oil producers are right behind you.' Bradley sipped at his drink. 'Have you heard anything about Reed Jarvis applying for special consideration to become an American citizen?'

'The Canadian?'

Bradley nodded.

'Why are you interested in him?' The Senator looked at him curiously.

'He's making an offer for Millennium Films and also the seven TV and radio stations that we own. I remember that Ted Kennedy sponsored a bill to get Murdoch a quick citizenship.'

'Are you for or against him?' asked the Senator.

Bradley shook his head. 'I don't know yet. I have to get more information on his offer.'

The Senator smiled and held his hand toward Bradley. 'Just let me know what you decide, I'll go with you.'

Bradley rose to his feet. 'Thank you again, Patrick.' He bowed to Roxane. 'Good to see you again.'

Roxane watched him walk away. 'I've heard some rumors that Bradley has big money troubles.'

Patrick laughed. 'So what else is new? Bradley is an old-time wildcatter. He's used to money troubles, but he's always been able to overcome them and come up smelling like roses.'

'I don't understand,' Roxane said. 'If it's true that he is in money trouble, why does he throw a party like this? It has to cost at least two hundred fifty thousand.'

'He's wildcatting,' Patrick answered. He gestured to the party. 'Look around you. There is enough money here on his guest list to pay off the national debt. Somewhere in this pie, he might come up with a plum.'

Roxane looked around toward the crowd then back to him. She smiled teasingly. 'Would you like some pussy pie? But, just remember, you'll have to lick your fingers, it's very, very juicy.'

It was drizzling lightly as the limousine entered the Tinker Air Force Base in Midwest City, fifteen minutes from Oklahoma City. An Air Force MP jeep pulled in front of them and gestured them to follow. They crossed almost to the far end of the air strip at the edge of the field.

Before them, they could see the plane. F-Zero-60 was painted on the tail. Around the plane were a number of uniformed ground crew men and just as the limousine pulled to a stop Brig. Gen. Shepherd, uniformed in a white flight jumpsuit, opened the door. He stuck his head into the back door of the car. 'Judge Gitlin, Chuck,' he said quietly, shaking their hands. 'We're ready to go.'

'Thank you, sir,' Chuck said.

The judge looked at the airplane. 'It doesn't look very big,' he said in a nervous voice.

'It's big enough,' the general answered assuringly. 'Enough room inside for the four of us.'

'You're piloting us?' the judge asked.

'I'm sitting co-pilot on this one,' the general said. 'I've got the best pilot on the base with us for this one. Lt. Col. Sharkey. He's already got two hundred hours on these planes.'

'Which one is he?' the judge asked.

The general gestured with his hand. The judge saw a man also in a flight jumpsuit. He was not very tall, maybe five eight, and very slight.

'He seems like a kid,' the judge said. 'If he's twenty that's a lot.'

'Twenty-one,' the general replied. 'That's about the age of kids we want for this plane. Their reflexes have to be fast enough to match the plane. After twenty-four, we move them over to other jobs.'

'Then why are you co-piloting?' the judge asked dryly. 'I was at your baptism, you're fifty if you're anything.'

'I figure that I'm going to wind up fired for doing this job as soon as the Pentagon learns about it, so I might as well have some fun with it.'

'You ever fly one of these bastards?' asked the judge.

'Five times, Judge,' the general said. 'Don't worry, I know how to handle it if I have to.'

'I'm seventy-three years old,' the judge said.

The general laughed. 'Better late than never, Judge. Let's go.'

The pilot was already in his seat and he turned around to shake their hands. 'Judge Gitlin, Mr. Crawford.'

They both greeted Lt. Col. Sharkey. A ground crew man climbed inside the plane and strapped the two passengers into their seats. He took the judge's white felt hat and fitted him into a flight helmet, then did the same to Chuck. The general slipped into his seat. 'Don't worry about the helmet,' he said. 'Sometimes it gets a little rocky taking off and landing and I don't want you to bump your heads.'

'It's not my head I'm worried about,' the judge said sardonically. He saw the swing out doors close shut. 'How long will this flight take?' he asked.

'Between an hour fifteen to an hour thirty,' the pilot said. 'Depends on the weather conditions at the landing point.'

'How many miles?' the judge asked.

'Eleven hundred and seventy miles.'

'Jesus,' the judge said. 'That's almost a thousand miles an hour.'

'About,' the pilot said. He began turning on switches. A hum came into the cabin. Slowly the plane began to roll along to the head of the landing strip, then he turned into it and there was a soft-blue lit path of landing lights outlining the strip. The plane stopped and waited like a bird ready to fly.

A hollow voice echoed from the overhead speakers. 'F-Zero-60. Hold position for five minutes. Two commercial flights are on your flight path.'

'Roger, tower, I read you,' the pilot answered.

'How do you control where you're going?' the judge asked, his voice echoing in his helmet earphones.

'I don't have to do anything,' the pilot said. 'I just take it up and put it down. The minute I reach my altitude for the flight, automatically the plane takes over. When we're about one hundred miles over the Pacific below Los Angeles, then it comes back to me and I start taking it down.'

'Jesus Christ!' the judge said. 'I guess the only thing we have left to figure out is how to stick a rocket up our asses and point us in the right direction.'

The hollow tower voice spoke to them. 'Clear for takeoff, F-Zero-60. Good flight.'

As the plane took off a loud pop echoed behind them as the airplane sped down the runway and it seemed like only a second before it was climbing vertically into the night sky.

3

The giant games room was situated about a half floor below the ballroom. Beyond that was the large rolling glass door that enclosed a complete gym loaded with the latest Nautilus equipment as well as mirrored walls in which aerobic dancers and exercisers could watch themselves in the heights or depths of their glories. Outside the windows was a large path that led the way to the swimming pool. As big as the games room was, it was packed with the performers who the Shepherds had hired for their party. The room was filled with the odor of grass, being smoked down to the fingertips. More than half of the performers were not only stoned, but drinking champagne as if it were tap water, and snorting, their noses burning with the ice-blue Peruvian being passed around.

Rainbeau sat in the corner of the room that his two giant black bodyguards had taken as his private territory. Next to Rainbeau was the beautiful blonde black girl whose wild frizzed long hair almost covered her face. She accompanied Rainbeau on the electric mandolin. Her sister, almost a carbon copy of her, played the bass guitar. Beside them was Jaxon the drummer, his pale white face frozen in ecstasy with the rush of cocaine, and Blue Boy, the piano player, who looked like a black copy of the Gainsborough painting. The group stayed to themselves. Neither talking, nor looking at anyone else in the room. With three videos in the top ten, they didn't have to bother with anyone. Besides, Rainbeau was angry that he was hired for the party and not invited to it. He was also angry that he had no choice. The deal he made with Daniel Peachtree gave him the right to do the song he wanted and they paid for the full cost of the video, and that came to a lot of money, almost as much as making a motion picture.

He heard her voice before he saw her. No one had a voice like hers. Pure cunt. He looked up to see her. She was standing outside his circle. 'Thyme,' he said. 'Come on over here.'

The bodyguards gave her some room to move. 'What are you doing down here?' she asked.

'Doin' a gig,' he said. 'You, too?'

She seemed puzzled. 'Not really, I came up with Peachtree on his private plane.'

'You're a guest?' he asked.

'I guess so,' she answered. 'It doesn't make sense. I saw Michael and Brooke Shields up there.'

'Michael doesn't work for Peachtree.' He looked at her. 'Neither do you, right?'

'Check,' she said. 'He's a fag shit.'

Rainbeau was silent for a moment. 'He laid a hundred grand on us for this gig.'

'It still ain't right,' she said. 'Probably you would do it for nothin' if he asked like a gentleman.'

Rainbeau nodded. 'Some people don't have no class,' he agreed. He gestured at her. 'What would be your pleasure? We have it all.'

'I want to sing with you,' she said, looking at his eyes.

'We got no song together, no rehearsal. Besides, you're a guest and I'm just a hired hand.'

'Horseshit,' she said. 'We can put something together that'll work for us in five minutes.'

'You'd do that for me?' he asked, a slight surprise in his voice.

'We're the same kind of people, aren't we?' she smiled. 'Maybe I'm black and you're Puerto Rican but we come from the same street.'

He stared at her silently for a moment. 'How did you find us down here?'

'One of the asshole security men thought I was one of the entertainers, he shoved me down the steps.'

'Balls,' he said. 'Where was Peachtree?'

'Probably somewhere getting his boyfriend to give him head,' she answered.

His eyes met hers. 'You mean it? What you said earlier?'

'Anytime, anyplace,' she said. 'We'll be great together.'

'I have an idea,' he said.

'Tell me.'

'You know my song, the first one I hit, "I'm Just A Boy"?'

'Every word,' she said.

'Okay, you sing, but instead of boy you say girl. Then I'll do your song, "The Boy I Love". Only I sing it the "girl". We know the music, the arrangements should be a piece of cake.'

She hugged him close to her. 'Oh, baby. I love you. Really I do.'

He kissed her cheek. 'Now, let's try to get it together.'

At exactly the stroke of midnight, a drum roll brought Bradley and Charlene to the center of the stage. The room went silent as Bradley took the microphone.

'Friends and honored guests,' he said, his faint midwestern drawl enhanced by the sound system. 'For many years in Oklahoma, Charlene and I had an annual party in honor of our first born. On this day in 1955, Charlene and I stood on the ground beneath the derrick, Shepherd Oil Well No. One, our first born, as the gusher shot the oil up into the sky, then falling and covering us completely with black gold. We were holding each other, screaming to each other, but the only thing I could remember about what Charlene said to me was, "Now, Bradley, you can finally buy a store-bought suit."'

A wave of laughter and applause filled the tent as guests rose from their seats. Bradley held his hands up and slowly the guests returned to their seats.

Bradley, holding Charlene's hand in a gesture of acknowledgement, smiled. 'To cap the story. I finally got my store-bought suit two years later after Shepherd Oil Company Well No. One Hundred came through and I needed a suit to go to the bank, because now that I had money I had to borrow money to pay my taxes.'

Again the crowd laughed and applauded. Bradley kept them

quiet. 'Thank you all for coming and now you can relax, have a good time and enjoy the show and dinner.' Charlene and Brad held up their hands and waved warmly to their guests.

The music started and the stage began to turn as if on a disc and Bradley and Charlene, together with the orchestra that had been seated on the stage before, began to disappear from view as the lights began to dim, into total darkness.

When the lights came on again, it was a completely new stage set and the music was blasting the rock and roll music of Rainbeau. Then the spotlight picked out a young man in mid air landing in front of the group, his half-naked body painted in colors and sparkling with sequins, the microphone already held in his hand. The room began to roar with applause as they recognized Rainbeau in his exciting showmanship style. A moment later, another singer appeared. Surprise roared through the room. Thyme stood beside him, in a white floating chiffon that silhouetted her beautiful dark nudity beneath the costume.

Reed Jarvis, leaning against a marble column, whispered almost to himself as they began their song and dance. He felt a numbness in his stomach. 'That's almost pornographic, I can't believe at a party like this.'

Daniel Peachtree, appeared beside him. 'Reed,' he smiled. 'This is Hollywood, not Winnipeg, Ontario.'

Reed turned to him. 'You don't look so good. What happened, you fall down a flight of steps?'

Daniel shook his head. 'I tripped over a cypress in the garden while I was looking for your girlfriend.' Then he looked at Reed. 'Who's that Jed Stevens? He says he's got two hundred million in with you.'

'He has the money if he wants in,' Reed answered. 'But it's not his money that's in my deal. He's just checking it out for his uncle.'

'Then he's not a partner with you?'

'Hell, no,' answered Reed, watching Thyme as she went into her solo number. 'I don't have partners, and he won't be a part of us after tomorrow.'

'That easy?' Daniel said sarcastically. 'I hear Bradley has

no intention of bowing out tomorrow. At least, he doesn't sound like it to me.'

Reed shrugged and glanced back at Thyme on stage, then back to Peachtree. 'I still want to fuck that girl,' he said. 'Have you talked to her yet?'

'I was trying to find her when I ran into the fucking cypress hedge in the garden. The first time I've seen her is right now, on stage.'

Reed looked at him. 'All I want to know is, can you arrange for me to fuck her or not?'

Daniel didn't smile. 'I don't know,' he said. 'The name of the game is money. If money doesn't tempt her she won't be a player.'

'I don't care what it costs, you just get her,' Reed said flatly.

Judge Gitlin sank tiredly into the easy chair in the upstairs library and looked up at Bradley. 'It's only two in the morning for you here in California but it's four in the morning for me.'

Bradley handed the judge a four-finger shot of corn. 'This will wake you up.'

The judge nodded. He emptied the glass. 'Another taste,' he said.

Bradley nodded and refilled the glass. This time the judge sipped it. He looked up at Bradley. 'That's a big do you're having down there.'

'Hollywood bullshit,' Bradley said. 'It's something you have to do.'

'Costs a penny,' the judge said. 'You have the money to pay for it?'

'That's up to you,' Bradley filled a drink for himself. 'I'm not only drowning in oil but the hyenas are eating on my flesh.'

'What about the money you owe to the bank already. Twelve million? And personally twenty-five million to me?'

'Down for a penny, down for a dollar,' Bradley said wryly.

The judge stared at him. 'I know you. You come from a long line of Indian traders. How can I get you the money when the federal and state auditors are climbing up my ass?'

'Fantasyland. The eight acres I bought at the far end of the marina, I had you hold it in trust for me. It was never turned over to the studio. As a matter of fact, Jarvis and I never even discussed bringing Fantasyland into the studio and television deal. At the time he wasn't interested. It was not until Disney said they were opening in France, did he even talk to me about it.'

The judge looked at him shrewdly. 'You never used any money from the picture company to develop it?'

'No. I never did anything with it. Just left it there fallow.'

The judge thought for a moment. 'So, maybe it's worth fifty or sixty million. The way I see it you have no choice. Take his four hundred million and run.'

'Take the option he offered you, that costs you nothing. If things look good, pick it up. If it looks bad, let him shove it up his ass.'

'I feel like an asshole,' Bradley said. 'I was going to show the movie business how to do it.'

'There're others who went for worse. You'll still get four hundred million out of it, you could have lost the whole damn pot. Sit tight. Oil will straighten up sooner or later, the real estate you own around the marina for Fantasyland will do nothing but go up. All you hurt is your pride.'

Bradley looked down at the judge. 'Is that it? Just pride?'

'Our family has never been known for being humble,' the judge smiled. 'Jes' tell that Jarvis fellow you'll take his money an' wish him luck. You stay in the neck of the woods you know best. Oil and land.'

'I guess you're right,' Bradley admitted. 'But, man, this business is real fun.'

'You'll have another shot,' the judge said wisely. 'Who says that Jarvis fellow is any smarter than you were? He can go on his ass just as easy. Then maybe you'll be able to get back in.'

'Okay,' Bradley nodded. 'I guess I'll catch up with Jarvis and tell him what I decided.'

'Tell him shit,' the judge said, annoyed. 'Let him wait until the directors' meeting tomorrow. Meanwhile, give me another taste.'

4

The Century City Hospital was almost hidden at the end of the Century City Building complex in the quiet corner of the Avenue of the Stars and Pico Boulevard. There were eleven stories comprising the hospital, the other floors were made up of various medical doctors, dentists, and various medical laboratories.

Dr. Fergus Maubusson, one of the most successful and well-known cosmetic surgeons, had an important suite, consisting of two complete operating rooms, one recovery room, two private consultation rooms, one for himself, and the other for his assistant and associate, Dr. Jon Takashima, another business office for the receptionist and bookkeeper as well as his three nurses, one of whom was always in his office twenty-four hours around the clock. Beyond that door was the small, quiet, softly lit entrance room. Appointments were very carefully policed so that no patient would ever meet another.

But this day was special. The entire morning appointments had been re-arranged because at five o'clock in the morning, Mr. Reed Jarvis had requested an emergency appointment with the doctor. When the night nurse had awakened the doctor, while holding Jarvis on the telephone line, the answer came without hesitation. What Mr. Jarvis wanted, Mr. Jarvis would get.

Dr. Fergus Maubusson, born Fred Markovits on the lower East Side of New York, had long ago decided that if he wanted to be successful in Beverly Hills the name was the game in a town that was built of names and bullshit. And he chose his name carefully: Fergus, because it was Scottish and the Scots were long known for conservatism, and, Maubusson

123

was French to sound off the feeling of the Gallic taste for cosmetics and beauty. And topped off with many genuine medical degrees, along with two years in the famed hospital specializing in cosmetic surgery in Lyon, France. The only photograph of importance in his reception room was of himself and Dr. Yves Pitanguy, who was usually considered the most important cosmetic surgeon in the world.

At the moment, he was seated on a high stool at the foot of his specially built operating table looking down at his patient, whose knees were held by stirrups, much like a gyn-ob used to examine his patients. He spoke without inflection, 'I've never seen a girl who could do a circumcision as surgically precise as this. She had to be Jewish.'

Reed stared across and up at the doctor, squinting at the blue halo from the light behind the surgeon. Reed was angry. 'It's nothing to laugh about, Doctor. What can we do about it?'

Dr. Maubusson was direct. 'First, we have to give you a tetanus shot. That might prevent any infection. Second, I would like you to bring in the girl that gave you this treatment. I want to check her out in case we're facing a rabid treatment as well as other complications.'

'Shit, Doctor,' Reed snapped. 'Isn't it bad enough that I ran into a vampire instead of a fucking cocksucker?'

'There could be well . . . ,' the Doctor said flatly. 'AIDS, for example. There have been many cases traced to prostitutes.'

Reed felt a chill running through him. 'Could that be possible?'

The doctor opened his hands expressively. 'Who knows? We don't even know how it happens. But whores could be carriers never even knowing that they have it.'

Reed looked at him. 'I don't know if I can get her to come in. She's a very well-known lady.'

'You can tell her we'll be completely confidential,' Maubusson said.

'She won't come,' Reed said surely.

'Maybe you should have her see her own doctor?'

'I don't think she would do that either,' Reed said. 'We

haven't parted in a friendly manner.'

'Tell her that you had a checkup this morning and that you tested a possible positive. That she should check herself for her own sake.'

Reed nodded silently, then looked up at him. 'Meanwhile, what can we do about this?'

'Two things for the moment,' said the Doctor. 'We load you with penicillin after we clean up the wound and bandage it. Then shoot you with a series of tetanus. It will be a series of about six shots. It will be uncomfortable for you. Fever and aches.'

'The hell about that,' Reed snapped. 'What will it do about my prick?'

'It may look a little different,' Maubusson said. 'But it will function normally.'

'What do you mean look a little different?' Reed asked.

'You've seen Japanese penises,' Dr. Maubusson said. 'Sort of slanted on the underside of the head and a little shorter.'

'Jesus!' Reed exclaimed. 'The damn thing is small enough. Is there anything you can do about that?'

'Sure,' Dr. Maubusson said smiling. 'I can build it up to any size you want. But first, we have to get you over this.'

Reed leaned back. 'Okay, let's go on with it. How much time will it take?'

'The procedure won't take very long but we have to keep you here for at least three hours in case you have any reactions to the tetanus shots.'

'Do I have to?' Reed asked. 'I have some very important meetings this morning.'

'If you're not carefully watched you could wind up with some very bad consequences. Possibly even a seizure.'

Reed thought for a moment. 'I'll arrange to hold the meetings until later in the day.'

'That makes sense, Mr. Jarvis,' the doctor said.

'But, I'll have to use your telephone,' Jarvis said. 'I'll have to get in touch with a number of people.'

'You can use my private office,' Dr. Maubusson nodded. 'No one will interfere with you.'

* * *

It was six o'clock in the morning and Daniel was having his morning coffee and getting ready for his usual morning call to the East Coast when the telephone rang. He picked it up. 'Peachtree.'

Jarvis' voice came through the receiver. He made no greetings, his voice was harsh. 'I'll be a little bit late, I should be able to make it by noon.'

Daniel was worried. 'Is there anything wrong?'

'Not with the deal,' Jarvis said. 'I have a personal problem that I can't delay.'

'Anyway I can help?' Daniel asked.

'No,' Jarvis said abruptly, then he quickly changed his mind. 'Can you get in touch with that nigger?'

'Thyme?' Peachtree asked.

'What other nigger did we talk about last night?' Jarvis said in an annoyed voice. 'I want to talk to her.'

'I'll get her to call you,' Daniel said.

'No,' Jarvis said. 'Just give me her number and I'll talk to her.'

'Hang on,' Daniel said, putting him on hold while he searched his computer file for the number. A moment later he went back on the line. 'Here it is. If she doesn't answer, call me back and I'll chase her down.'

'Okay,' Jarvis said shortly.

Peachtree spoke into the phone. 'Look, if there is a real problem, I can straighten her out.'

'It's my problem,' Jarvis said.

'What if Shepherd is pissed off when you're late? We've pushed him into the meeting for this morning,' Peachtree said.

'Tell him nothing. They can just wait for me,' Jarvis snapped. 'I'm only being polite to him about this deal, if he gives me any troubles I'll cut his balls off. He's out of money, no one else to go to except us.'

'I'll be in the office by eight o'clock if you want to reach me,' Peachtree said.

'Good,' Jarvis said and put down the telephone without even a parting word.

Daniel rose from the breakfast table, then turned and

picked up the telephone and called Thyme's number.

Her husky voice echoed in the receiver. 'Hello.'

'It's Daniel,' he said. 'Did Jarvis call you?'

'I just spoke to him,' she said angrily. 'That man's crazy.'

'What happened?'

'He started to beat up on me when I didn't want to fuck him.'

'Then what did you do?'

'What the hell do you think I did?' she said. Then she began to laugh. 'You should have seen his fucking face when I bit his goddam cock.'

'Jesus!' Daniel exclaimed. 'You hurt him?'

'Just a little,' she said, still laughing. 'I think I bit his fore-skin off. He was bleeding like a pig when he left.'

'Now we're both in trouble,' Daniel said. 'He's going to blow off your contract.'

'I won't be in any trouble,' she said. 'I already called Jimmy Blue Eyes. He told me if the asshole bothers me, he'll take care of him.'

'Just keep everything cool,' Daniel said, placating her. 'I'll get things straightened out.'

'You better,' she said flatly and hung up the phone.

5

It was one p.m. and the sleeting rain slammed against the penthouse thermopane windows in the World Resort and Casino in Atlantic City. In the large living room an old man leaned back comfortably wrapped in his blankets in a specially built barclaylounger. Around him several assistants looked down at him. The old man looked at his watch and then looked up at them. 'Get my nephew in California.'

'Yes, Don Rocco,' answered his secretary from her desk.

Jed was on the line in less than a minute. 'Weren't they supposed to close the deal by now?' Rocco growled, glancing at his wristwatch again. 'It's after ten o'clock in the morning there.'

'We've heard no word,' Jed said.

The old man sounded annoyed. 'The fucking Canadian is screwing us.'

'How can he, Uncle Rocco?' Jed asked. 'Without our money he can't swing the deal.'

'I heard that Milliken got him four hundred million from the Japs,' Rocco said.

'Want me to talk to Jarvis?' Jed asked.

'No. If he's trying to screw us there's only one thing to do,' the old man said. 'We screw him first.'

Jed held the telephone without speaking.

'I knew we should have put a blanket on the son of a bitch,' said Rocco. 'This way we never knew whatever the hell he was doing and we might have four hundred million screwed into this goddamn set-up before we know it.'

'Who do you want me to talk to?' Jed asked.

'They're having a directors' meeting at noon at the studio. I want you to talk to Shepherd, don't talk to Jarvis. Shepherd has to come up with eighty-five million for a production fund; if he doesn't make it, Jarvis has the right to pay him off in full. You tell Shepherd that you'll back him.'

'What makes you think that he'll believe me?' Jed asked. 'He doesn't know me from Adam.'

'He knows money,' Uncle Rocco said. 'You bring a bank check for the eighty-five million. He'll believe money.'

'Then where do we go after that?'

'We screw Jarvis. You talk to Milliken. He'll listen to you. After all, you're a good customer. You've already placed four billion bonds through him.'

'And what are you going to do?' Jed asked.

'I'll get my money back from him. After all, it's my bank who loaned him the money,' Rocco said.

'But you gave the money to a Canadian company,' Jed said.

'It was the Canadian Bank that gave him the loan,' Rocco said. 'We'll work it out or he'll lose his ass.'

'Okay,' Jed said. 'I'll get over to the meeting. Anything else?'

'Yes,' Rocco said. 'You tell Shepherd that under no circumstances does he make any further deals with Jarvis. We'll stay behind him all the way.'

'All right, Uncle Rocco,' Jed said.

Uncle Rocco suddenly changed the subject. 'What's the weather like out there?'

'Beautiful,' Jed said. 'Sunny and warm.'

'Damn,' Rocco complained. He got out of the barclaylounger and walked over to the thermopane windows and looked down at the sleeting rain to the boardwalk and ocean. He still had the telephone in his hand. He mumbled complaining to his nephew. 'There's no fucking luck. Here I am freezing my ass in the east while you're out there in sunshine and orange county getting fat and happy. We Sicilians have no luck.'

'You can move out here, Uncle Rocco,' Jed said. 'You can live like a king.'

'No,' Rocco said. 'I made my deal. I agreed to stay here. I move out there and it would be like Bonanno. Everybody agreed that he could move out there. His business would be protected. He'd have no problems. Then a few years later he started his car in his driveway and that was all. Boom! I feel safer in my own territory. At least, I know what's going on here.'

The fourteenth story of the high-rise building just inside the studio gate was known as the Gates of Heaven. The top floor was reserved only for Bradley Shepherd. The other executives were placed on the floors below, in accordance with their importance, the higher the position, the higher the floor. But everyone knew that below the ninth floor there were flunkies with titles instead of money and power, even though their large windows looked down on the sound stages and other offices of Millennium Films.

It was already eleven-thirty in the morning. Jed parked his customized Chevy Blazer where the guard at the studio gate had pointed him to park. Somehow, it didn't look out of place with all the splendor of the stretchout limos, Rolls, Mercedes, European sports cars and their American cousins, Cadillacs and Lincolns.

The guard in the large pink marble lobby sitting importantly behind the massive desk, looked at him with a surly expression. He asked Jed's business and then whispered into the telephone, and pointed to the first bank of elevators. 'First door, Mr. Stevens. That's the private elevator express to Mr. Shepherd's office.'

Jed stepped into the elevator. There were no buttons to press. The doors closed automatically and the touch of his weight on the elevator floor sped it up to the fourteenth floor. He stepped out of the elevator. A receptionist, who could be a clone of Meryl Streep, nodded to him coolly. 'Mr. Stevens?'

He nodded silently.

She pointed an elegantly manicured finger. 'Door One.'

'Thank you.' He walked to Door One and opened it. Behind the door, three secretaries were behind their desks. One of them rose from her chair and came toward him. 'Mr. Stevens?'

He nodded.

'I'm Sherry,' she said in a soft voice. 'I'm Mr. Shepherd's

personal secretary. He's in the directors' meeting at the moment, but he asked if you would make yourself comfortable in his office until he returns. In the meantime, may I offer you some coffee, tea?'

'Nothing, thank you,' he said. 'I have time, I can wait.' He waited until she left the office then walked over to the window and looked out. To the south and west he could look out over the studio and to the north and east was the seventy acres of bleak land beyond the marina that was planned for Fantasyland. He took a cigarette from his pocket and lit it. 'Shit,' he said to himself, thinking about the eighty-five million dollar cashier's check in his pocket. 'There has to be a lot of money out there somehow.'

He turned from the windows and looked down at Shepherd's desk. It was completely unmarred by a piece of paper, not even a telephone. He wondered how the man got his telephone calls. Maybe he had an Austin hearing aid stuck into his ear lobe with a button dial stuck in his pocket. Then he laughed aloud and dragged at his cigarette. 'Sherry,' he called out to the empty room.

The secretary's voice came from hidden speakers in the ceiling and walls. 'Yes, Mr. Stevens?'

'Could you come in for a moment?' he asked.

She appeared in a moment. 'What can I do for you?'

'Is there any way you can get Mr. Shepherd out of his meeting for a few minutes?'

'He's at a board meeting,' she answered.

'Then it's even more important that you have him speak to me.'

She hesitated. 'How important?'

'I have an eighty-five million dollar cashier's check made out in his name,' he answered.

Sherry was bright. 'I'll get the message to him.'

'Thank you,' Jed smiled. 'And, meanwhile could you have one of your assistants bring me a cup of black coffee with two sugars?'

Bradley sat at the head of the large oval directors' table. Silently, he glanced around the group. The only director absent was Jarvis. Brad spoke to Siddely, Jarvis' attorney. 'Where the hell is Jarvis?'

Siddely was nervous. 'I don't know,' he said in a hoarse voice. 'I've called everywhere I thought I might be able to reach him, but no answer. The last I saw of him was when he left the party. That was about two in the morning.'

'Reed said he would have a check for me,' Brad said. He turned to Daniel Peachtree. 'Have you heard from him, Daniel?'

'Reed has never been late to an appointment,' Peachtree answered nervously. 'Maybe he had a problem with his car.'

Sherry came into the boardroom and pressed a note into Bradley's hand. She waited a moment until he had scanned it. 'Any answer, sir?'

Bradley nodded to her silently. After she had left the room, he turned to Judge Gitlin who was seated beside him. 'Guess we might wait a bit more,' he said. 'Gentlemen, the bar will be open in the dining room next door for coffee and drinks. The judge and I will be in my office.' He smiled and glanced around the table. 'Just give me a call as soon as Jarvis shows up.'

6

The giant sign spread across the two-lane entranceway.
Between the lanes was a two-man guard shack, above it was
the sign that read 'MILLENNIUM FILM CORP. INC.'

Reed Jarvis gazed at the sign, as he sat back in his white
specially built stretchout limousine, complete with black-out
windows in the rear seat compartment. He felt secure in the
bullet-proof car that could not be penetrated even by a missile
launched from a bazooka. He spoke softly into his scrambler
telephone to Peachtree. 'I'm on the way,' he said, putting
down the telephone.

Despite his physical discomfort he felt good. The company
he was just entering represented three billion dollars of newly
invested American money. It was not only the film company,
it was twelve television stations, thirty radio stations, and real
estate that already had thirty-four high-rise office buildings,
apartments and hotels. Now there was also the cable company
and the video film rental and sales, sold in more than twenty
thousand retail stores across the country. And he had control
of all of it for only two hundred million of his own and eight
hundred million of syndicate money. All he had left to do was
to spin off the real estate and he would have more than enough
to take the syndicate out and Milliken and Drexel Burnham
and Lambert had agreed to guarantee his money.

They were all assholes, he thought to himself. It was not
important to him that they had lost more than a half billion
dollars in the last two years. There were assets to make it
back and even more. Little did they know what was on the
horizon. He would show them how to make this business
work. He glanced toward his chauffeur's compartment as the
driver spoke to the uniformed guard who had come out from

the guard shack to check them. Reed smiled to himself. This was only the first day, after that they would all know his car.

The guard nodded at the chauffeur, and holding a plastic card in his hand, he went behind the car and placed the card under the rear axle of the limousine. He nodded back to the chauffeur, and waved to him to proceed.

The guard stood outside the small shack until the limousine turned, and he stepped back into the guard shack and looked down at the two guards he had tied securely on the floor. Coolly, he removed his gun from his holster and carefully attached the silencer to his automatic, then he shot each of the guards in the forehead. Calmly, he walked out of the guard shack and onto the street outside the studio gate.

Quickly, he slipped behind the wheel of an unobtrusive dark green Ford and turned on the motor. Then he glanced back at the studio gate, checking the second sweep of his watch. At exactly the moment when the second hand reached twelve, he turned his car into the traffic as the deafening roar of the exploding bomb came to his ears from the studio behind him.

Daniel Peachtree walked into the boardroom where the other directors were sitting. 'I've just heard from Jarvis. He's in his car, on the way here. It should only be a few more minutes.'

Siddely smiled, relieved. 'Good, I never knew him to miss a meeting.'

The moment the words had fallen from his lips, the noise of an explosion echoed through the room, rocking the building momentarily.

Siddely was pale. 'What the hell is that? An earthquake?'

Daniel looked at the man's hands gripping tightly to the table. 'No way,' he said. 'I'm a Californian. I've been in a few earthquakes, they're not anything like that. Let's go out onto the balcony and see what's happening down there.'

The other directors quickly followed after him. They looked over the steel railing and down at the front of the office building. There was a large white stretchout limousine spread and twisted on the roadway below them, smoke poured out from inside it but it still held together like a swollen spoiled can of sardines. Around the roadway shattered glass was scattered both from the windows of the car and the windows of the large glass office entrances. The noise of a fire alarm screamed into the air and men in uniforms came running from the office building staring at the car.

'What the fuck happened?' one of the directors asked.

Daniel looked down at the mess below them, then he turned to the directors who were staring at him. His voice was as pale as his face. 'I guess we just lost Reed Jarvis. That was his limo. I recognize it.'

'That had to be a car bomb,' McManus, Bank of America's representative on the board, said. 'I've spent two years in Beirut and I've heard a few of them. I wonder who the hell could have done it?'

'I haven't the faintest idea,' Peachtree said. 'But that's not my job, that belongs to the police. I still have business to take care of.'

He walked back into the boardroom and picked up the first telephone. Quickly, he tapped out a combination of internal numbers.

A girl's voice answered. 'KFAN-TV.'

'News desk. Emergency,' he said shortly.

Siddely came up behind him. 'Aren't you going downstairs to see what's happened?'

'In a moment,' Daniel said. 'I want the TV crew outside before any of the other stations get out here to cover it.' He turned and spoke into the telephone. 'This is Peachtree. A limo just blew up in front of the Gates of Heaven. If we don't have our TV crew on this and on the air before any other station has it, I'll have a whole new staff running this news department tomorrow.' He waited a moment while the man spoke. 'I know nothing other than what I told you.'

He replaced the telephone onto the receiver and turned to the other directors. 'I just thought it was our own story, we should at least be the ones who get the scoop before anyone else.'

They stared at him. Sherman Siddely, who had put the whole deal together for Jarvis, lit a cigarette with a shaking hand. 'If it's really Jarvis inside that car, we're all in a lot of trouble.'

Bradley appeared in the doorway. 'It was Jarvis in the car,' he said, moving into the boardroom, Judge Gitlin and Jed Stevens following behind him. 'I just came from downstairs. The whole lobby is a mess, but fortunately, no one has been hurt there. The guard down there told me it was Jarvis' limo that had just stopped in front of the building.'

'Jesus,' Siddely suddenly paled. 'I can't believe it.'

'You need a drink,' Bradley said. He turned to the others. 'We all need a drink.'

Daniel opened the bar and took out several bottles. He placed a tray of glasses on the bar and began pouring whiskey into each of them. Silently, they all began swallowing their drinks. He sipped his own slowly and watched Bradley.

Bradley held his glass in his hand without sipping his drink. He met Daniel's eyes and nodded. 'I saw the TV crew moving on the scene. I figured that you called them.'

Daniel nodded. 'I thought since it was our story, we should be first on the air with it.'

'Good thinking,' Bradley said approvingly. 'What was it that you told me at the party? That Jarvis was going to appoint you the President and CEO?'

'That was what he was thinking about,' Daniel answered nervously.

Bradley nodded. 'It was a good thought. You have the job.'

Daniel's mouth was agape. 'I – I don't understand. I thought –'

Bradley interrupted. 'Don't look a gift horse in the mouth. I know a good idea when I see it. You can handle this business better than I can. You just proved it under fire. Turning a disaster into a triumph.'

Siddely flushed. 'But now, we have problems. Without Jarvis, where are we going to get the money to continue operating?'

'We'll manage,' Bradley said calmly. 'The main thing is not to panic. Let's adjourn this meeting until five this afternoon. I have a feeling we're going to be crawling with cops and press for a few hours.' He turned to Daniel. 'You're the CEO, so you're stuck with having to deal with this.'

'I'll call the PR boys in on it,' Daniel said.

'Good,' Bradley nodded. He turned to the others. 'We'll arrange to meet here again at five o'clock.'

Daniel came into Bradley's office, his face drawn and tired. 'The police want to talk to all of the directors. I told them that we were all shocked about this and they agreed they would wait and talk to us tomorrow.'

'Good,' Bradley said.

Judge Gitlin looked at Daniel. 'Do the police have any idea as to who might have done it?'

Daniel shook his head. 'They just feel that it was a professional hit. The killer also killed the two guards at the entrance shack. He took no chances that he could be identified.'

'I wonder if the killer was in the shack when I came in. I got here only about half an hour before Jarvis,' Jed said.

'Did you get parking instructions?' Daniel asked.

'Yes,' Jed answered. 'He stuck a sticker on my windshield.'

'Then you saw one of our own men. Maybe one of them that was killed,' Daniel answered. 'Meanwhile, the police are going to check on what Jarvis has been doing in the last few days. Maybe they'll learn something more about him that will give them a clue about this.'

'This publicity isn't going to help us. Our stock hasn't been doing that great in the market as it is. Now it will really go into the shithouse,' Brad said. 'Let's get back to the directors and see if we can find some way to counter it.'

Silently, they all filed into the boardroom. The directors were already there. Quickly, Bradley went to the head of the table. He remained standing as they took their seats. Briefly, he told them what Daniel had informed him on the police investigation. He was silent for a moment, then spoke. 'We're all in shock, gentlemen, so I think this meeting should be brief and to the point. There are two important problems facing us right now. The first problem is money to continue operating. Fortunately, I have been able to arrange a short-term loan of eighty-five million dollars. I think that can hold us for the moment. The second problem is up to all of us. We have to marshal our friends in the market to rally round us. I will ask each of you to help in this matter.'

A general assent came from the directors.

Bradley looked down to Siddely. 'Sherman, we have to know as soon as possible who will control Jarvis' stock and their intentions about it.'

Sherman looked at him, then at the other directors. 'As far as I know Jarvis had bought this stock in his name personally. I don't know the details of his will, but I do know his wife will be his only heir.'

'You can talk to her and find out what she has in mind?'

'I can try,' Sherman said. 'But one thing I do know, she hated him. They stayed married only because of the financial problems that would be created had they gotten a divorce. She's in Toronto and I'll get up there to see her.'

'Good enough, thank you,' Bradley said. 'Now for other important business. As you all may know, I have to devote more time to my own oil company, and I feel that it would be unfair to Millennium if I continue in the day to day operation of the studio. Therefore, I ask you to agree with me that Daniel Peachtree should be elected to the position of President and CEO of Millennium and I will move to the position of Chairman of the Board.'

There was a moment's silence as the directors looked at each other, then Sherman Siddely spoke up. 'I'm concerned only about the public relations of this change in management at this particular moment. I am afraid that the public might feel that you are running away from this situation and the difficulties that now face the company.'

'That's a crock of shit, Sherman,' Bradley said evenly. 'I know that you and Jarvis had already spoken to the directors about Peachtree's position. The only difference in this proposal that I'm bringing to the table is that I become the Chairman instead of Jarvis. Daniel will do a good job and I will be behind him and continue to support the company with its financial problems.'

Siddely's face flushed. 'Jarvis had a plan to refinance the company.'

'It might sound like cold ass,' Bradley said. 'But dead men don't make plans. All I can suggest is that you stay on top of his estate and make sure that we don't have any flap in that area.' He turned to the others. 'Now I will entertain a motion for the promotion of Peachtree and for me to become the Chairman.'

It took only moments for the motion to be seconded and approved. Bradley smiled. 'Congratulations, Daniel. Now your work will be really cut out for you. You'll have to send out press releases about the reorganization and also about the condolences we all feel about the Jarvis tragedy.'

Daniel glanced around at the directors. 'I already have the public relations people working on Jarvis.'

'Good,' Bradley answered.

'I'll send the releases out about the changes in our positions the day after,' he said. He looked at Bradley. 'The eighty-five million fund is firm?'

'I have it in the bank, we'll transfer to the company as soon as we complete the paperwork,' Bradley confirmed.

'That will help me a great deal,' Daniel said. 'I have several good opportunities for production in film and TV but the big problem is that the major agencies want to see our money.'

Bradley turned back to the board of directors. 'I suggest that we adjourn and let Daniel do his work. As for the rest of us, I have a feeling we're going to be driven crazy by the media and the police. There's no way we'll be able to avoid them. My advice to you is relax, tell them what you know and it will be over soon enough.'

Siddely shook his head. 'I still can't believe it. I don't know who would want to have him killed.'

'I do,' Bradley said. 'Me.'

7

'Congratulations, Mr. Peachtree,' his secretary greeted him as he returned to his office directly from the board meeting.

'Thank you, Gladys,' he smiled. 'How did you find out?'

Gladys laughed. 'The studio tom toms are faster than the speed of light.' She picked up a sheaf of telephone messages from her desk as she rose to follow him into his office. 'Thyme has called twice. She said that it's very important.'

'I'll call her,' he answered. 'Ask Mr. Shifrin to come to my office.'

'Yes, sir,' she said. She started to walk away, then turned back to him. 'Jack Reilly wanted to know if you would like him to have Mr. Jarvis' office redecorated for you before you moved in.'

Daniel looked at her. The king is dead. Really dead. Long live the king. 'I haven't really thought about it yet. Tell him I will let him know.'

'Yes, Mr. Peachtree,' she said. 'I'll get Mr. Shifrin for you.'

He waited until the door had closed behind her, then picked up the phone and dialed Thyme's private line. She answered. 'Thyme?' he asked.

'Yes?' She sounded nervous.

'Daniel.' He spoke in a low voice. 'I wanted to talk to you but I was tied up. You know about Jarvis?'

'I couldn't miss it. It's been all over TV. He must have been a real mess,' she laughed huskily. 'Christ, and how he was pissed off when I only bit off a little piece of his cock. I wonder what he's thinking about now.'

'Be serious, Thyme,' he said. 'The cops are going to find out that you saw him last night.'

'The cops were already here,' she said. 'That's why I called you.'

'What did you tell them?'

'The truth,' she said flatly. 'He took me home from the party and I invited him up for a nightcap. Instead he tried to deep throat me and I bit his cock. Then he called me some names and went away mad.'

'You told that to the police?' he asked incredulously.

'I learned that a long time ago. Don't lie to the police. They always find out if you do.'

'Did you tell them that I brought you to the party in my plane?' he asked.

'They already knew that,' she said.

'What else did they ask?'

'Nothing much,' she answered. 'If I knew of anyone who would do him in and I told them nobody except me. So they laughed and went away.'

'I hope you were straight when you talked to them. I don't think they would like it if you were high,' he said.

'Don't be an asshole, Daniel,' she laughed. 'They're homicide, not narcs.'

'You're going to show up in the papers,' he said.

'There's no such thing as bad publicity. Especially if it's a smell of scandal.' She laughed again.

'You're a real bitch,' he said in an admiring tone. 'There's nothing sacred for you.'

'You're no better,' she said. 'I don't see you crying.'

'We don't have any choices, do we?' he answered. 'We have to play the cards they deal us.' He glanced up as a knock came from the door and Neal poked his head in. He gestured to Neal to enter. 'Okay, Thyme, thanks for the call and keep in touch if there is anything I can do for you.'

'I'm cool,' she said. 'Rainbeau has invited me to spend a week with him at his home in Puerto Rico. Methanie and I are leaving tomorrow morning in his private jet.'

'You should have fun,' he said. 'I hear he has a fabulous place there.'

'It won't be just fun. We're planning an album and a video

together. He has a number of songs that we can work on,' she said.

'That makes it even better,' he said. 'Rainbeau is signed to our label.'

She laughed. 'But I'm not. You'll have to deal with my people.'

'Smart ass,' he chuckled. 'But I'm not worried about it. We'll work out.'

'I'm sure you will,' she said flatly. 'Especially after all we've been through together.'

'Bitch,' he laughed.

''Bye, baby,' she said and put down the telephone.

Daniel placed his telephone down and looked over at Neal. 'That was Thyme,' he explained. 'Everything is okay with her. We'll not have any trouble. The police have already spoken to her.'

'She didn't tell them that you arranged the date?' Neal was still anxious.

'She's a smart bitch,' Daniel answered. 'Always thinking but a little blackmail goes a long way.'

Neal smiled. 'I feel better already. It could have been very embarrassing for us.' He was still standing in front of the desk. 'Congratulations, Daniel. You've made it. I don't know whether to kiss you or shake your hand.'

Daniel laughed. 'For now, you can shake my hand. I don't know who will be popping into the office.'

'The power trip gave me a hard on that won't quit,' Neal said, rubbing his crotch.

Daniel stared at the bulge in Neal's pants. His mouth went dry. 'Take it out,' he said hoarsely. 'I want to see it.'

Neal quickly opened the zipper and his erect penis sprung, swollen before him. Without touching himself, he met Daniel's eyes. 'Say the word,' he whispered. 'And I'll come all over your desk.'

Daniel took a deep breath, his face flushed. 'Put it away,' he said nervously. 'This is no time to get crazy.'

'But I love you,' Neal said.

'Wait until we get home,' Daniel said. 'Right now, we have work to do.'

Quickly, Neal straightened his clothes and stretched back into the chair in front of Daniel's desk. 'Okay,' he smiled. 'I'm ready.'

'Is the presentation we prepared for Jarvis about changes in the company still at the printer's?'

'Yes,' Neal nodded.

'Get them all back and take them home. Make sure you have all of them and then put all except two of them into the shredder. Any asshole who might get a copy could blow us out of the water.'

'You mean all the work we put into it goes down the toilet?' Neal asked.

'Not really,' Daniel said. 'We'll simply rewrite it for Shepherd's point of view instead of Jarvis'. The program is just as good for one or the other.'

'But Jarvis had the money to carry it off. How do we know how much Shepherd has left?'

'I figure that he has the money,' Daniel said. 'He was too quick to move in during the meeting.'

Neal stared at him. 'Do you think Shepherd had anything to do with Jarvis' death?'

'I don't think so,' Daniel answered. 'I had a feeling that Bradley was ready to take Jarvis on at the meeting. The rest was coincidental.' He rose from behind his desk. 'Now get on your horse, you can make the printer's before he closes at eight o'clock.'

He waited until Neal had closed the door behind him then he asked his secretary to find Siddely for him. He found him in Jarvis' office. 'Sherman,' he said. 'I think we have to talk.'

'I was thinking the same thing,' Sherman answered. 'I'll be right down to your office.'

The attorney seemed as though he had regained his composure after the shock of the afternoon. He held his hand out to Daniel. 'Congratulations,' he said effusively. 'I am glad that Bradley has made the right choice.'

'Thanks, Sherman,' Daniel smiled. He gestured to a chair. 'We still have some problems. The most important is if there will be any flap from Jarvis' company or heirs.'

Sherman shook his head. 'I've already been trying to get in

touch with Mrs. Jarvis. But she's traveling in South America and nobody seems to know where she is.'

'That doesn't make me feel any better,' Daniel said.

'But there is another problem,' Sherman added. 'Jarvis had two hundred million of his own, but it wasn't enough so he took an under the table partner to advance him another two hundred million to begin the deal with Bradley. He was also expecting another four hundred to buy Bradley out. I don't know where he was going to get that money.'

'That's a lot of money. How could he hide it?' Daniel said.

Sherman looked at him. 'Jarvis was a strange man. He kept things to himself. Even I don't know who he was doing business with for that money.'

'Black money,' Daniel said flatly.

'Maybe,' Sherman said, holding up his hands. 'But we don't know.'

They sat there silently for a moment, then Daniel looked at him. 'All I can think is that we have to sit tight.' He reached for his first cigarette in six months. Deeply he sucked in the smoke, then coughed and choked. Quickly he put it out. 'Shit,' he said. He looked across the desk at Sherman. 'Do you think that Bradley might have been tied into it?'

'I don't think so,' Sherman said. 'Bradley was tapped out.'

'Bradley seemed very sure of himself. Even before the explosion,' Daniel said quietly. 'But there are two things I still don't understand. What were Judge Gitlin and Jed Stevens doing at the meeting with him?'

'Judge Gitlin is Bradley's attorney from Oklahoma. Jed Stevens I know nothing about.'

'I know about Stevens. He's the CEO of General Avionics Leasing Corporation,' Daniel said. 'He must be sitting on top of at least six billion. He leases commercial airplanes to half the airlines in the world.'

'Do you think Bradley brought him in?'

'Anything's possible,' Daniel said. 'That's just another thing we have to find out about.'

8

Brad dropped himself into the oversized chair behind his desk and looked across as Judge Gitlin and Jed sat in the comfortable chairs opposite him. He pulled the white handkerchief from his breast pocket and wiped the sweat from his brow. 'Jesus,' he said. 'Jesus.'

Judge Gitlin looked at him. 'We could use another drink.'

'Sherry,' Brad spoke into his intercom. 'The judge will have a shot of CC straight up. I'll have a Glenmorangie on the rocks.' He turned to Jed. 'And what will be your pleasure?'

'Coffee, black with sugar,' Jed answered.

A moment later Sherry came into the office and placed the drinks before them. Sherry turned to leave the office.

'Hold all calls,' Brad said.

She nodded and closed the door behind her. Brad lifted his drink. 'Cheers.'

The judge nodded and swallowed half his drink. Brad smiled and spoke into the intercom. 'I forgot, Sherry,' he said. 'The judge never takes one shot, he needs the bottle.'

Sherry returned quickly with the bottle of Canadian Club and left it on the desk in front of Judge Gitlin, then left.

Brad sat there silently for a moment then gestured to Jed. 'I'm puzzled. You came in out of left field. What brought you into this game?'

'I was at your party last night,' Jed answered.

'So were almost five hundred others,' Brad said. 'But none of them came in with eighty-five million dollars.'

'There's another thing I'm curious about,' Judge Gitlin said. 'The exact amount that was needed to keep him in the company. How did you know about that?'

Jed smiled. 'You have friends. I have friends. Friends talk. And I'm a gambler.'

'That's high stakes,' the judge said.

'You don't win with nickel bets,' Jed said.

'What do you expect to get out of it?' Brad asked.

'I don't know yet,' Jed answered. 'That's what we have to talk about.'

'Even with the eighty-five it will be tough with Jarvis in the deal. But you came in with the money before anything happened to him,' Brad said. 'I still don't know why.'

Jed smiled. 'Maybe I like your style. You throw a great party.'

The judge refilled his drink. 'You're a young man,' he said. 'Where do you get that kind of money?'

'I'm holding sixty percent of the stock of a company that I started. General Avionics Leasing Corporation which has six billion in assets.' Jed looked at them. 'So, gentlemen, you can see I can afford the game. Now, you just relax, I'm not going to take anything away from you. Maybe we'll be lucky and make a lot of money together.'

Brad turned to the judge. 'What do you think?'

'You have no choices,' the old man said. 'Besides, he reminds me of you. You're both crazy.'

'Jarvis' stake in this still worries me, now his estate still has an option of forty percent of Millennium's stock. How do we know what they'll do?' Brad said.

The judge spoke in a cold steely voice. 'You got yourself into that problem. You'll have to get yourself out of it.'

Jed turned to the judge. 'Brad will work his way out of it,' he said. 'I have faith.'

'Thank you,' Brad said. 'But we'll have to talk some more, after we have more facts in hand.'

'We will,' Jed said. 'But right now I have to get back to my office.' He rose to his feet and placed several business cards on the desk in front of Brad. 'You call me or I'll call you. We'll set up some proper meetings. Lawyers, accountants, the works.'

Brad looked up at him. 'But meanwhile don't you want a note for the eighty-five?'

Jed met his eyes. 'Do you have the money for it?'

'No,' Brad said.

'Then what difference will it make?' Jed smiled. 'We'll work it all out later.' He shook Brad's hand then the judge's. 'Gentlemen,' he said and left the office.

Judge Gitlin stared at the closed door. He turned to Brad. 'We better get a line on that boy. He's too relaxed for my taste. Also it's hard to trust a man who don't drink.'

Brad shook his head. He called Sherry on the intercom. 'Get me McManus at the Bank of America.' He nodded to the judge. 'You met McManus at the directors' meeting. He's been on our board since I got into Millennium. He'll check Stevens out for us.'

'When can we go home?' the judge said. 'Don't forget I'm an old man. I need some rest.'

Brad laughed. 'Then I'll tell Charlene to cancel your dinner date.'

'A dinner date?' the judge exclaimed. 'With who?'

'Zsa Zsa Gabor,' Brad answered. 'She likes older men.'

'I don't want to change Charlene's plans,' the judge said quickly. 'I'll be okay for dinner.'

Jed turned into the parking garage on the street level of the ten-story, green-mirrored glass building on Century Boulevard opposite the air freight area at LAX. He left his Chevy Blazer with the valet and walked to the elevators. He pressed the button for the seventh floor, taking him up to his office.

Kim Latimer, the attractive VP of Corporate Relations and Jim Handley, the always-worried-looking VP and Treasurer of GALC, were always waiting at the elevator door. It was crazy, but he could never get into his office unless one or the other of them were waiting at the elevator door. He was sure that they had paid off the parking valet.

'You've had a busy day,' Kim said.

'Kind of,' he answered as he started toward his office.

'What did you do with eighty-five million?' Jim asked. 'It left us short on the payment to Boeing.'

'It's safe,' he said. 'Pay Boeing out of the Rental Reserve Account.'

They followed him into his office. He looked down at the messages on his desk. He shook his head. Uncle Rocco was always the same. He never left any messages.

Handley looked at him. 'What happened to Jarvis?'

'He blew his top,' he answered wryly.

'Not funny,' the treasurer said. 'Does it affect us?'

'I don't think so,' he said. 'I'm dealing with Bradley.'

'How do we fit into this?' Jim asked.

Jed shrugged his shoulders. 'I'm not quite sure. I'm playing this one personally. I'll repay the company from my own account tomorrow.'

'Okay,' Jim said. 'I just want to protect you and us.'

'We'll be okay,' Jed said. 'Thanks.'

Jim left the office. Kim stood in front of his desk. 'Are you all right?' she asked.

'I'm okay,' he answered. He slipped into his chair. 'This has turned into a rough day,' he said. 'I'm tired.'

She came around behind him. 'Let me rub your neck and shoulders. It'll ease the tension.'

'Good,' he said. Her hands were gentle and warm against him. He rotated his head. 'That's like magic. It really helps.'

'Your Uncle Rocco called me on my private line,' she said.

He turned to her quickly. 'Why didn't you tell me before?'

She shook her head. 'Not in front of Jim.'

'What did he say?'

'He said that he will call you at home at midnight your time,' she said.

'What else did he say?'

'"Rico," he said. "They couldn't get him in New York, now they're putting together a grand jury to nail him in New Jersey."' She looked at him. 'He wants you to have your phones debugged. And sweep your apartment as well.'

'Get John Scanlon in Security and have him take care of it.'

'Are you in trouble?' she asked in a concerned voice.

'Not me,' he answered. 'But I am worried for my uncle.' He watched as she called Security then looked down at his messages. There was only one that was important. He picked up another phone. 'Let me talk to Rudy Mayer in Purchasing,' he said to one of the secretaries in his outer office.

Rudy came on the line. 'Yes, Boss.'

'What kind of deal does Aerospatiale want to give us on the A300s?'

'It's their new model. A300-200. Stretchouts. Carries four hundred passengers. You order ten and place them on US airlines, they'll give you a twenty percent discount and a twenty-year finance plan.'

'They give you any idea of the figures?'

'No,' Rudy said. 'They won't give any numbers until you tell them that you're interested.'

'Usually domestic airlines are cautious about foreign planes. But there is a market for them. Vacation season. Florida. Mexico. They're always short of space.'

'What do you want me to tell them?'

'Tell them I'm interested. I'll start talking to Eastern, American, Western and Mexicana,' he said.

'Mexicana isn't a US line,' Rudy said. 'Maybe they will be selling to them direct.'

Jed laughed. 'The Mexicans have no money. I can guarantee Aerospatiale.'

'Okay, Boss,' Rudy said. 'I'll get on it. Just one question. What do you do if Boeing is pissed off because you short them on 727-200s?'

'It all comes down to money,' Jed said. 'The A300 has a better payload and uses thirty percent less fuel than the B727. Maybe it's time Boeing stopped believing they're the only airplane in the world.'

He put down his phone and looked up at Kim.

Kim nodded. 'Scanlon said he would get on it right away.'

'Good,' he smiled. 'Come home, I'll shower and dress up. Then I'll take you out to dinner.'

'You have a deal,' she said. 'With one exception.'

'What's that?' he asked.

'I won't ride in that pickup truck.'

'Okay,' he smiled. 'We'll take the Corniche.'

'Lovely,' she smiled and picked up the telephone.

'Who are you calling?' he asked.

'Chasen's,' she said. 'Where else do you go out in a Rolls?'

9

'Why don't you come to bed?' Kim asked. 'It's almost two in the morning and you better get some sleep.'

'Uncle Rocco said he would call and he will,' Jed replied.

'It's five in the morning in the east,' Kim said. 'He's not a young man, he's probably gone to bed. He'll call you in the morning.'

'You don't know anything about my family,' Jed said. 'Uncle Rocco will call. He's not called the Capo for nothing.'

'Okay,' she said. 'Maybe he got tied up with something.'

The telephone rang. Jed looked at it in surprise. It wasn't his private phone, it was the hotel switchboard. Slowly he picked up the receiver. 'Stevens.'

The desk clerk sounded apologetic. 'Your uncle is here to see you, Mr. Stevens. He didn't give me his name.'

'My uncle doesn't need a name. He's my uncle,' Jed laughed. 'He's alone?'

'No, Mr. Stevens. He has two gentlemen with him.'

'Have one of the bellmen lead them to my cottage.' He put the phone down and looked at Kim. 'Uncle Rocco is here.'

'I better slip into something to wear,' she said.

'Take your time,' Jed said. 'I'll meet them in the living room.'

'My uncle isn't alone,' he said. 'He is with his secretary and bodyguard.'

'Uncle Rocco must be quite a man,' she said.

'He's old-fashioned,' Jed said. 'The Godfather never goes out without his staff.'

'If he's old-fashioned, what will he think about me?' she said, stepping into a pair of slacks.

'He called you, didn't he?' Jed asked.

'Yes,' she answered, slipping on a blouse. 'He wanted to talk to you.'

'He wouldn't have called you if he didn't believe you were okay,' Jed smiled. The doorchime rang. 'I'll get them,' he said.

He crossed to the entrance hall and opened the door. He slipped the bellman a fiver and led his uncle into the cottage. They looked at each other for a moment, then hugged and kissed each other on the cheek. His uncle was wearing a cashmere winter coat. 'Welcome to California, Uncle Rocco,' he said. 'Let me take your coat. It's warm here.'

His uncle nodded. 'I'm sweating,' he said as he slipped out of his coat. Then he gestured to his bodyguards. 'You remember Danny and Samuel?'

Jed nodded and shook hands with the men. At that moment Kim came into the living room. She smiled at them.

His uncle smiled at her. 'You're Kim, Jed's girl. I've spoken to you on the phone several times.' He took her hand and kissed it as an old-fashioned courtier.

He turned to Jed. 'She's very pretty,' he said and then in Italian, 'Siciliana?'

Kim laughed and answered him in Italian. 'No, I'm sorry, my parents were Scotch and Irish.'

'That's not too bad,' Uncle Rocco laughed.

'You must be exhausted,' she said. 'I can get you some coffee and sandwiches?'

'Just coffee, black and strong,' Uncle Rocco said.

'Right away,' she said and turned to the kitchen.

'You're looking good, Uncle Rocco,' Jed smiled.

'At my age you have to watch your diet,' his uncle said. 'Less pasta, less meat, more fish and green vegetables.'

'Vino?' Jed asked.

'Maybe later,' Uncle Rocco laughed. 'You are surprised to see me?'

'Yes,' Jed answered.

'It's family business,' Uncle Rocco said. 'We couldn't talk about this over the phone, so I chartered a plane.'

Jed looked at him silently.

'Do we have a place where we can talk alone?' his uncle asked.

'The den. No one can hear us in there,' Jed said.

Kim left two pots of coffee for them and closed the door behind her. Jed filled both cups and leaned back in the chair and looked at his uncle. 'Okay?' he asked.

'She makes good coffee,' Uncle Rocco said.

Jed nodded. 'You didn't come here for coffee.'

He chuckled. 'That's right.' He sipped more of his coffee. 'The Canadian got whacked,' he said.

'I know,' Jed said. 'I was there.'

'He was a bad man,' Uncle Rocco said.

'No worse than the others,' Jed said. 'Everybody gets greedy when it comes to money.'

'It's not only money,' Rocco said. 'He turned on his friends. That's against the rules.'

'I don't understand,' Jed said.

'Rico,' he said. 'He went to New York and told Giulani where I got all the money I loaned him. Now Giulani is getting the US District Attorney in New Jersey to prepare another case against me. They tried to get me in Manhattan, then in Brooklyn and lost. Now they're trying again.'

'What is that law about double jeopardy?' Jed asked.

He laughed. 'Don't be stupid. Each case is different. They're digging up other charges. The latest I hear from the grapevine, they're trying to tie me into the unions and the corruption in Atlantic City.'

'Can they make it stick?' Jed asked.

'I don't think they can. When I was offered Atlantic City unions, I turned it all down and gave it to the Scarfo family from Philadelphia. They wanted it. I told them they could be my guest. I was not interested in the day to day bullshit. I wanted to be like Frank Costello. An elder statesman.'

'Then what do you have to worry about?'

'Nothing, I hope,' he said. 'The only hard information they have was from Jarvis. But he can't go in front of the grand jury now. Dead men can't give testimony.'

Jed stared at his uncle in surprise. 'Don't tell me. You had him whacked?'

Uncle Rocco was indignant. 'Do you think I'm stupid? Then Giulani would really crawl up my ass.'

'He'll still try to nail you,' Jed said.

'Trying and getting are two different things,' Uncle Rocco retorted. 'Not that I wouldn't have liked to get the son of a bitch, but somebody beat me to it.'

'I need a drink,' Jed said, getting up. He looked down at his uncle. 'Would you like something?'

The old man nodded. 'Do you have any *vino rosso*?'

'Bolla Chianti,' he said.

'Vintage?' his uncle asked.

'Of course,' Jed smiled. 'I learned something from you.'

He walked into the living room. Uncle Rocco's men were sitting on the couch, a pot of coffee on the small table before them. He nodded and walked into his bedroom.

Kim was sitting on the bed, a newspaper spread out in front of her. She looked at him. 'Are you all right?'

'Fine. How about you?'

'I'm okay,' she said. 'A little bit nervous but okay.'

'Relax,' he said. 'Uncle Rocco wants *vino rosso* and I need a drink. I just came out to get it.'

'Want me to help?' she asked.

'No, I can handle it.' He went back through the living room to the kitchen. He took a bottle of wine and opened it. Then he went to the bar in the corner of the living room and picked up a bottle of Glenlivet and glasses, a bucket of ice, put them on a tray and went back to the den.

His uncle picked up the bottle of wine and checked the label. 'Eighty-two,' he said in a satisfied voice. 'A very good year. You really learned something.'

Jed smiled and helped himself to some scotch on the rocks while his uncle poured himself a glass of wine. His uncle held up his glass. '*Salute.*'

'*Salute.*' Jed sipped at his drink. He waited until his uncle finished his glass of wine and refilled it. He met his uncle's eyes. 'Do you have any idea who did it?'

'I have an idea,' Uncle Rocco answered. 'The hit was ordered out of Canada. The hitman was a French Canadian who works both sides of the border.'

'It ought to be easy for the police to pick him up then,' Jed said.

Uncle Rocco smiled. 'They'll never come near him. He's a real pro. By now he's probably on his way to Europe or South America.'

'You seem sure of that,' Jed said.

'That's where he'll be paid. France or Peru.' His uncle sipped more of his wine. 'If he's really smart he'll go to France. If he winds up in Peru, he'll be finished. He'll get whacked.'

'You know something that I don't?' Jed asked.

His uncle nodded. 'Alma Vargas.'

'The Peruvian girl?' Jed said in surprise. 'Where did she get into this?'

'She married Jarvis in France three years ago. He was getting ready to divorce her. She didn't like it. Jarvis was a very rich man. Now she's a very rich *putana*.' Uncle Rocco chuckled. 'You don't know how difficult it was for me to get her out of the country when you came back with her. She wanted to marry you.'

'Jesus,' Jed said. He poured himself another scotch. 'There goes your money.'

'Maybe not,' Uncle Rocco smiled. 'She still likes you.'

'Wait a minute,' Jed said. 'She's not going to give you back the money.'

'I know that,' Uncle Rocco said. 'All I want you to do is arrange for her to put Jarvis' interest in support of Shepherd.'

'Does she know that you gave Jarvis the money?'

'She introduced me to Jarvis. I thought he had a great plan.' He looked into his wine glass. 'Maybe I wasn't so smart but neither was Jarvis. That Peruvian *putana* was smarter than all of us.'

'Peruvian pussy,' Jed laughed.

'I don't understand,' his uncle said.

Jed looked at him. 'Many years ago when I was young. She stood naked on the deck of the boat in the Amazon. And she told me about Peruvian pussy. It was the best in the world, she said. But she never told me as well that it was the smartest.'

'What do you think?' Uncle Rocco asked. 'Will you talk to her?'

'Of course I will,' Jed replied. 'But we don't have to do anything. The money is already in the company and there's no way she can get it out. Believe me, Uncle Rocco, this is something I really know about. By the time I'm finished, Shepherd and I will control it all and she will have only a minority interest.'

The old man stared at him. 'You mean that?'

'That's my kind of business,' Jed answered.

Uncle Rocco sat there silently for a while, then he sighed slowly. 'I'm getting old,' he said. 'Ten years ago I would never have gone for a scam like this. It was too legal for me.'

Jed laughed. 'Legal or illegal. It's where they draw the lines. They're the same thing.'

'No,' the old man said. 'I'm too old. I've lost my smarts.'

'You're the same as you always were, Uncle Rocco,' Jed said gently. 'It's just a different game.'

Uncle Rocco shook his head slowly. 'I want you to come back to the family.'

'I've never left the family, Uncle Rocco,' Jed said. 'What is it that you want me to do?'

'I am getting old,' he said in a suddenly weary voice. 'I want you to help me.'

Jed reached for the old man's hand. He felt his uncle's hand trembling. 'Tell me, Uncle Rocco.'

'Get me out of these wars,' Uncle Rocco said huskily. 'I want to die in bed.'

THE LAST MAN OF HONOR

Salt Water Taffy. The Steel Pier. The auction houses that filled every other store on the boardwalk with phony antiques. The two passenger rolling chairs pushed back and forth along the boardwalk, pushed by a smiling black man who also acted as a tour guide for seventy-five cents an hour. The white sand covered with picnicking families and the vendors, mostly teenage kids, selling candy apples, Eskimo pies and popsicles. That was the Atlantic City I remembered when I was eight years old and spent two weeks at Aunt Rosa's in the small house she had rented at the far end of the boardwalk.

It was not anything like the monster hotel and casinos I looked down on from Uncle Rocco's penthouse that turned the million lights into Las Vegas on the boardwalk. I moved away from the windows and went back to Uncle Rocco's large mahogany desk. On the corner of the desk there was a large candy dish of Salt Water Taffy. I gestured to it. 'I never knew that you liked that.'

He smiled. 'Why not? The president has a jar of jelly beans on his desk.'

I laughed. 'Okay. But I remember when I stayed at Aunt Rosa's, she wouldn't let me have any. She said it would make cavities in all my teeth.'

Uncle Rocco chuckled. 'All women had funny ideas in those times. Did it ever give you any cavities?'

'I had a few cavities when I was a kid,' I said. 'But I don't know whether it was from Salt Water Taffy. I never got to eat that many.'

Uncle Rocco laughed. 'I eat them all the time and I don't have any cavities. All they do is stick to my choppers and I have to take them out and clean them.'

161

I laughed. 'I never knew you had false teeth.'

'I've had them a long time,' he answered. 'When I was young some son of a bitch hit me in the face with a baseball bat.'

'What did you do?' I asked.

'Nothing,' he replied. 'I was going to blow the bastard away but your grandfather stopped me. He was a Genovese and it would have started a war. That would have been really crazy because they would wipe us out. At that time the Genovese was the biggest family in New York. So my father sent me to the best orthodontist in Manhattan and I wound up with the greatest looking choppers in the world.'

I laughed. 'They're still pretty good.'

He nodded. 'This is about the fifth pair.'

I looked at him. 'We have some things to talk about.'

'That's right,' he said. The telephone rang and he picked it up. He listened for a moment, then answered. 'Send him in.' He looked up at me. 'I have to talk to this man. It won't take too long.'

'I can wait,' I said. 'Do you want me to leave the room?'

'No,' he answered. 'You can stand near the windows.' He opened a drawer from his desk and handed a Luger automatic to me. 'I know you know how to work one of these.'

I stared at him. 'You're expecting trouble?'

'Not really,' he said. 'But in my business –' He shrugged his shoulders.

I walked over to the windows as I slipped the gun into my jacket pocket. From the corner of my eyes I saw the man come through the door. A swarthy man of medium height, a dark and angry face, a tight-fitting suit.

My uncle rose from his desk and held out his hand. 'Nico,' he said smoothly. 'Good to see you.'

The man ignored my uncle's hand. 'You screwed me out of three hundred grand,' he said harshly.

My uncle was unruffled. 'You're a shmuk,' he said. 'If I wanted to screw you I would have taken you for three million.' Nico seemed to get angrier. 'It isn't the money,' he snapped. 'It's the principle.'

'What do you know about principle, you asshole?' Uncle

Rocco's voice grew cold. 'You screwed your father before he was cold on his death bed. What happened to the money your father wanted to divide between you and your uncle?'

'My uncle disappeared,' Nico said. 'We never could find him.'

'You made sure that nobody would look for him,' Uncle Rocco said, still cold. 'Especially in the pig farm you owned in Secaucus.'

'That's all horseshit,' Nico said angrily. 'That has nothing to do with this. You still owe me three hundred grand.'

Uncle Rocco stood up behind his desk. 'I am a man of honor,' he said quietly. 'I made an agreement with your father when I came down here, he took over the unions and he gave me five thousand a month for expenses. After your father died I never asked for the money. It was sent each month to me by messenger just as it came from your father.'

Nico stared at him. 'Nobody was authorized to do that.'

'That's your problem,' my uncle said flatly. 'Maybe nobody in your organization likes you.'

'I'll get rid of the son of a bitch,' Nico said.

'Still your problem,' Uncle Rocco said. 'You make sure that the five grand comes to me every month. Just as your father and I had agreed.'

'And if I don't?' Nico snapped.

Uncle Rocco smiled and sat back into his chair. 'As I said, I am a man of honor. I keep my word and I believe you will honor your father's word.' He paused a moment then smiled gently. 'Or you will find yourself joining your uncle in the pig farm.'

Nico stared at him. 'You're crazy, old man. I can hit you right here.'

I watched them and started to take the Luger from my pocket, but Uncle Rocco seeing from the corner of his eyes, shook his head. I let the gun stay in my pocket.

'Then you're more of a shmuk than I thought,' Uncle Rocco said easily. 'You'd never get out of here alive.' He laughed. 'I'm seventy-two, you're only forty-seven. You're getting lousy odds. Insurance companies give me four years, they give you twenty-seven.'

Nico sat there quietly for a moment. Finally he nodded. 'Don Rocco,' he said in a respectful voice. 'I apologize. I was angry.'

'It is nothing, my son,' Uncle Rocco said quietly. 'Just think before you act. You will find that life will be easier.'

'Yes, Don Rocco,' Nico said, rising from his chair. 'I apologize again.'

'Goodbye, my son,' Uncle Rocco said. He watched Nico leave the room, then he turned around to me. 'Now you know why I want you to get me out. I'm tired of dealing with these crazies.'

'Do you really think he would have done anything?' I asked.

'Who knows?' Uncle Rocco asked. 'But he won't get another chance. I have his first underboss already talking to the Feds. They'll get him.'

'You deal with the FBI?' I questioned.

'No,' he answered.

'But you had his man talk to the Feds.'

'That man came to me for advice. He knew I was a man of honor with much experience,' he said quietly. 'All I told him is that the Feds would not kill him and Nico would. What he decided to do was his own choice.' He held out his hand. 'Give me the gun.'

I placed the Luger on the desk in front of him. He placed it in the desk drawer. But not before he polished it with a soft rag. 'I don't want to have any of your fingerprints on it.'

'Thank you,' I said. 'And why did you have it unloaded? I might have been killed.'

Uncle Rocco smiled. 'No way. I have a sawed-off shotgun built into the desk aimed at the chair he was sitting in. He would have been blown across the Atlantic Ocean.'

I stared at him. 'You lie a lot, Uncle Rocco. What else have you lied to me about?'

He shook his head sadly. 'You're family. I am a man of honor. Whatever I tell to you is for your own protection.'

'What protection do I need?' I asked. 'I live a straight life. General Avionics is a respected company. All we do is buy airplanes and lease them to airlines. Everything is legitimate.'

My uncle looked up at me sadly. 'A Di Stefano is a Di

164

Stefano even if his legal name is Stevens. Maybe the world you live in doesn't know that, but the world that you were born into knows who you are. Even back in Sicily. That's why your father went off the mountain in Trapani. Old worlds don't die, their hatred and vendettas live on.'

I stared at him. 'You haven't retired, have you?'

He didn't answer.

'My father said that,' I said bitterly. 'Not to trust your word.'

Uncle Rocco looked straight into my eyes. His voice was husky. 'You have to believe me. I have never betrayed my family.'

'A man of honor,' I said sarcastically. 'I haven't heard that before. Where did you pick that up?'

His voice was cold. 'The five biggest families are in New York. They respect me. The Sicilian commission composed of the most important families, including the Corleonesi, and the Borgettos, honor me as the only American that is their equal. I have never betrayed their trust and respect.'

'If that is true,' I asked, 'why are you concerned that someone would kill you?'

'The older men are gone. The young are taking over and they're all greedy. They can't wait.'

'What do they want from you?' I asked. 'You tell me you're out of the business.'

Uncle Rocco shook his head. He tapped his temple with a forefinger. 'This is what they want. I am the only one left who can communicate between the old world and the new. They know that one word from me and they would be cut off from the old country.'

'Why should that bother them?'

'Ten to fifteen billion a year,' he said.

'The Sicilians have that much power?' I asked.

'They have a worldwide army. They have made deals with the Chinese triads and the Colombian cartels. That gives them thousands of soldiers. As well as the American government nailing them from all sides with the Rico Act.' He took a deep breath. 'It's not like it used to be. Once we were kings, now we're scrambling for crumbs. The Americans are getting weaker, each family is becoming smaller and smaller.'

I was silent for a moment. 'I still don't know what you want me to do.'

He stared at me. 'How much do you think your business is worth?'

'Maybe two or three billion,' I said.

'How much do you get out of it?'

'Over a million a year,' I answered.

He laughed. 'Chicken shit.'

I didn't speak, just looked at him.

'What if I could put you into a legitimate investment company with over twenty billion in cash and assets that you would own forty percent of, and earn you more than five million a year?' His voice was dripping with honey.

I met his eyes. 'And who would own the other sixty percent?' I asked.

He nodded. 'Other men of honor?'

I shook my head. 'Uncle Rocco, Uncle Rocco,' I said laughing. 'That's too rich for my blood. I'm happy in my own little store.'

'You're getting more and more like your father,' Uncle Rocco grumbled. 'I could have made him into a multimillionaire. But he went his own way.'

'He did all right,' I said. 'He had a good business and a good life. What more can any man want?'

Uncle Rocco shrugged. 'Maybe you're right.'

'He didn't need anyone's permission to retire.' I watched him silently for a moment as I sat in a chair on the other side of his desk. 'Now, how can I help you?'

'First, you take my offer to head up the investment company. After that we begin to buy companies with profit potential. Your company, Millennium Film Corporation, then Shepherd's oil companies, Jarvis' Canadian holdings. Outside of your own company they're all cash short and losing their assets but they can be bought up. Then there is a list of other companies we have looked at. It will be up to you to get them all together. It could be like RJR and Nabisco but cash-rich, not on borrowed monies.' He watched me intently, as if wanting to see my decision before I spoke.

'What do you think the government will do when they find out all of your men of honor are in a business like this?' I asked.

'They are not in the company. The company is nothing but legitimate businessmen, Japanese, Europeans, Arabs. The banks are all the big banks. Citicorp, Morgan Stanley, Chase. Stockbrokers, Merrill Lynch, Hutton, Goldman Sachs. Everyone completely straight and blue ribbon.'

'And what do you get out of it?' I asked.

'Out of this,' he said. 'I retire completely legit.'

I took a deep breath. 'Do you know that I love you, Uncle Rocco?'

'I know,' he said quietly.

'But, it won't work. It's like a daydream.'

'They are all men of honor. We made an agreement. We have all the money we need. Twenty billion clean. The government has no strings on it, all the taxes have been paid. We will have a legitimate business. For us the Mafia is over.'

'For you old men it may be over but the Mafia will never be finished. It's like the leaning tower of Pisa. It leans a little more each year but it never breaks.'

Uncle Rocco stared at me. 'What are you trying to tell me?'

'You have no choice, Uncle Rocco,' I answered. 'You have to stay here. You have too much in your head to walk away from them.' I met his eyes. 'How long do you think you would last?'

'Your father told me that same thing fifty years ago,' Uncle Rocco said.

'My father was right then,' I said. 'And his advice is just as good now.'

Uncle Rocco sighed. 'Then what do I do?'

'You seem to have everything under control here,' I said. 'Just do what you always did. Fuck all of them.'

'I still want to get Jarvis' piece back. It's a big number and I have some partners who want their shares back.'

'I told you I would help you with that,' I said.

'Good.' He smiled suddenly. 'Let's go down to my dining room. I have a surprise for you.'

Uncle Rocco loved surprises. This was a big one. Alma Vargas with her eleven-year-old daughter. Angela, named after her father.

Book Three

THERE ARE NO MORE GODFATHERS

1

Kim was angry. 'You're an asshole,' she said. 'What the hell do you care if your uncle loses two hundred or four hundred million? He has so much money that he won't even miss it.'

'He asked me to help,' I said. 'After all, he is family.'

'That's his con,' she said. 'He doesn't give a damn what happens to you. All he wants to do is get you into his spider web. You can take care of his business, he doesn't care what happens to the business you built and developed over the years. And you have enough money, you don't even need his help.'

'Calm down and come to bed, Kim,' I said. 'Everything will work out all right.'

'Sure,' she said sarcastically. 'You'll either wind up in jail or in the ground with the others.'

'I'm staying in my own business,' I said. 'All I'm doing is straightening things out. Then I'm out of there.'

'Meanwhile, you're out eighty-five million,' she said bitterly. 'I don't see where he's going to return the money to you.'

'He'll return it,' I said stubbornly. 'It's a matter of honor.'

'But you have already signed the agreement with Bradley. You've guaranteed him another four hundred million and his shrewd old lawyer set it up so that you don't get any stock in the company until all the money is paid in.' She stared at me. 'Where did your brains go? You don't work like that with General Avionics. You make sure that all the t's are crossed and the i's are dotted when you make any deal.'

'What are you getting pissed about?' I snapped. 'It's my problem, not yours.'

She turned away from the bed. 'And why are you talking

to Senator Beaufort to work out a US citizenship for that cunt?' she asked in a strained voice.

'Jarvis was going to get it before he got whacked. Now she has to get the citizenship or the FCC won't allow her to buy a share in the company because only Americans can own television or radio stations. They'd never okay my uncle with his record. Rupert Murdoch did it that way and that was a bigger deal than this,' I answered.

'And if it doesn't work?' she asked, not looking at me.

'Then Uncle Rocco winds up with the short end of the stick,' I said.

She turned to me. 'No, he doesn't.'

'What do you mean?' I asked.

'He's very smart. He's already got you on the hook,' she said. 'For almost five hundred million dollars. You'll have to sell General Avionics to pay that off.'

'He'll come up with the money,' I said.

She met my eyes. 'Like he came up with Angelo's kid. A child with sandy brown hair and green eyes like yours. Did Angelo look like that?'

I was silent. Angelo had black hair and dark brown eyes.

'Your uncle paid her to get out of the country when she wanted to marry you. You told me that,' she said.

I shook my head. 'I have a big mouth.'

'You were both fucking her,' she said.

'Not at the same time,' I said.

'Close enough,' she said. 'The kid could be yours.'

'Crazy,' I said.

Then I saw the tears drop down on to her cheeks. 'Men are so stupid.'

I reached for her hand. 'I'm not that stupid,' I said. 'I have you.'

She buried her face in my chest. 'I'm afraid,' she whispered huskily, 'that you're going to lose everything you worked for.'

'No way,' I said. I turned her face up to me and kissed her.

'She's a bitch,' she said. 'She's been completely done over with plastic surgery. Eyes, face, tits, tummy tuck, asslift, liposuction.'

I was surprised. 'How do you know?'

'You told me,' she said. 'You said she looked like she did twelve years ago. It doesn't work like that. Not for any woman. Especially after she's had a child.'

I started to laugh. 'I wonder if she had her cunt done too.'

'It's possible,' she said seriously. 'Would you like to check on it?'

'Not me,' I said quickly. 'I'm not interested in time travel.'

She reached down to hold me. 'You have a hard on,' she said. 'She's turning you on.'

'Bitch!' I kissed her and pulled her over on me. 'You cover me over with you and you don't think I feel it?'

'You're so bad,' she said.

'You're angry,' I said. 'Sit down on my face. I'll suck all the anger out of you.'

It was about three months before when I saw Uncle Rocco in Atlantic City and we had dinner with Alma and her daughter. The dining room was on the lower floor of Uncle Rocco's duplex penthouse. Alma was already there, seated at the small bar in the corner, looking out on to the ocean. She turned and rose as she heard us enter.

She smiled and held both hands out to me. 'Jed,' she said warmly.

I held her hands and kissed her on both cheeks. 'Alma,' I said. 'It's a real surprise.'

'Not really,' she said. 'I always knew sometime that we would see each other.'

'I can't believe it,' I said. 'You look just as lovely as you did when we first met. Really even more beautiful.'

She laughed. 'French makeup. It does wonders for one.'

'It takes more than that,' I said. 'I got older and heavier but you have found the fountain of youth.'

'Don't be silly,' she laughed. 'Then you were a boy, now you're a man. You look marvelous.'

'Thank you,' I said. 'Uncle Rocco told me you have a daughter.'

A faint shadow crossed her face. 'Yes,' she answered. 'I never knew that I was pregnant with Angelo's child.'

I met her eyes. 'Life is strange.'

'True,' she answered. 'The way we meet again. All because my husband dies.'

I still held her eyes. 'I don't know whether to give you congratulations or condolences.'

She didn't turn away from me. 'Maybe a little of both.'

A white-jacketed houseman came from behind the bar. He refilled her drink and looked at me.

'Scotch on the rocks,' I said.

He placed the drink on the bar in front of me and left the room. I held the glass up to her. 'Cheers,' I said.

'*Salute*,' she nodded. We sipped our drinks. 'My husband was a shit,' she said.

I was silent for a moment. 'But you married him,' I said. 'Why?'

'There were three reasons,' she answered honestly. 'One, he was rich, two, he had the hardest prick I ever felt, three, he asked me.' She laughed. 'He was crazy about my Peruvian pussy. He used to say my clit was almost as big and hard as his prick.'

'That sounds romantic,' I said.

'It was romance for him,' she said. 'But he was crazy. He really hated women. He wanted to destroy me. When he couldn't do that, he was going to divorce me.'

I was silent.

'I signed a prenuptial agreement. A million for each year we were married, but then at the end he also wanted to screw me out of that.'

'It doesn't make any difference now,' I said. 'You're his widow, you'll get everything.'

'It won't be that easy,' she said. 'He has two sons from a previous marriage. One is thirty-two, and the other, thirty. They're both officers in his corporation and the only inheritors of his estate.'

'How did you learn that?' I asked.

'His Canadian attorneys. He made his will seven years ago. If I cooperate, they said, they would see to it that I would get something out of the estate.'

'You're going to cooperate with them?' I asked.

'I'll break their asses,' she said angrily. 'I'll get my share.'

She took a deep breath. 'It might have been better if he had not been killed.'

'It doesn't make sense,' I said. 'I thought you went after him.'

A genuine look of surprise was on her face. 'Why should I do a thing like that? I knew that his sons were going to get all of it. It would have been easier for me to fight with him than his estate.'

'Then who killed him?' I asked.

'You don't know?' she asked.

I shook my head.

'Your uncle,' she said quietly. 'When he found out that Jarvis was going to screw him, he went into a rage.' She was silent for a moment. 'Godfathers don't forgive.'

Uncle Rocco had dinner at seven o'clock each night. The table was set for four people. It was beautiful. I never thought the old man cared about things like that. Candles. Tall stemmed glassware. English Coalport dishes and lovely French silverware.

He nodded as he came into the room and looked at Alma. 'Where's the baby?'

'She'll be here in a moment,' she answered.

'I arranged a special treat for her,' he said. 'Hamburgers from McDonalds.'

He turned to me. 'Have you seen the baby yet?'

Alma laughed. 'She's not a baby anymore. She's eleven years old.'

'She's still a baby,' he said. He turned to the door as the child entered. 'Angela,' he smiled, bending down to kiss her.

'Grandpa,' she giggled. 'Your whiskers tickled me.'

'The better to eat you with, my dear,' he laughed.

'You're not the big bad wolf,' she said. She looked at me. 'Are you my uncle?' she asked.

She had green eyes and blondish brown hair like my mother's. She was tall for her age and I was curious about her accent. She sounded British. 'I don't think so,' I said. 'Probably your cousin.'

'Grandpa is not your daddy?'

175

'No,' I answered. 'He is my uncle. Your father was his son.'

She turned to her mother. 'You said he was my uncle,' she said accusingly.

'In a kind of way, he is,' she explained. 'Your father and he were like brothers.'

She thought for a moment then looked up at me. 'May I call you uncle?'

'Of course,' I said.

'You have a funny name,' she said. 'Jed. None of the boys in my school have that name. Is that your real name?'

'Jed is an abbreviation,' I said. 'The full name is Jedediah.'

'That sounds like a biblical name,' she said. 'The pastor in Sunday school always told us about names like that when he read to us from the Old Testament.'

Alma cut in to the conversation. 'Angela goes to school in England,' she said. 'There are many things that puzzle her about Americans.'

But the child was stubborn. 'I've seen pictures of my daddy. He had black hair like yours,' she said, looking at her mother. 'Uncle Jed looks more like me than either of you.' She was silent for a moment, then turned to me. 'Did you ever fuck Mommy?'

None of us could find an answer for that. Her voice was sweet and innocent. 'Mommy went to bed with a lot of my uncles,' she said. She looked up at me again. 'There were sometimes she even went to bed with Grandpa.'

I glanced at Uncle Rocco. His face was red and flushed. I laughed and reached down for the child's hand. 'Forget about all this nonsense and let's have dinner.'

Dinner was perfect. The child had McDonalds' and we had *spaghettini al pomodoro al dente* and rare sirloin steak Sinatra with green and red peppers and onions.

2

Uncle Rocco looked at me quizzically as we walked up the staircase to his living room after dinner. Alma was taking the child to bed. 'What do you think of the baby?' he asked gruffly.

'She's pretty,' I said. 'And bright too.'

'She's Di Stefano,' he said.

'I'm sure,' I said.

'I gave her a trust fund for a million dollars,' he said.

I smiled at him. 'Fair enough. After all, she is your grand-daughter.'

'Maybe,' he answered. 'But it doesn't matter. She is a Di Stefano. And I know Angelo would have liked it.'

He watched me again as we reached the landing. I met his eyes. 'Uncle Rocco,' I said. 'You did the right thing. Angelo deserved it.'

'I had nothing left of him,' he said heavily.

I pressed his hand gently. 'You have now,' I said quietly.

I followed him into the living room and we sat down at a square glass card table. Next to his chair there was a wooden chest with three hand-painted decorated drawers. He took a key from his pocket and opened the top drawer. Carefully he lifted out a black enameled box. He placed it on the table and opened it.

'What's that?' I asked.

'Just a moment,' he said. Quickly he took out a number of glassine bags. He spread them out in front of him. 'This is the biggest business in the United States. More than GM and American Express combined. Over three hundred billion dollars retail.'

I watched him silently.

He tapped the small glassine bags and a little powder came

trom each. He pointed to the first powder. It was yellowish brown. 'This is Southeastern Asian heroin.' The next was pure white. 'This is Pakistani-Afghanistan heroin.' Following that was a blue-white crystal-like substance. 'South American cocaine.' The next bag held a small amount of shredded marijuana. 'This is from Colombia and Mexico.' The last bag he opened had a number of various colored pills and tablets that he spread on to the table. 'This is new,' he said. 'We call it designer drugs.'

'Okay,' I said. 'What has this got to do with me?'

'All of this is processed in Sicily. The families used to control the streets but now they are upset because there are many small dealers bringing in their own material and selling it on the street for less than the families.'

'How did that happen?' I asked.

'Men became greedy. The agreement with the families fell apart and war came. Many died and the government took advantage of the situation and moved right in. Now life is very different for the families.'

'You're retired, Uncle Rocco,' I said. 'You have nothing to do with it.'

He looked at me. 'I thought that. But now, they have other ideas.'

I looked at him without speaking.

'Many years ago,' he said, 'after the war, Luciano arranged that there would be a commission. Nothing could be done without the agreement of the commission. No territories could be invaded, no businesses could be taken out and most of all, no killing of capos or heads of families unless agreed to by the commission.' He took a deep breath. 'For years everything was quiet, we all did well and profited. And then everything fell apart.'

'Why was that?' I asked.

'Luciano died. Costello became the judge but he wasn't Lucky, he was good but he couldn't hold the line. Gambling, unions, street banking, business protection service, he could handle that. But then there were drugs. That was a new business. More money than anyone could ever imagine. And they became greedy and tore at each other like animals.' He fell silent.

'What do they want from you, Uncle Rocco?' I asked.

My uncle was quiet. 'The Sicilian commission knows that I am a man of honor. And so do the Americans. They both agree that they want me to be head of the commission. They say I would be the *Capo di Capi* and whatever I would say would go.'

'Jesus,' I said. 'What kind of money would you get for that?'

'More millions than you can ever imagine,' he said. 'But that doesn't matter. I don't want it. I told you before that I wanted to die in bed. If I do this I will die in a year. In the street. Like Castellano, Bonanno, Galante.'

'What can I do to help, Uncle?' I asked.

'You talk to them,' he said quietly. 'You tell them that I am an old man. I have problems with my head. I forget things. That I can't handle the complications of a responsibility like that. Tell them I am now getting ready to go into a rest home.'

'And they'll believe me?' I asked incredulously.

'Maybe,' he said shrugging.

'But they don't even know me,' I said.

'They know,' he said confidently. 'They knew your father. They knew that he was straight and honest. And they know that you are your father's son.'

'Oh, God,' I said. 'And when am I supposed to do this?'

'You have some time,' he said easily. 'After you straighten up the business with the film company.'

'I don't know when I'll get that finished. Jarvis' sons won't even return my offer for their stock.'

Uncle Rocco smiled. 'We'll get the stock,' he said confidently. 'It took my money for that stock. The money came from my Canadian bank. The bank has asked them to pay the money back. That's four hundred million plus interest and the Jarvis Corporation hasn't got it. They have agreed to turn over the stock to the bank in return for cancellation of the loan without penalties.'

Alma's voice came from behind us. I hadn't heard her come into the room. 'I also waived my suit against the Jarvis estate. They insisted on that.'

Uncle Rocco looked at her. 'You will still get three million from the estate. And if this all works out you'll get a good commission.'

'I want five million dollars,' she said.

He laughed at her easily. 'You're nothing but a Peruvian *putana*.'

She laughed with him. 'I'm also the mother of your grandchild.'

I looked at them then turned back to him. 'You're both having fun,' I said, 'but I'm the only one who is short on this deal so far. I laid out eighty-five million cash and went on the line for four hundred million and haven't received a penny back yet.'

Uncle Rocco met my eyes. 'If you're worried I'll give you the money the first thing in the morning.'

'Uncle Rocco,' I said, shaking my head in annoyance. 'You know I won't be here in the morning. I have to leave at five a.m. to be back at eight o'clock in the morning for meetings.'

'Then I'll send you the money when you return to LA,' he said.

'Sure,' I said. I knew he wouldn't send me the money tomorrow. That wasn't his way.

'I am a man of honor,' he said quietly. 'When you wanted to get money to start your business, I gave it to you. You will get this money too.'

'Fuck it,' I said. 'I really don't give a shit whether I get the money or not. After all, it's family.'

He nodded. 'Family. That is all that really matters.' He looked at his watch. 'It's ten o'clock,' he said. 'We can pick up the news on the Philadelphia station.'

He turned in his chair and clicked on the remote. The large screen lit up. The announcer's voice could not hide his excitement. 'Less than twenty minutes before coming on the air tonight, we learned that one of Philadelphia's gang lords was shot and killed as he stepped out of his limousine on his way to dinner at his favorite restaurant.' The picture suddenly changed from the face of the anchorman to the face of the man that had been murdered. The announcer was speaking over it, but Uncle Rocco was no longer interested. He turned off the set.

I looked at him. He knew that I recognized the man. He had been in Uncle Rocco's office earlier today. 'What happened?' I asked.

My uncle shrugged his shoulders. 'I told you that he was a shit. Nobody liked him. Sooner or later somebody was going to whack him.'

I was silent for a moment. 'And this is the world they want you to control?'

'I said I couldn't handle it,' he said. 'That's why I want out.'

I got out of my chair. 'I'd better get to bed,' I said. 'I have to wake up very early tomorrow.'

Alma smiled at me. 'I thought we'd have some time to talk a little.'

'We will,' I said. 'But I have to meet with Senator Beaufort about your citizenship application.'

'Goodnight,' I said. I bent over and kissed Uncle Rocco's cheek. His fingers brushed my cheek lightly.

'Sleep well,' he said. 'I love you.'

'I love you,' I said to him. And I know we believed it.

I kissed Alma's cheek. 'Goodnight, dear,' I said. 'And your daughter is beautiful.'

'Thank you,' she said and I left them in the living room while I went down the steps to where the guest bedrooms were located.

There were four guest bedrooms and mine was the last at the end of the hall. In a kind of way it was the best room of all. Large and at the corner of the floor. There were large french windows on the two far sides of the room that looked out on to a long terrace that reached along the building past each of the other bedrooms. I stretched out on the bed in nothing but my jockey shorts and turned off the light next to the bed. I cursed silently. Despite the blackout curtains over the windows, the light still came in from the cracks of the curtains. There was too much Las Vegas on the boardwalk outside. I turned on my side, facing the walls with my back to the windows. After a while, I fell asleep.

I don't know how long I had been asleep, but suddenly I felt a blast of cold night air and a flash of light coming from the drapes. I rolled quickly in the bed toward the windows. But the drapes had already fallen close.

Alma's voice came to me. 'Are you awake?'

'I am now,' I said.

'Let me get under the covers,' she said. 'I'm freezing.'

'Stupid,' I said. 'Why didn't you come through the door?'

'One of your uncle's guards is sitting in the hall,' she said. 'I'm freezing. Now can you let me in the bed?'

I moved over and she got into the bed and pulled the blankets over herself. She took my hand. 'Feel,' she said. 'I'm really cold.'

She guided my hand over her breasts. She was cold. Then she took my hand over her belly and down to her fur. She laughed. 'But my pussy is warm. It's always hot.'

'Great,' I said. 'So what else is new?'

'Do you have a hard on?' she asked.

'No,' I said.

'I can fix that,' she said.

'Wait a minute,' I said. 'What have you come over here for?'

'I wanted you to know,' she said. 'Angela is your child, not your cousin's.'

'No big deal,' I said. 'I'm sure Uncle Rocco figured that out.'

'I don't give a damn what Uncle Rocco thought,' she said, quietly angry. 'Don't you feel anything about your own daughter?'

I looked at her. 'She's not my child,' I said flatly. 'You made a good deal with Uncle Rocco, don't fuck it up.'

I felt her open hand stinging across my face. 'You cold-ass son of a bitch!' she snapped.

I shook my head to clear it, then I smiled at her. 'I'm disappointed. I thought you just came here for an auld lang syne fuck.'

'Fuck yourself!' she answered angrily and started to swing at me again.

This time I caught her arm. She tried to hit me with her other hand. Now she was overdoing it. I had a temper of my own. I belted her on the jaw. She tumbled backwards off the bed, falling face down across a chaise, her naked buttocks and legs hanging out of her silk robe.

I stood over her as she stared up at me. 'You have a hard on,' she said huskily.

'I have to take a piss,' I said.

A faint smile began to appear on her face. 'Piss on me,' she said.

'You're crazy,' I said. 'Go back to your room.'

She turned quickly and cupped my testicles in her hand. 'Your balls are heavy with come,' she said.

'Get out,' I said angrily, 'or I'll fuck you in the ass.'

She rose on the chaise and went on to her knees, her ass in the air dogfashion. Quickly she wet her fingers with her cunt and spread the moisture over her anus. 'Do it,' she said. 'I love it.'

I stood there for a moment. Then she grasped my hard with her hand and pushed it into her. I grabbed her by the sides of her buttocks to pull her to me.

Suddenly there was a noise and the bedroom door opened. Angela stood in the doorway, the hall light framing her. 'Is my mother here?' she asked in a soft voice.

3

Alma quickly rolled from the chaise to the floor and when she came to her feet her robe completely covered her. I still had half a hard so I turned my back to the child and pulled on my pants. Alma spoke angrily to the child. 'I told you never to follow me!'

'I didn't follow you, Mama,' Angela said quietly. 'I just wanted to tell you that the guard in the hall is dead.'

'You were watching television again,' Alma snapped.

The child was still calm. Quietly she opened the door wide. 'Look,' she said.

Angela was right. It wasn't television. The guard was still sitting in his chair, a look of surprise on his face, a neat bullethole in the center of his forehead, his gun lying on the floor underneath his outstretched fallen hand.

'What else did you see?' I whispered to Angela.

'I peeked through my door. There were two men. They ran up the steps to Grandpa's,' she answered.

'Take her with you to my bathroom and lock the door,' I said to Alma.

'What are you going to do?' she asked.

'First, I'm going to get the guard's gun,' I answered. 'Then I'll figure out something. You get into the bathroom now.'

I watched them go into the bathroom and heard the door lock click shut. I went to my bedroom door and looked out into the hallway. It was empty except for the dead guard. I stood silent, listening for any sound. It was quiet. Quickly I ran across the hall to the dead guard, grabbed his gun from the floor and ran back to my bedroom and closed the door behind me.

I checked the gun. It was a Berretta automatic special with

an eleven-cartridge clip. The clip was full, not a cartridge had been used. I locked the clip tight and opened the safety. Then I looked down at the telephone next to the bed. There were six intercom buttons. One was listed, 'Mr. Di Stefano's bedroom.' I picked up the receiver and pressed the button.

There were three slow buzzes and just as my heart sank into my shoes, Uncle Rocco's voice came on. 'What the hell do you want?' he asked gruffly.

'Are you okay?' I asked.

'I'm fine,' he snapped. 'Now what the hell do you want?'

'I want you to know that the guard down here has been killed,' I said. 'And two gunmen have gone up the stairs for you.'

'I haven't heard anything,' he said. 'I would have heard shots from my bodyguards outside in my office.'

'Maybe they've been whacked too,' I said. 'I heard nothing from the hall when they killed the guard. They must have had silencers.'

'Shit,' Uncle Rocco complained. 'Nobody fights fair anymore.'

'They'll be going into your room after you,' I said.

'No way,' he said. 'They can't get in. My bedroom is a safe room. Steel door under the wooden panel and steel panels in the walls. And all the windows are presidential bullet-proof glass.'

'What if they have plastic to blow the door?' I asked. 'That can open monster safes.'

'That would be embarrassing,' Uncle Rocco said calmly. 'But for them not me. They have to get through the door. I have two Uzis and a double sawed-off shotgun aimed right at them.'

'In Nam, they threw in tear gas before going in,' I said. 'You can't see to shoot anything when you're blind and choking.'

'Where's the *putana* and my granddaughter?' he asked.

'They're safe,' I said. 'I have them locked in my bathroom.'

'That don't mean shit if those assholes come after you,' he said. 'Get them to the fire stairs and have them go all the way to the main floor. The security men will take care of them.'

'But what about you?' I asked.

'Get them on the steps, then if you want to be a hero, come after me,' he said.

'Don't be sarcastic,' I said. 'I promised to help you die in bed and not with bullets. How do I get to you?'

'There's an outside staircase from the terrace on your floor up to mine. It comes up to the back of my office french doors. Do you have a gun?'

'I grabbed the guard's gun,' I said.

'That's a Berretta special,' he said. 'Do you know how to use it?'

'I know,' I said.

'Okay,' he said quietly. 'When you get up there, just shoot the sons of bitches in the back. Give them no warning or they'll blow you away.'

'Gotcha,' I said.

'Now put a sweater on when you go out on the terrace, it's freezing out there and I don't want you catching any cold,' he said.

'I have a sweater,' I said.

'Good,' he said. 'Now check your watch. You come in my terrace doors in seven minutes exactly and start blasting. At the same time I'll come out of my door with the shotgun. If you don't get them, I will.'

'I want you to stay in your room,' I said.

'Don't be stupid,' he said. 'This is family.'

The phone clicked off. I knocked on the bathroom door. 'Come on,' I said.

Alma opened the door, the child was standing beside her. 'What's going on?'

'Rocco said to get you off the floor.' I pulled my sweater on. 'Now follow me.'

It took me two minutes to find the fire staircase. I opened the door. 'Now get down to the main floor. Rocco said that the security men down there will take care of you.'

'And what about you?' Alma asked.

'Uncle Rocco and I have a plan,' I said. 'Now, get going.'

Angela looked up at me. 'Uncle Jed,' she said. 'You're a real hero.'

I laughed. 'Get going, honey.'

It was two and a half minutes to get to the terrace doors. I opened the door and the icy blast off the ocean almost took my breath away and my chest was screaming in pain as I slipped and slid up the ice-covered terrace steps. My hands felt almost frozen to the iron railing along the staircase. I don't know how I got there but my watch showed six and a half minutes as I crouched near the upper terrace doors.

Damn, I cursed to myself. Uncle Rocco said seven minutes. I still had thirty seconds to wait. Thirty seconds in windy icy hell. The Berretta turned into pure ice in my hands as I clasped it. Jesus, I prayed that I could squeeze my fingers to make that damn thing shoot. Fifteen seconds later, I rose from the crouch and leaned against the terrace window door. I tried to open the door knob but it was frozen and wouldn't open. I tried to kick the door. It still didn't move.

By this time the two bastards had their guns on me. I didn't know which prayers would give me the most protection. My mother's Adonai or my father's Blessed Mary, Mother of God. I saw the blue-white flashes from their guns, but I heard no sounds. Maybe I was already dead. But then I heard the faint ping of the bullets hitting the terrace windows. They never touched me.

Then I saw behind them, Uncle Rocco coming through his bedroom door, his shotgun in his arm. The sound of the two blasts even came through the windows. Uncle Rocco caught them both in the back of their chests as they turned to shoot at me through the window. They lay on their faces on the floor and Uncle Rocco stepped carefully around them to get to the terrace door. He dangled a large key in his hand then opened the terrace door with it.

'Get inside,' he said. 'It's freezing out there.'

'You bastard!' I said through chattering teeth. 'You could have got me killed.'

'Impossible,' he said. 'I told you that it was presidential bullet-proof glass.'

'What about pneumonia?' I asked, still shivering.

'Come to the bar,' he said. 'I have the best Sicilian grappa. One shot of this you'll be as good as new.'

I followed him to the bar. He poured me a shot and one for himself. '*Salute*,' he said.

'*Salute*,' I answered. The grappa burned down into my gut. I turned and looked at the two men on the floor then looked around the room. 'Where are your bodyguards?' I asked. 'I don't see them anywhere around.'

Uncle Rocco gestured to the two dead men. 'There they are.'

'I don't get it,' I said.

'They've been reached,' he said. 'Money is the root of all evil and it destroyed them.'

I stared at him. 'Who paid them off?'

He shrugged. 'Probably Nico. But I guess they didn't know that Nico was already gone. If they did, they wouldn't have tried it because there was no place to get the money for it.'

'Did you get Nico whacked?' I asked.

'No,' he answered. 'I am way above all those things.'

'The bodyguards,' I said. 'It doesn't make sense.'

'It made sense,' he said. 'They didn't have to do anything tonight. They could have whacked me in the morning when I came out for breakfast. They knew that nobody could have gotten into my bedroom.'

'What do you really need me for, Uncle Rocco?' I asked. 'It seems to me you do pretty good on your own.'

'I don't agree with that. If you stay in the business, sooner or later, they'll get you. I can't handle this excitement anymore, I'm too old for it.' He looked at me. 'You're family. Look down at the floor. Is this any way to live? You're going to have to get me out.'

I stared at him. 'I'll have another grappa.'

We both put away another shot. Now I felt nice and warm. 'How do we get this thing cleaned up?'

'I have connections downstairs. There'll be no word.' He looked down at the two men on the floor. 'There is only one thing that I feel badly about. That oriental rug on the floor cost me a hundred and fifty grand. It was only one of two in the world. And these two bastards ruined it.'

4

There was one thing special about grappa. Maybe it burns your guts out but it also blows the cobwebs from your brains. It turns your head into a 64K computer. I sat on the bar stool and watched Uncle Rocco talking on the telephone. In the room around us there were cleaning men working and straightening everything back to normal.

Uncle Rocco was speaking in Italian. I didn't understand Italian, but I had a 64K computer in my head and I knew exactly what he was saying. He told anyone he was talking to that they were assholes and none of them could follow the rules. And if they didn't obey the rules they would all wind up in the shithouse. Then he smiled, said, '*Ciao*,' and put down the telephone.

He gestured to me. 'Alma and the child are on their way up.'

'Good,' I said. 'I have to get some sleep. I have to catch a shuttle to New York for an LA flight.'

'You're not going,' he said firmly. 'We have a more important meeting here tomorrow.'

'I've made arrangements to conclude the contract with Aerospatiale at my office tomorrow,' I said. 'I have a half billion on deposit with them and if I don't sign, I can blow it all.'

'You won't blow it,' he said confidently. 'But if you don't make this meeting tomorrow you will blow it.'

The 64K grappa computer clicked in. 'Uncle Rocco,' I said, 'I thought you asked me to be here for family business, but that wasn't it, was it?'

Silently he poured grappa into our glasses. 'Drink,' he said.

'You're my uncle,' I said angrily. 'I came up here tonight

ready to die for you if I had to. But you're not being honest with me. You're just playing Godfather.'

'There are no more godfathers,' he said quietly. 'We are all nothing but honest businessmen.'

'What is the business?' I asked sarcastically. 'Death?'

'I didn't look for it,' he said. 'They were children playing games. They saw too many movies.'

I stared at him for a moment. 'I don't get it. What does your meeting tomorrow have to do with my agreement with Aerospatiale?'

'The meeting is with Europeans,' he said. 'They have more influence with Aerospatiale than you as an American. And your biggest competitor is a Dutch company who is bidding on the same deal.'

'I know that,' I said shortly. 'Tell me what I don't know.'

'The Dutch company will buy you out for three billion,' he said. 'Cash.'

'Two years from now,' I said. 'My business will be worth five billion.'

'The magic word deregulation has doubled the number of airlines of three years ago. You did well because they needed you. And now labor costs, maintenance and fuel are beginning to rocket,' Uncle Rocco said seriously. 'Seventy percent of the new airlines are underfinanced and loaded with junk bonds, Shylock interest payments. The industry is already discounting fares like crazy just to keep their head above water. A small recession and you'll wind up with more repo'd aircraft than you can stick up your ass.'

'It ain't going to happen,' I said. 'The market is still climbing and all the business forecasts are upbeat.'

'I've been around a long time,' he said quietly. 'And there's one thing I've learned. Life is a roller coaster. Everything that goes up, comes down.'

'But sooner or later it goes up again,' I said. 'History taught me that.'

'Right,' he agreed. 'But you have to be careful that you don't get caught in the downside.' He gulped his grappa. 'If you get three billion for your company, how much do you net?'

I rolled the numbers over in my head. 'Between six hundred and six hundred and fifty million after taxes.'

A new respect came into his face. 'You're rich.'

'I'm not in your class, Uncle Rocco,' I said.

'But you did better,' he said heavily. 'You never had to shovel society's shit since you were fifteen, you never had to do hard time for eleven years of your life or murder to save your life or to gain respect from the society. And you never had the dead pictured in your eyelids when you went to sleep.'

I placed a hand on his arm. 'But it was many years ago, Uncle Rocco,' I said. 'It was another time, another world.'

'But I'm still alive,' he said quietly. 'And for me it's still the same world. That's why I want to get out of it.'

It was my turn to fill the glasses with grappa. '*Salute*,' I said. We gulped our drinks. The large entrance door opened and four men in overalls carried in another large rug and placed it on the floor in place of the one that had been covered with blood.

I stared down at it, then turned to Uncle Rocco. 'I thought you said that there were only two rugs of this kind in the world.'

He smiled and nodded. 'That's true. But I wasn't going to take any chances if anything would happen to it. So I bought the two of them.'

'What are you going to do with the other one?' I asked.

'I'm shipping it to Pakistan,' he answered. 'It was made there over two hundred years ago but the Pakistanis are the only ones who can clean and repair it even now.'

I climbed off the bar stool. My legs were a little wobbly. 'I'm going to bed,' I said.

Alma came into the living room. She had already dressed. She looked at Uncle Rocco. 'Are you all right?' she asked.

He nodded. 'Everything's okay.'

She turned to me. 'Angela is already asleep.'

'Good,' I said.

'She adores you,' she said. 'She thinks you're a hero.'

I laughed. 'She's a child. When she grows up she'll think I am stupid.'

It was Uncle Rocco who interrupted. 'You are a hero. You came to save my life.'

'I was stupid,' I said. 'You didn't need any help.' My head was beginning to hurt. 'I better get to bed, I'm getting dizzy.'

'I'll help you down stairs,' Alma said quickly.

'No, thanks,' I replied. 'I'll manage.'

She turned to Uncle Rocco. 'Did you tell him that I was going to Los Angeles?'

I stared at Uncle Rocco. 'You didn't tell me.'

He held his hands outstretched. 'I forgot.'

'Oh, shit,' I said. Then I weaved out of the room and managed to half fall down the staircase. The three security men that were posted on the floor helped me tumble into bed. The ceiling spun around and I went out. Grappa. I couldn't believe it. I didn't wake up until noon the next day.

Uncle Rocco was sitting on the edge of my bed when I opened my eyes. 'How do you feel?' he asked.

I felt my head exploding and I squinted at the light. My mouth was stuffed with cotton. 'Awful,' I mumbled.

He reached to the night table and picked an empty tall glass and a pitcher filled with a reddish brown drink loaded with ice cubes. He poured a glass and handed it to me. 'Drink it. You'll feel better.'

I held it close to my mouth. A terrible smell came to my nose. 'What the hell is it?' I asked.

'Bloody Mary and Fernet Branca,' he said. 'Swallow it.'

I drank it quickly. I began to get nauseous. 'It tastes like shit,' I said.

Quickly he refilled the glass. 'Again,' he ordered.

Automatically I did as he said. Suddenly I could breathe again, my eyes cleared and my headache disappeared. 'Jesus,' I said. 'Who taught you that formula?'

He laughed. 'It was my mother's anti-grappa medicine.'

'It works,' I said. 'I'll grab a shower and get dressed. What time did you say that we'd have a meeting?'

'I've already had the meeting. There was no way I could wake you up,' he said.

'Then what the hell happened?'

'Everything is all right,' he smiled. 'I told them that you said you would take care of it.'

'Take care of what?' I asked.

He smiled. 'Buy control of Fantasy Films.'

'I don't know anything about that business, what am I going to do with it?' I asked.

'Turn it over to them,' he said.

I thought for a moment. 'And what happens if I decide to hang on to it?'

'That's what Jarvis wanted to do,' he answered.

'Then I have no choice,' I said.

'And neither do I,' Uncle Rocco said. 'I'm the *patrone*. We'll both be dead.'

5

I pulled the Blazer into the garage of my office building and stopped in front of the parking attendant. He came out of his small booth and smiled at me. 'Good morning, Mr. Stevens.'

'Good morning, John,' I said.

He looked at me. 'Miss Latimer is waiting for you in the garage floor waiting room at the elevator.'

'Thank you, John,' I said and crossed toward the elevator corridor. I opened the door and she was alone in the small room. She stubbed out a cigarette in the small sand box next to her.

'What's wrong?' I asked. I never saw her smoking in the daytime.

'You didn't tell me that cunt was coming to the meeting,' she said angrily.

'I told you all of them would be here. She's one of the principals,' I said. 'I couldn't leave her out.'

'I don't trust her,' she said.

'You're jealous,' I said. 'Forget it. It's only business. After today you won't see her anymore.'

'Maybe I won't,' she asked. 'But will you?'

'Don't be silly,' I said. 'I won't either.'

'I am jealous,' she admitted. 'She really is special.'

'Yesterday's style,' I laughed.

She looked at me. 'You mean that?'

'You're today's style,' I said, kissing her. 'You're my baby.'

She nodded, smiling. 'I'm sorry. I got upset.'

I started toward the elevator. 'Everybody up there?' I asked.

'All there,' she said. 'And they were early. Shepherd, his attorney, Gitlin and McManus from the B of A, Peachtree and his assistant Shifrin. The cunt and her banker from

197

Canada, the team from D B & L, Siddely. The attorney representing Millennium then Jim Handley from our office with our accountant, Dave Bliss. I thought I'd fill in as secretary and notary.'

I smiled at her as the elevator went up. 'Bitch,' I said. 'I should have known that you'd find a way to get yourself into the meeting.'

She looked up at me. 'I'm not crazy,' she smiled at me. 'I wasn't going to leave you alone in the room with that woman.'

I could see the curiosity on their faces as I entered the meeting. I stood at the head of the table, Kim sat to my left, her tape recorder and her stenotype placed in front of her.

'Good morning, Mrs. Jarvis and gentlemen. First, I want to thank you for your attendance at this meeting at such short notice. As you know, for the last few months I have been studying the operations and problems of Millennium and I genuinely believe we now have to face the moment of truth. The company is hocked up to its ass and its income cannot support its operation for another two weeks. Under these circumstances even Section 11 won't help us. We have no inventory or assets to live on until we get well. All that faces us is Section 13 or a public auction. Neither of which will do any of us any good. Everything will be lost.'

They were all silent for a moment, then Judge Gitlin spoke quietly. He was sharp. 'If the company busts,' he said, 'there are only two real losers. Mr. Shepherd and Mrs. Jarvis. They each have four hundred million in it.'

'True,' I said. 'But Shepherd owes me eighty-five million. I don't see where he's paying me back.'

'You told him that you would support him,' the judge said quietly. 'You knew that you would be on the line for the four hundred.'

'It wasn't on paper,' I said. 'And you never told me how much the company was in the shithouse.'

'We'll sue your ass off,' the old man said.

'I have an eighty-five million dollar note that Shepherd signed. I have a better lawsuit than you have.'

'You're nothing but a crook,' the judge said pleasantly.

'*C'est la vie*,' I answered. 'Life changes.'

Mr. Kinnard, Alma's Canadian banker, looked at me. 'How do we fit into this?' he asked.

'I don't know,' I said. 'That loan was given to the late Mr. Jarvis. I understand that his stock was given to the company as collateral.'

'But you tell me that this company is worth nothing,' he said.

'All I can give you is my sympathy,' I said.

'Jed, you're nothing but a prick!' Alma snapped. 'I thought I could depend on you.'

'Personally, you can,' I said. 'But this is not personal, Alma, this is business.' I had to admire her. She was giving one of the greatest Academy Award performances I had ever seen. A woman scorned. Not a conspirator from the beginning.

'Wait a minute,' Shepherd said. He looked shrewdly at me. 'You didn't ask us to this meeting just to tell us that the company is broke. We all know that. You have something else in mind.'

I smiled at him. 'You're guessing right, Brad.'

'You want to take the company over,' he said.

'No, Brad,' I said. 'I want to buy it.'

'You're crazier than I was,' Brad said.

'Maybe I'll be lucky,' I said. 'I'll give you fifty percent on the dollar for your interest.'

'It won't work,' Brad said. 'My agreement with Jarvis is to pay him off at one hundred percent.'

'Jarvis is dead,' I said. 'Mrs. Jarvis might be agreeable.'

Alma looked at me then at the Canadian attorney, Mr. Kinnard. 'What do you think?'

'Fifty percent would be better than nothing,' Mr. Kinnard said.

Alma nodded to me. 'You have a deal.'

'You heard her,' I told Brad.

Brad gestured to Judge Gitlin. 'What do you think, Judge?'

Judge Gitlin smiled wryly. 'There's something screwy in this deal but we don't have the time to dig it out. Take the money and run.'

I rose from the table. 'Thank you, gentlemen. Now I'll ask

the attorneys to draw up the agreements as quickly as possible. I have the money already in an escrow account for you.'

Bradley looked at me, his face flushed and angry. 'You screwed us, didn't you?'

I was silent.

'I thought that you had come in to help us,' he said.

'I did,' I said. 'But I didn't know that you were already dead in the water. Jarvis had shoved the harpoon up your ass. If it wasn't for me you would have absolutely nothing. Now you can go back and put your own house together.'

Silently, Bradley left the room with Judge Gitlin. I turned back to the table. 'Alma, you and Mr. Kinnard, begin putting your papers together.'

Alma nodded. 'We'll arrange it.'

'Thank you,' I said. I watched them leave the conference room. I turned to the table. Peachtree and his assistant were staring at me.

'Daniel,' I said, 'you're still the president of the company. I have faith in your knowledge and ability even though you are a son of a bitch. I'm transferring one hundred million dollars to the company operating account and I expect you to begin production as soon as possible. I have also appointed Jim Handley, as executive vice president and chief financial officer of the company. I ask you both to go through the company and clean it up. I expect you both to live up each other's asses.'

Peachtree looked at me. 'Thank you, Jed. But, as you know, I do not have a contract as yet.'

'Okay, you'll have one tomorrow morning,' I said. I met his eyes. 'How much money do you want?'

Daniel shrugged. 'I haven't thought about it yet.'

'Then think about it,' I said. 'And we'll sit down and work it out.'

'I need ten million dollars tomorrow,' he said. 'I have the opportunity to take the distribution of *Star Island*. Every studio in town has the hots for it, but the producer is an old lover of mine. He knows we'll give him a fair share.'

'That's your job,' I said. 'Do it.'

'What about Jim Handley?' he asked.

'Jim will handle the finances, you both work together.'

'Good enough,' he said. He rose from his chair. 'I have work to do. I'll get back to the studio.'

We shook hands. I smiled at him. 'Have a nice day,' I said.

He laughed. 'You too,' he said and left the conference room with his boyfriend.

I leaned back in my chair and lit a cigarette. 'Jesus,' I said. I felt as if I had gone through a wringer. I was still waiting for Uncle Rocco's money.

Jim Handley leaned toward me. 'What do we do next?'

'Borrow,' I said. I turned to Ron Schraft, who headed the three man delegation from D B & L. 'Can we market a billion dollars of high yield bonds?'

Ron was young, but he was bright and very close to the source. He came directly to the point. 'No chance,' he said. 'Mike says the numbers don't work out.'

'We have the assets,' I said. 'Real estate is worth at least four hundred million and earns us forty million a year. One hit movie and we'll be swimming in money.'

'Millennium has lost four hundred million a year during the last two years,' Ron said. 'There was no hit movie. Besides, Mike doesn't have any faith in the movie business.'

'I think he's wrong,' I said.

Ron gestured with his hands. 'But Mike likes you and wants to do business with you. If you merge Millennium into General Avionics, he thinks he can sell five billion high yield bonds for you.'

I stared at him. 'That's shit,' I said. 'General Avionics doesn't need any money, I'm not going to put into hock for the picture company.'

Ron was calm. 'It's just an idea,' he said. 'Mike just wanted to help.'

I rose to my feet and held my hand out to him. 'Thank him,' I smiled. 'This is not the kind of help I need.' We shook hands politely and they left the conference room.

'Sons of bitches,' Handley said.

'It doesn't mean anything,' I said. 'It's just business for Mike.'

Sherman Siddely turned to me. 'I was talking to McManus

and we agreed that B of A isn't going to help.'

I laughed. 'When did you ever know of a bank that would lend you money if you really need it?'

McManus laughed. 'You're right. But B of A has forty million of negative loans in movies that died.'

'Come on, Mac,' I said. 'B of A has blown hundreds of millions in negative loans in the film industry over the years. Forty is a drop in the bucket. Besides the only reason you made the loans to Millennium is because you thought that Shepherd would transfer his oil company's accounts over to you.'

McManus grinned. 'Smart ass,' he said.

'Why don't you be a sport and split the *Star Island* negative deal with me? Five million isn't that much.'

The banker smiled. 'And what do you give me for it?'

'New business from General Avionics,' I said.

'Do you mean that?' he asked.

'I keep my word,' I said. 'And besides that I will guarantee you the first money out of the picture if it pays out.'

McManus turned to Siddely. 'What do you think?'

Siddely nodded. 'Peachtree knows what he's doing. I'll put my money on him. If Shepherd ever had production men as good as that fag, he wouldn't have fallen into the shit.'

McManus turned to me. 'I'll check it with my home office. I think it's a deal.'

'Thanks,' I said. 'Every little bit helps.'

Siddely turned to me. 'Jarvis knew what he was doing. He had Peachtree really checked out.'

'Too bad he wasn't smart enough to check out his car,' I said.

'Jarvis chased the wrong girl,' Siddely said. 'She had a Las Vegas gangster boyfriend.' He looked at me. 'I didn't know that you had known Mrs. Jarvis?'

'She was married to a cousin of mine a long time ago,' I said.

'I tried to get in touch with her,' Siddely said. 'But she would never even talk to me.'

'I don't know anything about it,' I said. 'I hadn't even heard from her until she contacted me about this deal.'

'That was a stroke of luck,' Siddely said.

'Not bad,' I said.

Siddely looked at me. 'Jarvis offered me the job as vice president and general counsel for Millennium.'

I met his eyes. 'If you're still interested in it, you've got it.'

He hesitated then held out his hand. 'We'll do well,' he said.

I smiled. 'I know we will.'

Finally the meeting was over and I went back to my office. I walked over to the small bar in the corner of the room and had myself a scotch on the rocks.

Kim watched me. 'How do you feel?'

'Tired,' I said. I swallowed half the drink. 'Get Uncle Rocco for me.'

'What do you want him for?' she asked.

I stared at her. 'He promised five hundred million dollars and I haven't seen a penny of it.'

6

He was sitting in my office when I returned from lunch. He rose from his chair and smiled at me. 'Mr. Stevens,' he held out a business card.

I read it quickly. It was a European type card, much larger than the American business cards.

LEONARDO DA VINCI
Director Financial Transactions
Super-Sattel EuroSky Broadcast Corporation
Canale 21
Liechtenstein

I looked puzzled.

'My apologies, Mr. Stevens,' he said. 'I did not mean to intrude into your office, but Mr. Di Stefano assured your secretary that it would be all right.'

Silently I walked to my desk and called Uncle Rocco on the speed dialer. His voice was husky. 'Congratulations,' he said. 'I heard that you completed the deal.'

'What do you have? Spies in my office?' I snapped. 'First, you know about the deal by the time I come back from lunch, then you have a man invited to my office without asking my permission. Don't you have any respect for privacy?'

'It's family,' he said. 'There is no such thing as privacy with a family. Besides this has nothing to do with privacy. Leonardo is only there to balance our finances.'

'Okay,' I said. 'How?'

'Relax,' Uncle replied. 'Just leave it to Leonardo.' The receiver clicked off and I put down the telephone.

Da Vinci was a tall man, about six three, broadshouldered,

like an athlete, blue-eyed, black hair and a neatly trimmed beard. He wore a black silk suit, Italian cut, white shirt and black tie. He held out his hand and smiled. 'Just in case you're wondering,' he laughed, 'I have no talent as an artist.'

I laughed with him. 'Then how come the name?'

'I thought it would be a more interesting name than Leonard Davidson,' he answered. 'Something about the name Da Vinci always impresses people.'

'It impressed me,' I said.

He took an envelope from his inside breast pocket and gave it to me. I opened the envelope and quickly scanned the accounts listed on it. It held all the advances I had made to Shepherd and all the new commitments I made for Millennium Films. The total added up to five hundred and ninety-five million.

He looked at me. 'Do you find the figures correct?'

I nodded. 'Yes. But I don't understand how you discovered them so quickly.'

'It is part of our business,' he said. 'Now that you have agreed with the amounts we'll now begin to settle our accounts.'

'Good,' I said. 'Then I'll ask Jim Handley, my financial vice president, to join us. He can help us direct the money into the correct account.'

'Excellent,' he said.

'By the way,' I asked. 'Will the checks you give us be drawn on US banks or foreign?'

'Checks are old-fashioned,' he said. 'We'll transfer the money directly into your bank accounts.'

Handley came into the office while Da Vinci was opening his thick clumsy attaché case and spreading it on my desk top. Quickly, Da Vinci set up a laptop computer and connected it to a ten-inch satellite disk, both powered by four six-volt batteries. Quietly he flipped the power switch and light spilled into the screen. The screen was blank until he turned the disk direction and then letters came in blue on the screen. 'EUROSKY CANALE 21.'

He turned to me. 'We're ready for business.'

I introduced them. Handley was curious but he was very

clever. He didn't ask questions. Quickly, I told him what was being done.

He turned to Da Vinci. 'Isn't this against the law?'

Da Vinci shook his head. 'Not if you notify your bank in advance that you will make certain deposits in this fashion. After all, banks transfer and deposit between themselves in that manner.'

'What connection does Mr. Di Stefano have with EuroSky? And why does EuroSky want Millennium?' I asked.

'As far as I know,' Da Vinci answered, 'Mr. Di Stefano is one of the investors in EuroSky. And EuroSky is a new company created for the new open market of international television in Europe. EuroSky has already placed four satellites over Western and Eastern Europe, and they are in direct competition with the British companies of Murdoch and Thames for the continental European market. And Millennium is one of the last companies that has over fifteen hundred feature films plus many other film subjects for distribution.'

'Is it clean money?' Handley asked.

'Yes,' Da Vinci said. 'The money is coming from Lloyds Bank of England and Crédit Suisse in Geneva.' He paused for a moment. 'In order to transfer the money to your accounts, I would appreciate it if you gave me the account numbers of each of the banks you want money transferred to.'

I looked at Jim. 'Okay, give him the numbers.'

Jim was still nervous. 'If we give you the account numbers wouldn't it be possible that you could make withdrawals from these accounts without our knowledge?'

Da Vinci smiled. 'No, not if you notify your banks that this method is to be used only for deposits into your account.'

'Okay,' I said. 'Let's go.'

The whole transaction took only about fifteen minutes and then Da Vinci looked at me. 'You've got your monies.'

Jim looked at him. 'How do we know? I don't have any confirmation.'

Da Vinci laughed. 'Call your banks, they'll tell you.'

'Okay,' Jim said and walked over to my desk and picked up the telephone. It took him another twenty minutes to verify the deposits. He looked very impressed as each bank confirmed that the money was already deposited into the accounts.

Jim turned to me. 'The first eighty-five million dollars you advanced to Shepherd is your own money, and I have authorized that money to be placed in the reserve account.'

'Good,' I said.

Jim continued. 'We will then pay the other sums agreed to at the meeting.'

I listed the payments to Jim. 'The payments to Mrs. Jarvis and Mr. Bradley will be paid as their paperwork is completed. As was agreed with Peachtree, one hundred million dollars will be put into the production account and a separate amount will be deposited for the acquisition of distribution rights to *Star Island.*'

'Okay,' said Jim. 'I've got it. Now I'll get back to my office, and start getting things organized.'

Jim left and I watched Da Vinci put his computer and his equipment back into his attaché case. He placed the attaché case on the floor and looked at me.

'Are you planning to stay on with Fantasy?' he asked.

'I don't think so,' I said. 'I know nothing about this business. The entertainment business is another world.'

Da Vinci smiled at me. 'It's no longer an entertainment business. It's now communications. It is becoming a new world.'

I looked at him. 'General Avionics is a big enough world for me,' I said. 'I'm not greedy.'

Da Vinci shrugged his shoulders. 'That's up to you.' He looked at his watch. 'It's late, almost five o'clock. If you don't have any plans tonight, why don't you join me for dinner?'

'I have no plans,' I said.

'Good. Suppose we meet at The Palms on Santa Monica Boulevard at eight p.m.'

'It's a date. I'll bring a girl.'

Da Vinci smiled. 'And so will I.'

I waited until he had left my office and then called Uncle Rocco again. 'It's all finished,' I said to him. 'Now what do we do?'

Uncle Rocco laughed into the receiver. 'I still want you to think about my earlier proposition. We have a very big investment corporation and you could do very well with it.'

'Is that company invested in EuroSky?' I asked.

'Of course,' Uncle Rocco said. 'We own it all. We have some of the most important motion picture and broadcasting people in Europe to operate EuroSky.'

'How much did that cost you?' I asked him.

'Not that much,' Uncle Rocco said. 'Maybe eleven billion dollars, but we will get more than fifty percent of that amount back because we are leasing space on our satellites in Europe to telephone and other communication companies. They should give us about a billion a year of income.'

I laughed. 'I don't know what you need me for. You're doing very well on your own.'

They were six deep standing at the bar at The Palms at eight p.m. I had no problem getting in and getting a table, because Kim had called and made a reservation for us. I saw Da Vinci at the bar, holding a drink. He saw me and came over with a worried expression on his face.

'Have you spoken to Mr. Di Stefano in the last hour?' he asked.

'No,' I said. 'I spoke to him earlier this afternoon after we had completed our business. But not since.'

'I am a little concerned. I tried to telephone him a few times and there is no answer at his apartment,' Da Vinci said.

'That is strange,' I said. 'There is always someone at his apartment.'

'There's been no answer,' he said quietly.

'Let me try to get him,' I suggested. At the same time, my beeper went off. I looked on the tiny screen and saw a number that was unfamiliar to me.

I turned to Kim. 'Have a drink at the bar with Mr. Da Vinci, and I will return this call and then try to locate Uncle Rocco. I'll only be a minute. I'll use the car phone.'

I was lucky. The nice thing about having a Corniche is the valet always parks the car in front of the restaurant. I slipped the valet a fiver as he unlocked the door. I got into the car and picked up the telephone receiver. First, I called Uncle Rocco's telephone number. I let it ring six times, but there was no answer. Then I dialed the other number. To my surprise, Uncle Rocco answered.

'What took you so long?' he asked gruffly.

'What's happening?' I asked. 'Where the hell are you?

'I'm in the Air France first-class lounge at JFK.'

'What the hell are you doing there?' I asked.

'I got word there's a contract out for me,' he said.

'Do you know who ordered it?' I asked him.

'I have an idea,' he said. 'But I'll have to clear it in Europe. Meanwhile, I've got to stay undercover. So, I'm renting a yacht in the South of France. I'll stay on the boat until I get everything straightened out.'

'How do I get in touch with you?' I asked.

'I'll let you know where I am and you arrange to meet me there as soon as I call,' he said.

'I thought you said you were out of this business?' I questioned.

'I am out of the business,' Uncle Rocco said. 'The trouble is there's some assholes that won't accept it. That's why I want you to straighten them all out.'

I groaned into the telephone. 'Okay, Uncle Rocco,' I said. 'Call me. I'll be there. Meanwhile, you take care of yourself.'

'I will,' Uncle Rocco said.

The phone went dead in my hand and I put it back on to its cradle. I went back into the restaurant.

Da Vinci looked up at me. 'Did you try to reach Di Stefano?'

'I got no answer from him either.' I shrugged. 'Let's have dinner now. We won't hear from him until tomorrow.'

Da Vinci looked at me. 'Where do you think he is?'

I began to hear warning bells echoing in my head. 'Mr Di Stefano loves opera. He probably went into Manhattan to the Metropolitan Opera. He must have let his staff off for a couple of hours until he returns home.'

Gigi, the manager of The Palms, led us to a table. We sat

down and ordered drinks. 'I thought you were bringing a date?'

'I had invited Mrs. Jarvis, but I was stood up,' he answered. 'I couldn't reach her by telephone either.'

7

The nice thing about The Palms is that you can really eat if you have an appetite. The pot-bellied waiter had his apron tied around his middle. 'We have a special tonight,' he said. 'Lochness Monsters,' he laughed. 'Six-pound lobsters!'

Kim smiled at him. 'No way we could ever finish one of those.'

I looked at her. 'How about splitting a four pounder and then splitting a rare New York steak, french fried, loaf of onion rings and cottage fries.'

Kim cut in, quickly. 'We'll start with Gigi's salads.'

I turned to Da Vinci. 'What are you going to have?'

'I'll have a New York steak, medium-rare,' he said. 'And a side of spinach and a baked potato.'

'How about a bottle of Chianti?' the waiter suggested.

'Good enough,' I said.

The waiter took off, and we sipped at our drinks. 'How did you meet Mrs. Jarvis?' I asked.

'I was her account manager at her bank in Paris,' he said.

'Was she married to Jarvis at that time?' I asked.

'No,' he answered. 'About the time she was married, I went to work for EuroSky, and we lost touch.'

'How did you tie up with EuroSky?' I asked.

He laughed. 'They needed a banker who knew computers. At that time, there weren't many of us that had a knowledge of computers in Europe.'

'Didn't EuroSky advance money to Jarvis for Millennium Films?' I questioned.

He looked at me with a completely open expression. 'If they did,' he said, 'I knew nothing about it, because I was just assigned to this project a couple of weeks ago.'

The waiter brought out our salads as we were eating the freshly-baked bread on the table. We had just picked up our salad forks when a small group of people passed us on the way to their own table. I recognized the exotic black singer, Thyme, who I had seen at Bradley's party. One of the men with the group paused at our table and looked down at Da Vinci.

'Leonardo,' he said. 'I didn't expect you in town this soon.'

'I had some special business,' he said. 'But I was planning to get in touch with you first thing in the morning.'

The well-dressed, good-looking, middle-aged man nodded to him. 'You can reach me at the hotel tomorrow morning because I'm returning to Las Vegas in the afternoon.'

Da Vinci nodded. 'I'll be in touch.' And the group moved on to their table.

I looked at Da Vinci. I thought it was curious that he didn't introduce us to his friend.

Kim looked at us. 'That black girl is Thyme. She has the number one hit on the charts right now. And I've heard that her boyfriend is a Las Vegas gangster.'

Da Vinci smiled and continued eating his salad.

Service at The Palms was efficient. Our food came through in short order. We ate, and by nine-thirty p.m. we had finished. When the waiter brought the bill for the meal, Da Vinci reached for the check. I put up my hand. 'No way,' I said. 'This is my town.' And I paid the bill.

We walked outside. Da Vinci asked the valet to call him a cab.

'Don't bother,' I said. 'I'll drop you off. Where are you staying?'

'I'm at the Beverly Rodeo,' he said.

'Jump in,' I said, as the valet opened the car door for Kim.

I dropped Da Vinci at the Beverly Rodeo Hotel. Da Vinci's jacket swung open as he stepped out of the car.

'We'll be in touch tomorrow,' Da Vinci said.

'Okay,' I answered. And watched him go into the lobby of the hotel. I moved the car away from the curb and into the traffic.

I looked at Kim. 'He's got a gun in a shoulder holster.'

'How do you know?' she asked.

'I saw it when he got out of the car,' I said. 'It doesn't make sense to me. Why does a computer banker need a piece?' I was silent for a moment, and shook my head. 'Nothing makes sense.'

'You're tired,' Kim said. 'Let's go back to the apartment and you can relax. Maybe you need a jacuzzi. It's been a rough day.'

I nodded. I still didn't tell her about Uncle Rocco leaving the country.

'But first, I have an idea.' I said. 'Call Alma at the hotel, tell her I'm coming over to talk to her.'

Kim picked up the car phone and dialed Alma's hotel. She asked for Mrs. Jarvis.

The desk clerk spoke into the phone. Kim hung up the receiver and looked at me. 'She's checked out.'

'Okay,' I said. 'I guess there's nothing we can do. Let's go home.'

It was about eleven-thirty p.m. when Kim and I were sitting in the jacuzzi. I leaned back into the foamy, bubbling water.

Kim looked at me. 'I've come to a decision, Jed. I'm quitting my job.'

'What the hell for?' I asked her. 'You have a great job.'

'I don't need a job,' she said angrily. 'I need a relationship. I thought we had one, but all we have is a fuck every now and then.'

'I have many problems,' I answered.

'You had more problems when we first started this business,' she said. 'But you still had time for us.'

'We'll have it,' I said. 'I just need a little more time, to get through all of this.'

'I don't know,' she said. 'In another year I'll be thirty years old, and my mother always says that if you're not married by the time you're thirty, you're an old maid.'

'Oh, Jesus,' I said. 'You're still a kid.'

'You're not that young, either,' she said. 'I think we better decide what our future is going to be.'

'I know what our future is,' I said. 'We'll get married, just like everybody else.'

'Do you mean that?' she asked, wide-eyed.

'Of course I mean it,' I said. 'But don't push me.'

She got out of the jacuzzi. 'Where are you going?' I asked.

'I'm going to shave my pussy,' she said. 'I want to feel young again.'

I stepped out of the jacuzzi and put on my terrycloth robe. 'Come on to bed,' I said. 'We'll practise a little.'

She looked at me. 'Don't you want me to shave my pussy?' she asked.

'It doesn't bother me,' I said.

'Then you better shave your beard, or you'll scratch my clit.'

'Oh, balls,' I said. 'Let's go to bed.'

The telephone began ringing. She reached for it and listened into the receiver and then turned to me.

'There's a limo in front of the hotel,' Kim said. 'Your niece, Angela Di Stefano, is waiting to come up here.'

Kim slipped into a terrycloth jumpsuit and I put on a pair of jeans and a t-shirt. The doorbell rang and I opened the door. Angela was standing there, and a bellboy was standing behind her with two valises.

'Uncle Jed,' she said in a small voice.

'Yes, sweetie,' I answered.

'My mother told me to stay with you for a few days.' She looked apprehensively up at me. 'Is that okay?' She didn't know if she was welcome.

'Come on in, honey,' I said and took her hand. 'Where is your mother?'

'She had to go on a business trip,' she answered.

'Where?' I asked.

Angela looked at me. 'I think she's going to France.' She turned and saw Kim and gestured to her. 'Is she your wife?'

I smiled at her. 'She's my fiancée,' I answered. 'We're getting married very soon.'

Angela was very smart. 'She's a very pretty lady,' she said.

I introduced them to each other. Kim smiled at Angela. 'Have you had dinner?' she asked.

'I haven't had much,' she answered.

'C'mon, let's have something to eat,' Kim said and they walked together into the kitchen.

I called Peachtree on the telephone while Kim was putting Angela to bed in the guest room. It was near midnight, and I apologized for calling that late.

'I need some information,' I said. 'I remember that you escorted Thyme to Brad's party.'

'That's right,' Peachtree answered.

'I also heard somewhere that her boyfriend was a Mafia gangster out of Las Vegas.'

'That's right,' Daniel said. 'His name is Jimmy Pelleggi and he used to be Sam Giancanni's representative in Las Vegas.'

'Does he still have anything to do with the casinos?' I asked.

'I don't think so,' Daniel said, 'because the gaming commission got all the Mafia out of the gambling operations.'

'Then what do you think he's doing in Vegas?' I asked.

'What I hear is that he runs drugs and prostitution. He's a tough man,' Daniel added. 'They call him Jimmy "Blue Eyes" because his eyes are like ice blue.'

'What does he have to do with Thyme?' I asked.

Daniel laughed into the telephone. 'He follows Giancanni, after all, and Giancanni had Phyllis McGuire under his wing for a long time.'

'Do you know anything about a man called Leonardo Da Vinci?'

'The artist?' Daniel asked.

'No,' I said. 'He's a European banker and I know that he knows Jimmy Pelleggi.'

'I don't know anything about that,' Daniel answered.

I thanked Daniel and put down the telephone. For the first time I felt frustrated that I couldn't get in touch with Uncle Rocco. There was a peculiar set-up going on. I knew now that Jimmy 'Blue Eyes' was in the drug trade. And I remembered that Alma also was in the drug trade. And I knew that Da Vinci had contact with both of them. Something was going on, but I didn't have the answers.

Kim came into the living room. 'Angela has gone to sleep.'

'Good,' I said. 'I think that we should do the same. It's been a long day.'

Kim looked at me. 'Why do you think Alma took off for France in such a hurry?'

'I don't know,' I said. 'But I have a feeling it has something to do with Uncle Rocco. He's taken off for France also tonight. He may be in real trouble.'

8

Kim and I were having coffee and Danish for breakfast.

Kim looked at me. 'We have to get someone to take care of Angela when we go to the office. We can't leave her alone.'

'I didn't think about that,' I said. 'Do you know anyone that could do it?' I asked.

'My sister has three kids,' she said. 'She'll know someone that can help.'

'Get in touch with her,' I said. 'We need someone right away.'

The telephone rang. Kim answered it. She said it was Da Vinci.

'Good morning,' I said.

'Good morning,' he answered. 'Have you heard anything from Alma?'

'Not a word,' I said.

'Well, I have,' he said. 'I heard that she left her child with you.'

'It was a surprise for me,' I said. 'She showed up after we came home from dinner.'

'Did she say anything about where her mother had gone?' he asked.

'No, she only said that her mother told her to stay with me for a few days,' I answered.

Da Vinci was annoyed. 'I have two valises of Alma's that I was supposed to give her. Now I don't know what to do with them.'

'What's in them?' I questioned.

'I don't know, it belongs to Alma. She never mentioned what was in them.' He hesitated a moment. 'Is it okay if I drop them off with you, and you can give them to her when she returns.'

'I don't know why not,' I answered. 'After all, I have to return her kid to her also.'

'I'll drop them over to your apartment today,' Da Vinci said. 'Because I have to return to Liechtenstein today.'

'Okay,' I said. I put down the telephone and looked at Kim. 'Da Vinci has two valises for Alma,' I said. 'I told him he could leave them here.'

She picked up the phone and called her sister. She spoke to her for a few minutes, then replaced the phone on its cradle and turned to me. 'My sister has a girl that can take care of Angela. She's sending her right over.'

'Thank God,' I said.

Angela came into the breakfast room. 'Good morning,' she said.

'Did you sleep okay?' I asked her.

Angela nodded. 'Really well.'

Kim looked at her. 'What would you like for breakfast?'

'*Petit pain au chocolat*, and coffee,' Angela smiled.

Kim laughed. 'Number one, we don't have *petit pain au chocolat*, number two, you're too young to drink coffee.'

Angela frowned. 'My mother always lets me have coffee.'

'Look,' Kim said, 'this is America, in America kids drink milk, not coffee. I can't get a *petit pain au chocolat*, but I can get chocolate donuts. But I think you should eat something more substantial,' Kim said, sounding motherly. 'How about ham and eggs, or pancakes and sausages?'

Angela looked at her. 'Pancakes and sausages sound good,' she said brightly. 'But if I don't have a cup of coffee, I won't be able to stay awake for the whole day.'

Kim laughed. 'Okay, but very weak coffee.'

'Okay,' Angela said. 'I'll have *café au lait*.'

'Okay, that's fine,' Kim said, and called room service.

Angela looked over at me. 'What are we going to do today?' she asked.

'I've got someone coming over here to stay with you. Kim and I have to go to work,' I answered.

Angela nodded. 'You both sound exactly like my mother,' she sighed.

I rose from the table. 'I've got to shave and get dressed,' I said, and left Angela sitting there with Kim.

Jim Handley was waiting for me when I came into my office.

'I've got some word from Aerospatiale,' he said.

'What's the word?' I asked. He didn't look happy.

'It doesn't look good. The Dutchmen have offered them more money.'

'That's crazy. Aerospatiale offered us the deal,' I said.

'What can I say? This is just what they told me,' he said.

'I think that the only thing we can do,' I said, 'is send them the down payment.'

Handley looked at me. 'You haven't even spoken to the other airlines yet. How do you know how much you can take a shot at? Twenty percent down on that many planes will cost a minimum of a quarter of a billion dollars,' he said. 'And we haven't got it right now.'

'We're fucked,' I said. 'Someone has gotten a line on our cash. That's why the Dutch company made the offer.'

'What are we going to do?' Handley asked.

'We'll fuck the Dutch company,' I said. 'We'll buy them.'

'But they want to buy you,' Handley said.

'They want to buy us, we want to buy them,' I said. 'They'll give us three billion dollars. I'll offer them five billion for their company.'

'Where are you going to get the money?' Handley asked.

I didn't tell him that Uncle Rocco wanted me to head up a tremendous, probably one of the biggest, investment companies in the world. And if I did what Uncle Rocco wanted, I would have the money. Instead I told him that if it didn't work, we could always merge, or we could get Milliken to sell junk bonds for us and get the money.

'And what are you going to do about Millennium Films?' he asked. 'EuroSky has already advanced you 595 million. How do we get any money out of that?' he asked.

I leaned back in my chair. 'They advanced me all the money, but Fantasy still winds up as my company.'

'So how are we going to pay back the advance?' Handley asked.

I smiled. 'For years, I've been watching Kerkorian sell MGM and UA over and over again. And at the end of it, he always ends up back in control of the company. What he sells is pieces,' I said.

'So?' Handley said.

'It's very simple. I sell them the foreign distribution rights to the film library. That's still fifteen hundred feature films plus other film inventory,' I said.

Handley looked at me. 'I thought you didn't want to stay in the film business.'

'It doesn't matter,' I said. 'Didn't we talk about the fact that their real estate and property could sell for as much as four hundred million dollars. That's not bad.'

A strange respect crossed Handley's face. Then he smiled. 'Jed,' he said. 'You're turning into a real prick.'

Kim entered my office an hour and a half later. 'My sister sent me the nanny. And I made arrangements for her to take Angela to Disneyland,' she said.

'That's nice,' I said.

'Also, after they had left for Disneyland and I was getting ready to come to work, Da Vinci came and left two large aluminum valises at the apartment,' she said. 'He told me that we can give them to Alma when she returns.'

'Fine,' I said. 'Did he say anything else?'

'Only that he was catching a flight this afternoon for Europe,' she answered.

'Well,' I said, 'I guess that takes care of that.'

The phone rang and my secretary came on to the intercom. 'A Mr. Pelleggi is on the phone for you,' she said.

I picked up the telephone. 'Yes, sir,' I said.

'We didn't meet last night,' Pelleggi said through the receiver. 'But I saw you with Da Vinci, and I was wondering if you had a number for him.'

'I'm sorry,' I said. 'As far as I know he is on his way back to Europe.'

'Damn,' Pelleggi said. 'Do you have any information about Mrs. Jarvis?' he asked.

'No,' I said.

He hesitated for a moment. 'I'm a friend of your uncle's. We've known each other for many years.'

'I'm glad,' I said. 'I'm very fond of Uncle Rocco.'

'I'm also one of the investors in a company with Mr. Di Stefano,' he said.

'Yes?' I said.

'It is very important that I get in touch with your uncle,' Pelleggi said.

'As far as I know, he's still in Atlantic City,' I said.

'I got no answer at his apartment,' he said.

'I'm sure he'll show up in a short time,' I said. 'If I hear from him, I will ask him to get in touch with you.'

'I appreciate that,' Mr. Pelleggi said, and hesitated again. 'By the way, did you know that Alma's husband, Reed Jarvis, hit on my girlfriend the night of Bradley Shepherd's party?'

'I know nothing about it,' I said. Which was the truth.

'The son of a bitch is lucky he got himself killed before I could do him in. I wouldn't have made it that easy for him,' he said.

'Well,' I said. 'All's well that ends well. Now all we have to do is keep our noses clean.'

There was silence, then he laughed. 'You call me Jimmy "Blue Eyes". I like you. You're just like your uncle.' And he hung up the phone.

9

It was late by the time I left the office. Kim had left early, because she wanted to check on Angela and make sure everything was okay. When I got to the downstairs parking lot, it was empty. All the attendants had gone for the day.

I jumped into the Blazer, and left the garage. I turned on to Century Boulevard. A voice came from behind me in the back seat.

'Señor Stevens,' a man's Spanish-accented voice said. 'It's been a long time.'

I looked in the rear-view mirror. 'It has been a long time,' I said. The last time I saw the man was in Peru. 'Captain Gonzales.'

The man smiled. 'You remember the name correctly, but it is no longer Captain. I am now a General.'

'Congratulations,' I said. 'Why didn't you come up to the office?'

'I didn't want anyone to know that I was here with you,' he answered.

'What can I do for you?' I asked.

He smiled. 'Señorita Vargas called me yesterday, and asked me to get in touch with you because there are some big troubles.'

I pulled over to the side of the road and turned to him. 'General Gonzales, why don't you get into the front seat. It's easier for us to talk that way.'

General Gonzales hadn't seemed to change much. He was still slim and dapper as before. He had a little gray in his hair. But his pencil-line moustache was still black.

I moved back into traffic. 'Did Alma say what kind of trouble?'

'She couldn't go into detail. But I know it has something to do with *la cocaina*,' he answered.

'I thought she was through with that business. After all, she married a very rich man and she has a lot of money.'

'That's true,' Gonzales said. 'But she's under a great deal of pressure from the Mafia. They want her to open up her South American contacts for them.'

'Christ,' I said. 'Nothing seems to change.'

Gonzales nodded. 'She told me that she will be in touch with you, and we'll find out what we need to do.'

I looked at him. 'Do you know of my uncle, Mr. Di Stefano?' I asked.

'I know of him,' Gonzales said. 'But we have never met.'

I looked at him. 'I think that she and my uncle are together in Europe trying to straighten out the problems.'

He turned and looked out the window. 'You'll have to let me know the minute she contacts you,' he said.

'Okay,' I said. 'Where are you staying?'

'I haven't checked into a hotel yet,' he answered. 'I just arrived here.'

I looked over at him. 'Then come home to dinner with me and then we'll find a place for you to stay.'

He nodded. '*Gracias, señor.*'

I turned north on to the freeway to Sunset Boulevard, and then east to the Bel Air gates.

Gonzales looked at me. 'Do you have bodyguards following you?' he asked.

'No,' I said.

'There are two men in a black Ford that have been behind us since you pulled out of the office garage,' he said.

I looked in my rear view mirror. But I couldn't see anything.

Gonzales opened his jacket and took out an automatic. 'Just in case,' he said quietly.

'I wonder what the hell is going on?' I said, as I pulled past the hotel entrance to my bungalow.

We got out of the car, but I still didn't see anyone. We went into the apartment. Angela saw me as I came through the door and then she saw Gonzales.

She smiled and spoke in Spanish. '*Buenas noches, Tio!*'

226

He bent over to kiss her. 'Angela,' he said in English. 'You're becoming a very big girl.'

She smiled and then turned to me. 'I would like to get a "Big Mac" for dinner.'

At that same time, Kim came from the other room. 'The nanny says she's been eating hamburgers and french fries all day at Disneyland,' she said.

'What the hell do I know,' I said. 'If she wants a "Big Mac" let her have it. Kids are a pain in the ass.'

I introduced Kim to the general. I told her that he was just up from Peru, because I had called him.

'I think we should have dinner in,' Kim said. 'I think we'll hear from either Alma or your uncle this evening.'

'I still want a "Big Mac",' Angela said.

'Okay,' I said. I turned to Kim. 'Ask the nanny to go out and get one for her.' And then I turned to Gonzales. 'You'll join us for dinner and I'll call the desk and get you a room, here at the hotel.'

We ordered from room service and while we were sitting at the bar having a drink, Jimmy 'Blue Eyes' called me.

'Have you heard anything from your uncle?' he asked.

'Not yet,' I answered.

'I put two bodyguards on you,' Jimmy said. 'I hope you don't mind.'

'You worried me a little bit,' I said. 'I saw two people following me from my office.'

'They are my men,' he said. 'I told them to stay near in case you had any problems.'

'Why should I have any problems?' I asked.

'Da Vinci is going to screw you,' he said.

'How is he going to screw me?' I said. 'He's nothing but a fucking messenger.'

'He's more than a messenger,' he said. 'He's a hit man.'

'Who is he after?' I asked. 'He didn't bother me.'

'He's after your uncle,' Jimmy said. 'I'm guessing that's why he went back to Europe. I have a feeling that your uncle has gone to Sicily to talk to the commission.' Jimmy 'Blue Eyes' was quiet for a moment. 'Did Da Vinci leave anything with you?' he asked.

'Yes,' I said. 'He left two valises that he said belonged to Alma.'

'Okay,' Jimmy 'Blue Eyes' said. 'Sit tight, I'm on my way over.'

We were in the middle of dinner when the desk clerk called and told us we had a visitor, Mr. Pelleggi.

'Bring him over,' I told her. We opened the door for Jimmy 'Blue Eyes' and he looked at Gonzales.

'Who the hell is he?' he asked.

'He's a friend of Alma's from Peru,' I answered.

He looked at me. 'Is he okay?' he asked.

'He's on our side,' I answered.

'Good,' he said. Jimmy opened the bungalow door and asked his two bodyguards to come in. And then turned back to me. 'Where are the valises that Da Vinci left?'

I looked at Kim. 'Where did you put the valises?'

'In the guest closet,' Kim answered.

I opened the door and took out the two valises. They were 28-inch aluminum valises.

Kim spoke to the nanny and asked her to take Angela to her room.

Jimmy gestured to one of his men. 'Open it.'

The man took out a big pocket knife. He pushed the flat side of the blade against the valise lock and hit it. The lock fell open. He lifted the top of the valise.

We looked inside. It was packed with cellophane wrapped bags of white powder. Jimmy had his man jab one of the packages. Jimmy bent down and took some of the powder on his finger and tasted it.

'That's heroin,' he said.

Kim turned to me. 'What are you doing? You're going to wind up in jail.'

I looked at her. 'Look, this isn't my business.'

I turned to Jimmy. 'Now what do we do?'

'This was part of the deal, Da Vinci was to bring heroin from Sicily in return for cocaine from Colombia,' he answered.

'What has this got to do with Uncle Rocco?' I asked.

'Your uncle has been out of this business for a long time.

And there are some people who want him back into it,' he said, and told his men to lock up the valises.

'How much heroin do you think is in there?' I asked.

'I think each valise has about forty kilos,' he answered.

'What's that worth?' I asked.

'Wholesale about seven million dollars,' he said. 'On the street after it's cut, maybe one hundred and fifty million dollars.'

'Now what happens to it?' I asked.

Jimmy smiled. 'I'll take care of it,' he said. 'Can I use your phone?'

'Be my guest,' I said.

Jimmy punched international numbers into the telephone. In a few seconds he was talking to someone in Italian. I didn't know what he was saying. He talked some more. He hung up the phone and turned to me.

'Da Vinci is already in Sicily,' he said. 'I think it is important that as soon as we hear from your uncle, we let him know that.' He then gestured to his two men and they took the valises out.

Jimmy 'Blue Eyes' held out his hand. 'Keep in touch, I'll leave two men here in case you need help,' he explained. 'You never can tell what those shitheads will do.' He shook his head. 'Now that the pizza connection trial is over, there is a whole group of new "zips" moving in and I think they are after the old men. The only way they can be controlled is by the Sicilian lords.'

I watched as they left the bungalow. I walked over and sat down at the bar. I leaned back in my chair and looked at General Gonzales. 'What do you think?'

The Peruvian general smiled and spoke quietly. 'They're all crooks,' he said.

10

It was eleven o'clock and we had finished dinner. We were having coffee. The general looked across the table at me. 'Do you have a gun?' he asked.

'No,' I answered. 'I don't need one here.'

'I think you need one now,' he said. He reached inside his jacket and handed me a small 9 mm automatic. 'Keep this, just in case,' he said.

'Why, do you think there will be a problem?' I asked.

'I have a feeling that something is not quite right,' he answered.

'What do you mean?' I asked.

He looked at me. 'Jimmy "Blue Eyes" didn't seem surprised that the heroin was here at your bungalow,' he said. 'It didn't take him long to take off with the valises. How much did he say that it would be worth? Seven million dollars?' he said.

'Yes,' I said.

The Peruvian nodded his head. 'That is not a bad night's work.'

'What are you saying?' I asked.

Gonzales replied. 'He said they were exchanging *cocaina* for heroin. But, he didn't tell you where the *cocaina* was coming from. I have a feeling that we will hear more from the Mafioso this evening.'

'He said he would leave two men here as bodyguards,' I said.

Gonzales smiled curiously. 'I don't know whether they are bodyguards or executioners. Jimmy "Blue Eyes" is playing with seven million dollars. If I were he I would not leave any witnesses behind.'

I thought for a moment. 'Maybe you're right.'

The telephone began to ring. Kim answered it, then looked at me. 'Your Aunt Rosa is on the phone,' she said.

'Aunt Rosa?' I asked. 'I haven't heard from her in a long time.' I reached for the phone. 'Aunt Rosa, how are you?'

'I'm fine,' she answered.

'You're up very late,' I said.

'I just remembered,' she said. 'Your father used to always send flowers for your grandparents' anniversary mass in Palermo,' she said. 'I thought it would be nice if you would send flowers this year.'

I thought for a moment. This was the first time I had ever heard about this. I knew Aunt Rosa was telling me something.

'I don't mind,' I said. 'When do I need to send the flowers?'

'The mass will be in Palermo in three days,' Aunt Rosa said. 'We have a cousin who is a florist in the Villa Igiea Grand Hotel. He'll know where to send the flowers.'

'Good,' I said. 'I'll arrange it right away.'

Aunt Rosa's voice was very serious. 'Don't forget. It's really very important.'

'Don't worry, Aunt Rosa, I'll take care of it,' I said.

'You always were a good boy,' she said. 'I know you will. Goodnight.' She put down the phone.

I turned and looked at Kim and Gonzales. 'Now we know where to meet Uncle Rocco,' I said.

Gonzales looked at me. 'I think it would be a good idea if I stay here in the bungalow with you. After all, I'm a professional and I'll know how to handle any trouble.'

'All I can offer you is the sofa, since Angela is in the guest room.'

'That's no problem,' he answered.

'Where are you going to meet your Uncle Rocco?' Kim asked.

'In Palermo in three days. So we'll arrange our travel plans in the morning. Let's go to bed now,' I said.

At three o'clock in the morning the telephone rang again. I picked it up. This time it was Alma.

'Is Angela with you?' she asked.

'Yes,' I said.

'Is she all right?' she asked.

'Yes,' I answered. 'Where are you?'

'I'm in Paris,' she said. 'Did General Gonzales arrive?' she asked quickly.

'He's here now,' I said.

'Good, let me talk to him,' she said.

I went into the living room. He was sitting on the couch, wide awake. 'Alma's on the phone,' I said.

He picked up the phone and spoke to her. I listened for a moment and I realized they were not speaking in Spanish. It was probably a Peruvian argot.

Finally, he said to her, 'Okay, I'll be there too.' He put down the telephone.

'What did she say?' I asked.

'She has arranged to rent a yacht in Antibes, and she and your uncle will take the yacht to Palermo. Your uncle thinks that it is the safest way for them to travel.'

'Did she say anything about us meeting there?' I asked.

'Yes,' he answered. 'She confirmed your Aunt Rosa's message.'

'Good enough,' I said. 'I'll arrange to get the plane tomorrow.'

He looked at me. 'What do you want to do about the bodyguards outside?'

'Screw them,' I said. 'If they don't bother us, we don't bother them.'

I went back to the bedroom. Kim was sitting up in the bed looking at me.

'What's happening?' she asked.

I smiled at her. 'You're going on a honeymoon. We're going to Europe.'

We arrived in Palermo the day before I was to meet Uncle Rocco. The hotel was comfortable and Kim and I had a nice suite. Gonzales had a room across the corridor from us.

At seven p.m. we went downstairs to the cocktail lounge to have a drink.

'It seems like a quiet town,' I said.

The general nodded. 'It reminds me of some of the towns in Peru. They always seem to be quiet, but there are problems below the surface.'

The waiter came to the table. Kim wanted a bottle of Asti Spumanti. The general and I had scotch.

During the day we had lunch at a restaurant not far from the hotel. This evening we had decided to have dinner at the hotel. The menu was completely Italian. Pasta, pasta, pasta.

We were sitting quietly, not talking, when I heard someone talking behind me.

'Mr. Stevens.'

I turned around. It was Jimmy 'Blue Eyes' standing there with his two bodyguards.

'Do you mind if I join you for a drink?' he asked.

'Be my guest,' I replied.

He moved into a chair. 'I didn't expect to see you here,' he said.

'Neither did I expect to see you here,' I said.

'Are you meeting your uncle?' he asked.

'I haven't had any messages, I'm just traveling a little bit. And I've come to attend the anniversary mass for my grandparents,' I said. 'What brings you here?'

'Business,' Jimmy 'Blue Eyes' said.

I didn't want to ask him what the business was.

Jimmy 'Blue Eyes' smiled. 'I know this town very well. Why don't you let me take you to dinner tonight?'

'If it's not an inconvenience to you,' I said.

'Not at all,' he said. 'It would be my pleasure.'

I looked at him. 'By the way, you mentioned the other day that Da Vinci was in Italy already,' I said. 'Do you think he might be here?'

Jimmy 'Blue Eyes' shrugged. 'I don't know. But anything is possible. I think we should keep our eyes open,' he said. 'I will pick you up in the lobby at eight-thirty.'

'You've got a date,' I said.

Jimmy rose from his chair and left the cocktail lounge with his bodyguards following.

I looked at Gonzales and Kim. 'What do you think?'

Gonzales didn't look happy. 'I think we're in trouble. We don't know who's on our side.'

Jimmy 'Blue Eyes' picked us up in a Mercedes 600 limousine. And it took us about twenty minutes to reach the outskirts of the city to the restaurant. The restaurant was in what used to be a private mansion. We sat on the terrace overlooking the water.

After we had been seated for only a few minutes the waiters brought a large plate of antipasto to our table. Jimmy 'Blue Eyes' ordered two bottles of red wine. I opened a package of breadsticks and started to laugh.

'What are you laughing at?' Jimmy asked.

I handed him the wrapper from the breadsticks. Printed on the outside was 'Made in Brooklyn, New York.'

Jimmy smiled. 'It's a small world,' he said. 'Tell me, what do you think your uncle is planning to do now?'

'As far as I know,' I said, 'Uncle Rocco wants to retire and stay out completely.'

Jimmy shook his head. 'They'll never let him do it totally. He knows too much.'

'He's an old man,' I said. 'I think they could let him have his last few years in peace.'

Jimmy didn't say anything. He looked at Kim. 'The food is very good here. They have wonderful veal and great fresh fish. Anything you want you will find very good,' he said.

'I like fish,' Kim said.

I looked around the restaurant. There were about twelve tables on the terrace. It was empty except for our table. 'They don't seem to be very busy,' I said.

'It's Sicily, nobody eats before midnight,' Jimmy said. 'We're Americans, we came early.'

The waiter came and gave us menus. I couldn't read a word. It was all in Italian. 'I think I would like some veal,' I said. 'With a side of fettuccini.'

'I'll have whitefish,' Kim said.

'I'll have fish, too,' Gonzales said.

Jimmy looked at the waiter. 'I'm going to have mussels.'

I didn't say anything. I hated mussels. To me just looking at them made me nauseous.

Suddenly the sun was gone and it was dark. The waiters were putting candles on all of the tables.

We were on our main course and Jimmy 'Blue Eyes' seemed in a good mood. He gestured to me. 'You don't realize how important Sicily is,' he said. 'We're a poor country. And a poor people. But somehow we have managed to work our way to a level of importance. Don't forget, if it wasn't for us, there would not be a Las Vegas. And I've spent my life keeping everything there in order.'

'But you don't have the casinos anymore,' I said.

He laughed. 'We don't need them. There are many other businesses that make a lot more money for us.'

I looked at him. 'Aren't you worried that someone will take it away from you?'

'People have tried,' he said. 'But nobody has been able to do it.'

He looked toward the door. 'What the hell is going on?' he said, and looked toward his bodyguards.

Gonzales and I turned to follow his gaze. There were two men coming from the restaurant to the terrace. The bodyguards looked frightened and disappeared. Jimmy reached into his jacket as I pushed Kim out of her chair and on to the floor. I rolled on top of her to protect her from harm.

I didn't see if Jimmy 'Blue Eyes' got his gun out of his jacket. But an Uzi seemed to place a tattoo on his body. The two men turned toward us, but this was where Gonzales was really a professional. He had two Colt 45 Automatics. One in each hand. He blew off the head of each of the two men.

'Jesus,' I said.

Gonzales spoke, disgusted. 'They're assholes. If they were going to hit, they should have hit everybody at the same time.'

I got up and we helped Kim to her feet. She looked very pale and nauseous. 'Don't look at them,' I said.

Gonzales spoke. 'Let's get out of here before the police show up.'

I looked over at Jimmy 'Blue Eyes'. He was lying on his stomach with blood soaking his jacket from the bullets that had gone right through him.

Gonzales and I held Kim by her arms, as we started to leave. I looked down at the two gunmen. One of them was Da Vinci.

'Da Vinci is not going to play his computer games anymore.' As a matter of fact, he had a very stupid expression on his face.

The restaurant staff didn't say a word as we went out the front door. I looked for the bodyguards. I didn't see them anywhere. The Mercedes was still there, with the keys in the ignition.

'Let's go,' I said. And we managed to find our way back to the hotel.

Gonzales looked at me. 'I don't know who they were after, Jimmy "Blue Eyes" or you.'

11

Uncle Rocco didn't show up at the hotel until seven in the evening. By that time, I was ready to get out of Sicily. Palermo was not the most exciting city in the world.

He came to our suite. 'How was your trip?' he asked us.

'The trip was fine, but I didn't realize that I was going to get in the middle of a war,' I said.

Uncle Rocco smiled. 'I'm sorry. I heard about it.'

'How did you hear about it?' I asked.

'The commission,' he said. He looked at me. 'You know that Da Vinci was after you as well as Jimmy "Blue Eyes".'

'Why the hell was he after me?' I asked.

Uncle Rocco shook his head. 'They thought that was the way they could get at me. But it doesn't matter now. I've got everything resolved. I've had the meeting with the Sicilian Commission, the head of the most important families in Sicily. They've sent the okay to the five families in New York.'

'What does that mean?' I asked.

He looked at me. 'I'm out. Now, all we have to do is to have you take over Inter-World Investments.'

'And where do we meet with them to do that?' I asked.

'Back in New York,' he said. 'Their offices are in the financial district.'

'Then what the hell did I come to Sicily for? To get myself shot at?'

'No,' Uncle Rocco answered me. 'We have a dinner in your honor to attend tonight. The commission wants to look you over.'

'What happens if they don't like me?' I asked. 'Do they kill me?'

'Don't be silly,' Uncle Rocco said. 'This will be a very pleasant evening.'

I met his eyes. 'I'll feel better if you can give me a machine gun.'

He laughed. 'You won't need it. We've got all the protection we need.'

Kim looked at me. 'I've got to get a dress. I didn't know we were going to have an important dinner to attend.' She looked at Uncle Rocco. 'Is Alma going to be dressed up?'

'Of course,' he said.

'Where can I get a dress?' she asked.

'Don't worry. All the stores are open until ten p.m. And we won't have dinner until midnight,' he said.

General Gonzales looked at him. 'I'd like to see Señorita Vargas.'

Uncle Rocco nodded. 'That will be no problem. You can join me when I leave here and return to the boat. She's there.'

The general nodded.

Uncle Rocco looked at me. 'You better go out to the stores, too. You have to have a tuxedo. This is really a formal occasion.'

'How many people will be there?' I asked.

'About twenty-four or twenty-five people,' Uncle Rocco answered. 'They're really curious to meet you. Most of them knew your father, when we were young.'

'Where will the dinner be held?' I asked.

'Here, at this hotel, I arranged for one of the private party rooms,' he said and looked at me. 'You don't look very happy.'

'I'm still not sure that I like this whole idea,' I said.

'Don't be so nervous,' he said. 'Just remember, you and I are family.'

General Gonzales followed Uncle Rocco as he left the suite.

I looked at Kim. 'Call the concierge. He'll probably know the best stores to go to.'

Kim and I started to laugh after we were dressed for dinner. We had to rent our clothes at a wedding boutique. Even though my tuxedo was Giorgio Armani, it was still a three-year-old style. Kim had on a very Sicilian long lace gown.

She laughed. 'I think we can go to the Mayor's office and get married in these clothes.'

'Anything's possible,' I said. 'I haven't seen a tuxedo like this in a while. What the hell, when in Sicily, do as the Sicilians do.'

I looked at my watch. 'Christ, we're early. We have another hour to kill before dinner. Let's have a drink.'

There was a knock at the door. I opened it. It was Uncle Rocco. He looked fantastic. And why shouldn't he, he, at least, had brought his own tuxedo.

'Where are Alma and Gonzales?' I asked.

'They are not coming to dinner,' he said.

'I thought you said Alma was coming?' Kim asked.

'I changed my mind,' Uncle Rocco said. 'In Sicily at business dinners the women are not invited.'

'Then why am I going?' Kim asked.

'First of all, you're American. Second of all, I told them that you were Jed's fiancée and that you also understand Italian which is helpful to Jed,' he answered.

'Okay,' I said. 'Let's have a drink.'

'A short one,' Uncle Rocco said. 'Because we need to be in the private dining room before our guests arrive.' He turned to Kim. 'That's a very pretty dress.'

She smiled. 'I feel like a Sicilian bridesmaid.'

He laughed. 'What the hell, nobody will know the difference.'

At a quarter to twelve we were in the private dining room. Exactly at midnight the other guests began arriving.

Respectfully, Uncle Rocco introduced me to each man as he arrived. Four of them were older men and in wheelchairs. They were each wheeled into the room by a younger man.

The table was set in a u-shape. Uncle Rocco sat at the head of the table. I was seated on his left, and Kim was next to me. On Uncle Rocco's right was one of the older men who was seated in his wheelchair.

I had been introduced to each of them, but there was one problem. When they spoke to me I couldn't understand a word and Rocco tried to translate for me, but he was also busy talking to the other guests. So Kim tried to help translate, but she only knew Italian, not Sicilian. But they were very polite about it and spoke in Italian so that we could communicate.

When I spoke to each of the older men, they spoke to me about my father. How much they had respected him because he was one of the few men who went his own way. They also said that they were pleased that I had followed in his footsteps.

Kim leaned over and whispered to me. 'What these men said about your father is really very nice.'

'Yes,' I said. 'But don't forget one thing. Probably all of them are killers.'

By two o'clock in the morning dinner was over, and we were all toasting each other.

Uncle Rocco made a speech. I didn't really catch all of what he said, but the feeling I got was that he was thanking them for allowing him to retire with honor.

The man in the wheelchair on his right said a few words and handed Uncle Rocco a velvet covered jewelry box.

Uncle Rocco opened the box. He took out a beautiful diamond-studded Patek Phillippe watch. He nodded and kissed the old man on each cheek and then turned to the other guests.

It was hard for me to believe, but I could see tears rolling from his eyes as he thanked the other guests.

Everyone applauded, and began to rise from their seats to depart. A young handsome man came to the table and stopped in front of Uncle Rocco. Uncle Rocco smiled and held out his hand. The man said something in a harsh voice and pulled a gun from his jacket and shot at Uncle Rocco.

Automatically, without thinking, I jumped over the table and wrestled the young man to the floor. At the same time, there were two other men right beside me. They held him down and took away his gun.

I got up and moved quickly to Uncle Rocco. He was leaning against Kim. He looked very pale.

'Have somebody get a doctor,' I said.

The two men pulled the assailant to his feet. The old man

in the wheelchair that had been seated at Uncle Rocco's right
was speaking in a very rough voice. He then took a gun from
his own jacket and shot the assailant in the head.

I pulled open Uncle Rocco's jacket.

He looked at me. 'I wanted to die peacefully in bed, not by
a bullet.'

I looked down at him and smiled. 'You're not going to die
because of this wound. You've just been shot in the shoulder.'

The old man in the wheelchair turned to me and this time
I was surprised. He spoke to me in perfect English.

'I apologize,' he said. 'It is men like this who bring dishonor
to all of us.'

We were in the hotel suite and Uncle Rocco was groaning
while the doctor picked out the bullet from the flesh of his
shoulder.

He quickly swabbed the bullet hole with iodine and dressed
the wound then put a sling around Uncle Rocco's neck and
carefully placed his arm inside. He spoke in Italian to Uncle
Rocco.

'What did he say?' I asked Kim.

'He told him to keep his arm still and the bandages needed
to be changed every day for the next few days,' she said.

'That's not bad,' I said.

The doctor took out a hypodermic needle and loaded Uncle
Rocco with penicillin. He spoke again to Uncle Rocco in
Italian.

Again Kim translated. 'He said that's enough for the
moment and that he should take two aspirin every four hours
for the pain.'

The doctor stood up and put his instruments back into his
case. He turned and spoke to Kim in Italian. She nodded and
turned to me.

'He said that he would come by in the morning to check
on him.'

'Ask him how much I owe him,' I said.

Kim spoke. The doctor smiled and answered quietly in
English. 'One thousand dollars.'

I looked at Kim. 'This is an expensive doctor,' I said.

The doctor understood what I had said and he turned to me. 'I've not reported this to the police and that alone is worth something.'

I opened Uncle Rocco's jacket and took out his wallet. Quickly, I counted out ten one hundred dollar bills and handed them to the doctor.

'Thank you,' I said.

'No problem,' the doctor said. 'You are welcome.' And he left the suite.

Uncle Rocco stared at me. 'You didn't have to give him that much money. He would have taken half, in Sicily you always bargain.'

'Why should I bargain,' I asked. 'It was your money,' I smiled.

'Shit,' Uncle Rocco said.

I pulled up a chair next to the bed and looked at him. 'Now, why don't you tell me what was going on here tonight? Every time I'm around you somebody is shooting at you,' I said. 'The only problem is that they may be shooting at me as well.'

Uncle Rocco stared back at me. 'They're assholes.'

'I don't care who they are,' I said. 'I want you to tell me what we're going to do about it.'

Uncle Rocco shook his head. 'You're not going to do anything about it. The men of honor will take care of them.'

'How can you be sure?' I asked Uncle Rocco. 'Maybe they are the ones after you.'

'Don't be stupid,' Uncle Rocco said. 'Now we're all in legitimate business together.'

'Do you want to stay here at the hotel tonight?' I asked. 'I think you would be more comfortable here than on the boat.'

'That's a good idea,' he said. 'Besides it's very late and I think that we all need some sleep. Tomorrow we'll talk to Alma and Gonzales. After the doctor dresses my wound again, we'll start for home.' He looked at me again. 'You'll have to stop in New York at Inter-World Investments. They have two floors of offices at 80 Broad. You can start meeting your executives.'

12

The doctor arrived at ten o'clock in the morning to change Uncle Rocco's bandages. He took Uncle Rocco's temperature and seemed satisfied. He had no temperature. He quickly gave Uncle Rocco another injection of penicillin and carefully replaced his arm in the sling.

'You're pretty good,' he spoke in Italian to Uncle Rocco. 'All you have to do is keep changing the bandages daily, and give your shoulder a rest for a while and it will be as good as new.'

Uncle Rocco thanked him, and walked him to the door and he left. He came back and sat down at the table where we were having our coffee. 'Have you heard anything from Alma yet?' he asked.

'No,' I answered.

'That's strange, I'm surprised that she hasn't called or come over looking for me,' he said. 'I'll call the boat.'

'Do you have a number?' I asked him.

Uncle Rocco nodded. 'Yes.' He took a piece of paper out of his pocket and gave the number to the hotel operator. He waited a few moments as he listened to the phone ringing. He looked at me with a worried expression. 'There's no one answering. There should be an answer.'

'Maybe she and Gonzales are on their way over here,' I said.

'I think we should go over to the boat,' he said.

'Okay,' I said and called the concierge for a car. Fifteen minutes later we were on the quay in the harbor where the boat had been docked. The *Empress of Beaulieu* was a 120-foot motor yacht built by the Chantier D'Esterel in Cannes.

We got out of the car and looked up at the boat. We saw

no one. Uncle Rocco silently took a gun out of his jacket. 'Let's go aboard,' he said.

He looked at Kim. 'You better stay down here.'

'Why? Do you think there is a problem?' she asked.

'I don't know,' he said. 'But I don't take any chances.' He looked at me. 'Do you have a gun?'

I did. The 9 mm that Gonzales had given me. I followed Uncle Rocco up the gangplank. We boarded the boat and walked through the salon and then to the bridge.

Uncle Rocco held his hand up in front of me and gestured. There was a sailor crumpled on the floor under the wheel.

Uncle Rocco turned back and led me down a small spiral staircase that led us to the cabins. As we reached the corridor, I looked down. General Gonzales was lying on the floor, two bullet holes in his head. Quickly, Uncle Rocco opened the first cabin door. Alma was sprawled across the bed, her throat was cut, blood was spread all over the sheets. I felt nauseous.

Uncle Rocco pushed me back into the corridor and up the staircase. I looked at him. 'Why?'

He shook his head grimly. 'It's the drug trade. I told her not to try to play games with it. She wanted out, but she was trying to make a final killing.'

I still felt sick. 'What do we do now?'

We left the boat and were still silent when we reached Kim. I took her hand and we crossed from the quay to the street and got back into the car to go to the hotel.

Kim looked at me. 'What happened?' she asked as we sat in the back seat.

'They're dead,' I whispered.

A look of horror crossed her face. She began to cry. 'Oh my God,' she said. 'What will happen to that sweet little child?'

That was four years ago. We spent several weeks in New York, while I met with Inter-World executives. Then we went back to California.

A month after that, Kim and I were married in Las Vegas. And I lost $32,000 dollars at baccarat.

A month after we were married, we adopted Angela and

two years later we had our own child. A boy. I named him after my father, John.

Meanwhile, Uncle Rocco left Atlantic City and moved back to New York City. He rented the house he had sold me. He seemed to enjoy his life. But I had a feeling that he missed the action.

I worked all the time, and in a few years, Inter-World climbed near the top of the Fortune International 500. And became as well known to the public as IBM.

It was late one evening that Aunt Rosa called me. She was crying.

'Rocco is on his death bed and he wants to see you before he goes.'

I was in New York the next morning. Aunt Rosa was sitting outside the bedroom crying. Her two daughters were sitting with her. Inside the bedroom, there was a young priest praying and he had already given Uncle Rocco his last rites.

He was gasping for breath. A nurse was sitting in a chair next to the bed and had him connected to a heart monitor. He was feeding oxygen into his body with a portable oxygen tank.

I looked at him. His face was pale and he seemed to be in extreme pain. I touched his hand carefully so that I would not disturb the IV on the back of his hand.

He turned slowly and looked at me. I didn't say anything. After a moment he spoke. 'I'm really fucked,' he said.

I tried to cheer him up. 'I've seen people in worse condition.'

'I'm sure you have,' he said. 'But, they were dead.'

'Uncle Rocco, what are you complaining about? You said you wanted to die in bed. Well, here you are.'

'You are really a prick. After everything I have done for you,' he said. 'I've made your life. You're one of the richest men in the world.'

I smiled. 'That's not true. I just owe more money than anybody else.'

He laughed. 'You're really Sicilian. You may be half Jewish, but you are Sicilian,' he said quietly. 'You are family. You are the son that I lost.'

'But, you never lost a son,' I said. 'You've always had me.'

'At one time,' he said, 'I really hated you.'

'Why?' I asked.

'I know,' he said. 'That you shot Angelo.'

'I saved him from pain,' I said. 'Because I loved him and he told me that I should help him because I was family.'

Uncle Rocco was silent for a moment. 'I know that,' he said finally. 'Alma told me many years ago. She told me that you tried to save him. But there was no way that you could.'

I didn't answer.

He moved his other hand. 'I have a ring on my finger, take it off.'

Slowly, I moved the ring off his finger. It was an old-fashioned, heavy, gold ring with a large square diamond set in the center.

'Put it on,' he said. 'I want you to have it. I was going to leave it to Angelo. But you are Angelo to me.'

Silently, I slipped the ring on to my right hand. It felt very heavy.

'The doctors told me,' he said. 'That I will not wait too long.'

'Doctors do not always know everything,' I answered.

He smiled at me. 'I really don't give a shit,' he said. 'I don't want to wait.' He squeezed my hand and closed his eyes. His eyelids opened and he was gone.

It was the day after his funeral and I was sitting at the dining room table in Uncle Rocco's apartment, with a number of papers spread out on the table around me.

I had the last check from the Chairman. I was arranging to transfer them to Uncle Rocco's foundation.

The maid came in. 'There are some friends of Mr. Di Stefano's to see you,' she said.

'Ask them to come in.' I answered.

There were three old men. I remembered I had seen them at the funeral. I had not spoken to them there.

They spoke to me about Uncle Rocco who they knew since they were young. They also had known my father. They felt sad because there were not many men of honor now.

'But Rocco,' one of them said to me, 'was an extraordinary man. He never betrayed the trust. He truly was a great man of honor.'

I thanked them for coming. They rose to leave and one of them saw the ring Uncle Rocco had given me. He reached to hold my hand. 'I know that ring,' he said. 'It was your uncle's ring and it was his father's ring, your grandfather's. It was a symbol of a true Don.'

Before I could move my hand from him, he bent down and kissed the ring. A moment later the other two did the same. They looked up at me and there were tears in their eyes.

'May God be with you, Don Jed,' they said and they left.

I sat there for a few moments and looked down at the papers. The tears began falling from my eyes.

I knew that I was a very ordinary man. And I was an American, not Sicilian. But to these three old men, I was the **Godfather**.

MORE TITLES BY HAROLD ROBBINS AVAILABLE FROM NEW ENGLISH LIBRARY PAPERBACKS

☐	00083 4	The Adventurers	£5.99
☐	02794 5	The Betsy	£4.99
☐	00106 7	The Carpetbaggers	£5.99
☐	05768 2	Descent from Xanadu	£4.50
☐	03877 7	Dreams Die First	£4.99
☐	05350 4	The Dream Merchants	£5.99
☐	05315 6	Goodbye, Janette	£4.99
☐	00674 3	The Inheritors	£4.99
☐	03159 4	The Lonely Lady	£4.99
☐	04981 7	Memories of Another Day	£4.99
☐	00067 2	Never Leave Me	£4.50
☐	00076 1	Never Love a Stranger	£4.99
☐	02330 3	The Pirate	£4.99
☐	00946 7	79 Park Avenue	£4.50

All these books are available at your local bookshop or newsagent, or can be ordered direct from the publisher. Just tick the titles you want and fill in the form below.

Prices and availability subject to change without notice.

Hodder & Stoughton Paperbacks, P.O. Box 11, Falmouth, Cornwall.

Please send cheque or postal order for the value of the book, and add the following for postage and packing:

U.K. including B.F.P.O. £1.00 for one book, plus 50p for the second book, and 30p for each additional book ordered up to a £3.00 maximum.

OVERSEAS INCLUDING EIRE – £2.00 for the first book, plus £1.00 for the second book, and 50p for each additional book ordered.

OR Please debit this amount from my Access/Visa Card (delete as appropriate).

Card Number ☐☐☐☐☐☐☐☐☐☐☐☐☐☐☐☐

Amount £ ....

Expiry Date ....

Signed ....

Name ....

Address ....